Mango Motel

A Mango Bob and Walker Adventure

by

Bill H. Myers

www.mangobob.com

Chapter One

"Where's the gun?"

I was handcuffed to a table and had been asked the same question at least ten times in the past hour. Each time, I answered the same way. "I don't know anything about a gun. What's this about?"

I'd been walking back to my RV a little before midnight when two police cars rolled up. One stopped in front of me, one behind.

The cop in the car behind me got out and shouted, "Get down on the ground!"

I wasn't sure he was speaking to me so I turned toward his voice. That was a mistake. He pulled his gun and aimed it at my chest. He repeated the command. "Down on the ground!"

This time, I didn't hesitate. I dropped to the hard concrete, lay on my belly and spread my arms.

While the cop kept his gun aimed at me, the one from the other car rushed over and cuffed me. I knew better than to struggle. I also knew to keep my mouth shut.

They yanked me up off the ground and shoved me into the backseat of the car in front. Before they closed the door, I asked, "What's this about? Why am I being arrested?"

Instead of answering, the cop who was closest pulled out a small card from his pocket and said, "You have the right to remain silent. Anything you say can and will be used against you in a court of law. You have the right to speak to an attorney and to have an attorney present during any questioning. If you cannot afford a lawyer, one will be provided for you at government expense."

He put the card away. "Do you understand?"

I nodded and repeated the question I had asked before. "What's this about? Why am I being arrested?"

The cop smiled. "They'll tell you downtown."

The youngish looking officer said nothing as he drove me across town to the Saint Augustine police station. Inside, he handed me off to a man I assumed to be a detective. Unlike the cop who brought me in, he wasn't wearing a uniform. He was in slacks, a white shirt with a skinny tie, and an unbuttoned sport jacket.

The detective led me into a small room, sat me down in front of a metal table, and chained the cuffs to an eye bolt in the center of it. They weren't taking any chances of me getting away.

Without saying a word, he left the room, leaving me alone. Across the table, on the far wall, a large mirrored window reflected my image. I was pretty sure it was one-way glass. There'd be people on the other side watching me.

The security camera in the corner would likely record audio and video of everything that happened in the room. I reminded myself to act innocent.

Twenty minutes later, the same detective who had chained me to the table came in and sat across from me. His first words were, "Where's the gun?"

I shook my head. "I don't know why you're asking me about a gun. I haven't touched one in years. What's this about?"

Instead of answering my question, the detective repeated his. "Where's the gun?"

I shook my head again. "I'm not answering any questions until I know what this is about. Tell me why I was picked up. Tell me why you're asking about a gun."

He frowned. "Don't play dumb. You know why we're asking. You know what you did. Save yourself some trouble and tell me what you did with it."

We were back to the same question. One that I couldn't answer. Not without knowing why it was being asked. I crossed my arms and repeated what I had said earlier. "I'm not answering any questions until I know what this is about. Tell me why I was brought in. Tell me why you're asking about a gun."

He didn't answer. He stared at me for a few minutes, waiting for me to say something. When he realized I wasn't going to talk, he got up and left the room.

Fifteen minutes later, a second detective came in and took a seat across from me. He looked to be about fifty wearing a rumpled white shirt with a thin, black clip-on tie. He looked tired. I could see it in his eyes and, later on, hear it in his voice.

After introducing himself as Detective Booker, which I thought was a good name for someone in his line of work, he asked if I would like something to drink. I was thirsty, but I planned to pass on the refreshments until I found out how long I'd be in the station.

"No, I don't need a drink. I won't be staying long."

He smiled then re-read me my rights. When he was done, he asked if I understood them. It was the second time I'd had my rights read that night. "Yeah, I understand."

Before I was put in the cop car earlier that evening, I'd been frisked and they had taken my wallet. It was now sitting on the table in front of me. The detective opened it and pointed to my driver's license.

"Mr. Walker, you're here because there was a shooting. We have an eye witness who saw you go into the room with a gun and saw you come back out after he heard a shot.

"Our witness did the right thing. He called 9-1-1 and stayed at the scene to be interviewed. He told us everything and that's why we picked you up. You were the guy with the gun.

"But that's not all. When we searched the room, we found physical evidence that clearly shows you were there. Probably buying or selling drugs.

"So we know what you did. That's a done deal. The only thing we don't know is what you did with the gun. You want to tell me?"

I shook my head. "I didn't shoot anyone and there is no gun."

The detective crossed his arms and leaned back in his chair. He sat there looking at me; then leaned forward and said, "Look, we know you ditched it. If some kid finds it and hurts himself or uses it in a crime, it'll be on you. You don't want that. So tell us what you did with it."

I couldn't tell him anything. It was true that I had been near the room in question. But I hadn't carried a gun and hadn't shot anyone. They had the wrong guy, but I didn't have an alibi. I was there when it happened. I'd been walking away from the scene of the crime when they picked me up.

I was innocent, but I couldn't tell them why I had been there. Too many people would get hurt.

But there was no way a witness saw me go into the room with a gun. It hadn't happened. When the witness recanted, I'd be home free.

But I was wrong. Things only got worse.

Chapter Two

Seven Days Earlier.

It was Saturday morning and I was waiting for my psychic, sometimes psychotic, friend Abby to call me. She had texted earlier in the week about me meeting her in St. Augustine for something she was working on.

She hadn't gone into detail. Just that she'd be calling and I should be ready to roll. That's the way Abby is. Short on details, long on deception.

I knew going in she wouldn't be telling me much about whatever we would be doing. But I figured it had something to do with Boris, our friend in Key West. Some say he was once the head of the Russian Mafia's southern branch. I didn't know if it was true or not. It wasn't something I was going to ask him.

I'd helped him out of a mess several months earlier, and he was very appreciative. Money and support, any time I wanted it, even if I didn't ask for it. He was quite generous when he wanted to be.

I was pretty lucky when it came to my financial situation and didn't need his money. I'd gotten a solid severance package when I was laid off from my corporate job and received an unexpected windfall shortly thereafter.

My wife, or I should say ex-wife, filed for divorce the same day I lost my job. She got the house, her car, and half our savings. I got the other half and my freedom.

Needing a place to live, I bought a thirteen-year-old motorhome, drove it to Florida and have been calling it home ever since. Thirty-five and living in an RV, just me and my cat. A big orange bobtail named Mango Bob.

The cat wasn't my idea. A woman I was seeing was moving into a new apartment and asked me to take care of her cat until she got settled in. She had promised it would be "Just for a few days."

She'd said as soon as she got settled in, she'd come back for the cat.

But she never did. I didn't want to take him to the shelter so I ended up with him, instead of the woman. It was probably for the best.

After a rough start, Mango Bob and I learned to tolerate each other. He learned that life in the motorhome wasn't so bad. He had someone to feed him, clean his litter box, and on occasion entertain him. He's learned to enjoy the trips we take together and seems to look forward to seeing new places as we travel and camp. Our travels have mostly been in Florida, making new friends and a few enemies along the way.

One of those new friends is Abby, and, as I said, I was waiting for her call.

I'd been up since daybreak, thinking she'd call early. It would be a long drive in the RV to Saint Augustine and I wanted to be on the road before the traffic got too crazy.

It was nearly ten in the morning before I heard from her. Instead of calling, she sent a text with a cryptic message. "Calling in 5. Pick up."

I wasn't sure why she'd sent a text. It would have been easier to just call. A text wasn't necessary. But Abby is strange that way, so I waited for her to dial my number.

Had I known then how the call would change my life, I'm not sure I would have answered.

Chapter Three

Five minutes after getting the text, my phone chimed with an incoming call, caller ID "unknown". I expected as much. Abby prefers to use a burner phone; she doesn't like to leave a trail. I answered on the second ring. "This is Walker."

She hated it when I answered that way. She said giving my name out before I knew who was calling was a mistake. She said you never knew who was on the other line and if you gave out your name first, you might be locked into talking to someone you'd rather not.

Still, knowing it was her calling, I answered, "This is Walker."

I expected the voice on the other end to chide me about using my name, but that didn't happen. The voice, clearly not Abby, said, "Walker, I hope you don't mind me calling. I spoke to Abby about it and she said you wouldn't. I hope that's true."

Abby hadn't told me who would be calling. She just said answer the phone, and I did, assuming it would be her. But it wasn't.

The caller's voice was familiar, but I couldn't place it. It was the voice of an older woman, one that I'd heard before. But it wasn't someone who I'd had long conversations with. She had a slight European accent but spoke clearly with perfect English.

I didn't want to embarrass myself or the caller by asking

who she was, so I just said, "Abby said I should expect a call. She didn't say who'd be calling though."

The caller hesitated for a moment then said, "Walker, I apologize. I thought she would have told you it would be me calling. But it appears she hasn't. I'm Marissa. Marissa Chesnokov, Katrina's mother. Boris's wife."

I'd only spoken to Marissa once before. And only briefly. Kat had introduced us when I was visiting Boris at home. My impression was she was well educated, polite, yet not afraid to share her feelings or opinions. I was lucky she approved of my then relationship with Kat, her daughter. It could have been trouble if she hadn't.

That relationship with Kat had gone nowhere. I had been her boy toy for a couple of weeks but not much longer. She had since moved on, but we were still friends. As such, my first thought when Marissa introduced herself was something bad had happened to Kat. Or Boris.

"Is everything okay? With Katrina? Boris? You?"

She didn't hesitate with her answer. "Oh, they're both fine. Katrina is in Daytona, hanging out with a race car driver. Boris is out on his boat, doing whatever he and his buddies do when they're out on the water.

"This call is not about either of them. It's about me. I need a favor and I don't want Boris to know about it. Before I tell you what it is, I want to know how you're doing. Abby told us about the accident. It sounded awful. We were all worried you might not pull through.

"She told me today that your recovery has gone well. We know she was at your side in the hospital and then stayed with you for a month to help you sort things out. She's a good person."

14

It was true Abby had taken care of me after the wreck, but whether she was a good person or not depended on your definition of "good". If you crossed her, she could make your life miserable.

But if she liked you, she'd treat you fairly, and might even go out of her way when you needed help. I counted myself as one who considered her a good person. There would be others who wouldn't agree.

Marissa interrupted my thoughts. "I trust you are doing well?"

It was a question I had asked myself many times since the accident. I had suffered a concussion and was still having some side effects. There were two that concerned me the most. One was the occasional inability to remember familiar words. Easy ones like sedative and glacier.

Forgetting words was worrisome, but I could deal with it. I rarely had long conversations with anyone and when I did, the words that I'd forgotten rarely came up.

What bothered me most was the double vision. It would come on randomly and when it did, I wouldn't be able to see well enough to read or recognize faces. My vision would be perfect for days, but then, out of nowhere, things would go out of focus. It would be anywhere from a few minutes to sometimes an hour before I could see clearly again.

So far, the blurry vision hadn't been a big problem. It seemed to come on mostly when I was exposed to bright fluorescent lights. The kind they have in Walmart and other big box stores.

I'd be okay for a while, then start to feel like I was walking downhill, and soon after, everything would go out of focus.

If I were pushing a shopping cart, I could hang on to it

until I could see again. But if I didn't have a cart, I'd have to find a place to sit. My doctor had warned me I'd sometimes get double vision and not to worry about it unless it lasted more than a few minutes.

I didn't know how long he considered a few minutes but if it were more than ten, I was already in trouble. I should have talked to him about it. But I hadn't. The episodes were getting further and further apart. I figured they'd soon go away. It wasn't a big problem. At least not yet.

But I was a little worried about driving long distances. If my vision went while I was behind the wheel of my motorhome, rolling down the highway at sixty-five, it could be bad. Not being able to see well enough to keep an eight-ton vehicle in between the white lines could have deadly results.

So far, it hadn't been a problem. But I hadn't been driving much, preferring to stay close to home—the small strip of concrete where my motorhome was parked.

I was thinking about this when Marissa asked, "So, are you well enough to travel?"

Without hesitation, I said, "Yes."

Chapter Four

I was still on the phone with Marissa Chesnokov, the wife of a suspected mob boss. She had asked if I was well enough to travel, and I told her I was.

Satisfied with my answer, she said, "Walker, I need to ask you a favor. But before I do, it's something that Boris can not find out about. If he does, it might mean a few people get hurt. Not you but other people. People you don't want to know.

"So before I tell you more, would you be willing to do something for me without Boris finding out about it? If you don't think you can or should, I'll understand."

She paused and I took the opportunity to ask, "If Boris finds out about this, will I become his enemy?"

He was a powerful man and I suspected his associates didn't take kindly to those who chose to undermine or deceive him. I didn't want to give him a reason for me to meet those associates. But I wanted to help Marissa if I could, so I waited for her answer.

"Boris won't be upset with you. He might be upset with me but not you. And if you're successful with what I'm going to ask, he'll be quite impressed. If you fail, he'll respect that you at least tried.

"Either way, I plan to tell him everything after this runs its course. I'll paint you as the knight who agreed to help a damsel in distress."

Since it sounded like I would be in the clear no matter what, I said, "I'm in. Tell me what you need me to do."

"Good, I was hoping you'd say that. But if after you hear what I'm about to ask, if you want to change your mind I'll understand."

She paused, giving me time to respond. Since it seemed like she was waiting for my answer, I said, "That sounds fair."

I heard her take a deep breath, then, "I need you to find a man before others do. He's the son of a close friend, Anastasia Raines.

"She and I grew up together in the old country and after Boris and I moved to Florida, she followed. We're like sisters, and together we learned about living in this new country. I see her almost every day, and we talk about what's going on in our lives. Mostly about our children, the weather, and our aches and pains.

"She has a thirty-year-old son, just a few years younger than you. He lives with her and has done so on and off for most of his life. When her husband passed two years ago, he moved in with her full time.

"The kid is bright but not sure what he wants to do in life. Right now, he mostly plays video games. It's not that he doesn't want to work; it's just that he has a hard time keeping a job. He's been hired for many jobs in Key West, and soon after fired from those same jobs. He blames it on his bosses. He says they always have it out for him. They make him work more than he wants to and they get upset if he doesn't show up on time or misses a few days.

"His mother's worried about his lack of direction and has been encouraging him to wean himself off of her financial support. She's told him she won't be around forever and he needs to be able to take care of himself after she's gone. She also told him he'll never find the right woman as long as he's living in his mother's house.

"So, after much encouragement, he decided to go out on his own. He heard about the success of the Wiener Girl's food truck and liked the idea of making eight hundred to a thousand a day selling food to tourists.

"He was ready to go all-in on owning a truck in Key West until he found out that getting a permit was almost impossible. But he didn't give up. He searched the web and found a truck in Saint Augustine. A taco truck with high cash flow and low overhead.

"It was profitable, had all the necessary permits and a good location. Most importantly, he had contacted the owner and she had said she would consider selling it if the price were right.

"He thought it would be a perfect fit. He'd be able to move out of his mom's home and walk into a profitable business of his own. All he needed was enough money to buy it.

"The asking price was thirty-five thousand, and that was about thirty-four thousand more than he had.

"With his job history, there wasn't a bank in Florida that would loan him the money. He had no credit, no collateral, and a spotty work history. Loan officers knew that if they expected to be paid back, they needed to deal with someone else.

"That's when things took a wrong turn. Eager to raise the money he needed, he reached out to an alternative lending source. A man named Stephan Madicof. Known on the streets as Mad Dog.

"At one time, Madicof had worked for Boris. I don't know in what capacity, but my feeling was he couldn't be trusted. To me, he was bad news, someone ready and willing to stab you in the back the first chance he got.

"Boris put up with him. At least until a valuable asset being transported by Madicof disappeared.

"He denied any wrongdoing, but Boris soon learned that Madicof had lied. He had sold the asset and kept the money himself. Boris could no longer trust him and did what he needed to do. He let him live but kicked him out of his organization.

"Madicof stayed in Key West and built an underground business, making sure to stay out of Boris's way. He knows if he were to cross Boris again, it would be harmful to his health.

"So Madicof keeps a low profile and makes his money by offering high-interest loans to people who've been turned down by the banks. People like my friend's son.

"These are the kind of loans where there's no paperwork required, just a promise to pay on time and proof of collateral equal to twice the amount being loaned. The kind of collateral that doesn't leave a paper trail. Gold, diamonds, drugs and the like.

"Anastasia's son didn't have anything he could offer, but he knew who did. His mother had a five-carat diamond ring, a twenty-carat necklace, and several gold coins from the Atocha that had been given to her husband by Mel Fisher.

"Without telling her, he offered these as collateral. He assured Madicof he could get them if they were needed.

"Madicof knew the coins were worth more than he planned to loan the man and the diamonds would be icing on the cake.

"If her son failed to make payments on time, Madicof would be sitting pretty. So he agreed to loan him fifty thousand dollars to be paid back at the rate of five thousand a month for eighteen months.

"Had her son not been in such a rush to get the money, he would have realized he was agreeing to pay back almost twice what he was borrowing. If he missed a payment, the full amount would come due, along with the collateral he had promised.

"He didn't tell his mother any of this. He just told her he'd found a business he was going to buy in Saint Augustine and he was moving there. He said he'd found a place to stay and gave her his new address.

"That was two months ago. Earlier this week, two of Madicof's collectors showed up at Anastasia's home, looking for her son. He had missed the first two payments and they were there to collect the money and the collateral.

"She told them she knew nothing about the loan or the promised collateral. When they threatened her, she mentioned she was a friend of Boris and that he wouldn't be too happy if they hurt her in any way.

"The collectors knew Boris could bring a world of hurt down on them, so they backed off but not before telling her they were going to find her son and he was going to repay the money, either in cash or blood.

"That's when she decided to tell me. She's afraid her son is in over his head and is going to get hurt. She asked me if I knew anyone who might be able to find him before the collectors do and get him out of harm's way.

"Normally, I'd ask Boris to look into this. But he's been

looking for an excuse to settle things permanently with Madicof and I didn't want him to do something in haste that might attract the wrong kind of attention.

"So I started thinking about who I could trust to find my friend's son. The first person I thought of was you. You've proved yourself by finding my daughter when she was in trouble, and you helped Boris with the computer thing.

"I believe you have the skills needed to find this guy, and I trust you to do it discreetly.

"Does this sound like something you would do for me? Find my friend's son before he gets hurt? If you're interested in taking this on, I can text you the son's photo along with his new address. I can pay whatever you want."

I didn't want her money. I didn't need it and if Boris found out I was taking money from her, he wouldn't like it.

I wasn't going to do it to get paid. I was going to do it because she asked me to.

"I can start today. Text me the details. What's the son's name?"

Her answer made me laugh.

Chapter Five

"His name is Waldo. Waldo Raines."

I wasn't sure I had heard her correctly. "You said Waldo, right? And my mission is to find Waldo? Like the guy in the puzzle books?"

Marissa didn't understand. "I'm not sure what you mean by puzzle books. Are they something I need to know about?"

I shook my head, even though I was on the phone and she wouldn't be able to see me do it. "No, it's not important. Just a silly game from days gone by. Text me the details and I'll be on my way."

Before I ended the call, I asked, "Will Abby be meeting me in Saint Augustine?"

I figured she would be since she had spoken to Marissa and given her my phone number. We'd already planned to meet and this was probably the mission she had been reluctant to tell me about.

"No, Abby is not getting involved. She's too close to Boris and there's a chance she might get hurt if this thing goes south. I've haven't told her anything about it. I've got her going to Savannah to work on something else.

"You'll be doing this on your own. I've been told you prefer it that way."

It was true that I liked working these kinds of missions solo, but with Abby it was different. She had proven herself to be a valuable asset, someone who had an uncanny ability to find missing persons. But if this was something that could get her hurt, I didn't want her along.

Marissa promised to text me all the details, including Waldo's photo and last known address. She said she was calling on a burner phone and I could use the number to let her know how things were going.

We ended the call with her telling me to be careful. She said Mad Dog's men had a tendency to hit first and ask questions later.

That was good to know. The doctor who had treated my concussion said to avoid blows to my head. I was all-in on that. I didn't want to take a punch from anyone, anytime.

But sometimes doing your best to avoid something is the surest way to face it head-on.

Chapter Six

Because I thought I'd be driving to Saint Augustine to meet with Abby, I was already packed and ready to go. I had unhooked the RV from shore power, locked all the compartments, brought in the slides, and secured the bathroom door so it wouldn't hit Bob when he visited his litter box.

He had been uneasy most of the morning. Pacing around, voicing his concern with pitiful meows. He had trotted up to me, put his foot on my shoe, and meowed in a way that suggested he was saying, "Not again."

I understood why he might be feeling that way. Our last trip had not gone well. The motorhome had been destroyed and Bob went missing for more than two weeks. Out in the wild with no one to take care of him.

Since getting him back, he had stayed close to me. He didn't like it when I left for any reason and would be waiting at the door when I returned.

His two weeks trying to survive in the wild had been traumatic and he didn't want to go through it again.

I didn't blame him. I didn't want to go through it again either.

I had replaced my destroyed motorhome with the same make and model I had before. It was a few years newer, had three slides instead of just one and a larger bed in the back.

Other than that, it was the same. Same drive train, same

floor plan, and same sounds while on the road. I assured Bob it would be a safe trip and he had nothing to worry about.

But I wasn't so sure. It would be the first long trip in the replacement motorhome and the first since my concussion. The motorhome looked to be in good condition, but you never know for sure. Things could and often do go wrong. Flat tires, overheating, slides that wouldn't go in or out. The kind of problems that could leave a person stranded on the side of the road.

Then there was the question of my blurred vision. That was my biggest concern. If it happened while I was driving, I'd have to get off the road in a hurry. And that's not always easy to do in a thirty-two-foot motorhome. Especially when driving Florida's two-lane back roads where gators lived in the ditches.

But I'd promised Marissa I was going to help her, and that's what I planned to do. I plugged Waldo's last known address into the GPS, fired up the motorhome and headed out.

Eight minutes later, we were on I-75, going north in three lanes of heavy traffic. Just about everyone else was running ten miles over the speed limit. But not us. We stayed in the far right lane, making it easy for drivers in a hurry to get around the big motorhome.

I was making decent time, and if all went as planned I'd be in Saint Augustine well before dark.

But I should have known better. Things never go as planned on I-75 in Florida.

Chapter Seven

We'd gotten through Sarasota and the traffic tie-up at the University Town Center Mall without any problems. The motorhome felt good on the road, and the Ford V-10 was purring like a kitten.

But because the motorhome was new to me, I pulled off I-75 at the Ruskin rest stop and got out to make sure we weren't leaking anything. I didn't want to be dragging a brake, losing air in any of the tires or leaving a trail of sewage behind us.

A quick walk-around showed that all was well. No problems with the motorhome and I was feeling pretty good when I got back in and started it up. Bob, who had been hiding in his pillow fort in the back on my bed, came up front and joined me.

After he settled in on the passenger seat, I put the motorhome in gear and got back on I-75 heading north. It didn't take us long to get up to speed, and we were soon humming along at sixty-five. But not for long.

Thirteen miles later, about three miles south of the intersection of I-4 and I-75, all six lanes of the highway, both north and south, came to a full stop. The road had turned into a parking lot. I figured it was an accident. Probably near the Orlando exit. Undoubtedly caused by a driver in a hurry to get to the mouse kingdom.

I had checked Google maps before leaving and it showed

two routes to Saint Augustine from my home base. The first was to take I-75 to I-4 and follow I-4 to I-95. That way was all interstate and, in theory, would be the fastest way to go.

But not on a Saturday. I-4 is jammed up on normal days, but on weekends, the crowds heading to Disney World and the other theme parks turn I-4 into a demolition derby. Too many cars with too many people in a hurry to get to the same places.

The second option was to stay on I-75 all the way to Ocala then get on US 301 and follow the back roads to Saint Augustine. It would take longer that way as there were a number of small towns with stoplights and speed zones that would slow your progress.

But it would be less stressful than the high-speed traffic on the interstates. That was the way I had chosen to go. If I had a blurred vision episode, the small towns would give me a place to pull over and rest. On the interstate, I'd be a sitting duck if I pulled over onto the shoulder with cars doing eighty just a few feet from my door.

As I was thinking about the route I'd be taking, traffic ahead of me started moving again. It was mostly stop and go at first as inattentive drivers slowed to take photos and videos of the wreck that had caused the traffic jam.

But after everyone put their cell phones away and started driving, we got back up to speed and made our way past the mess of I-4.

According to the GPS, we would arrive at our destination, Waldo's last known address, around seven that evening.

And we would have, had it not been for the sinkhole.

Chapter Eight

We'd almost made it to Ocala when we hit the next traffic jam. As with the first, all six lanes, north and south, had come to a full stop. Ahead of me, as far as I could see, a sea of brake lights as drivers waited for the road to clear.

After twenty minutes, no one had moved. We were all still stopped, wondering what was causing the problem.

With traffic at a standstill, I couldn't see any reason to keep the engine running. It would be a waste of fuel. I turned it off, unbuckled the seat belt and got up to stretch. Bob stood and stretched with me, chirped once, and trotted to the back bedroom. For him, it was nap time.

It had been eight hours since I'd eaten breakfast. Since it looked like we wouldn't be moving anytime soon, and being a little hungry, I decided to do something about it. I started to open the fridge but thought maybe I should first check the news to see how long we might be stuck waiting for the traffic ahead of us to clear.

I turned on the dash radio, set it to AM and turned to News Radio FLA from Tampa. I'd listened to the station before and knew they had news and weather at the top and bottom of the hour.

It was about four minutes until five, so I didn't have to wait long to get the bad news.

The lead story was about a sinkhole that had opened up on I-75 just south of Ocala. The announcer was saying,

"Folks, if you're caught up in the traffic on I-75 between exits 329 on the south and 341 on the north, you might want to pull out your pillows and get comfortable. It looks like you're going to be there for a while.

"According to Florida Department of Transportation, they've closed I-75 near there and rerouted northbound traffic. Unfortunately for those of you who have passed exit 329 but not yet reached 341, the sinkhole will be keeping you from going further.

"DOT is telling us that you'll have to sit it out until they can get their experts on site and decide what to do about the sinkhole. They say to expect a six-hour delay. Maybe more.

"Meanwhile, state police are doing their best to reroute traffic. They are telling us that cars stuck between the two exits have no option except to wait it out. They are advising drivers to stay off the shoulders as they will be used by emergency vehicles.

"For those of you between the exits, settle in. It's going to be a long night."

I shook my head.

With the sinkhole blocking my way, it looked like I wouldn't be making it to Saint Augustine before dark. I might not even make it before sunrise the next day.

Still, being in a motorhome meant I had food to eat, a bed to sleep in, a bathroom when I needed it, and a TV to keep me informed. People stuck in cars ahead of and behind me wouldn't fare so well.

Fortunately, the weather wasn't bad. A little overcast and cool enough to survive without needing to run air conditioners. The cool weather would be the saving grace for people stuck in their cars.

I watched the sea of brake lights ahead of me slowly go out as drivers were getting the news that we'd be stopped for a while. They were turning off their engines to conserve fuel and hoping the people in the cars next to them would be doing the same thing. No one wanted to get carbon monoxide poisoning because they were surrounded by cars at idle with their motors running.

It wasn't long before the news spread and drivers killed their engines. Almost eerily, the constant hum of thousands of tires rolling down the pavement at seventy went away, and the highway was suddenly quiet.

But not for long.

In the distance, I heard a helicopter heading in our direction. Probably a news copter from the Tampa Fox affiliate. If it were their copter, they'd soon be streaming live video to their viewers, providing wall-to-wall coverage of the sinkhole and traffic jam.

Like everyone back home, I wanted to see what this latest disaster wrought.

I turned on the TV across from the couch and tuned to the local Fox affiliate; they were the only nearby station with a copter. As I expected, they had a live view from the air with running commentary from a reporter who was in the passenger seat. He was saying, "You heard me right, I-75 is shut down north and south between exits 329 and 341. Traffic in both directions is backed up for at least thirty miles.

"From what we've been told, the sinkhole is about twelve feet wide, starting on the shoulder of the northbound side and extending to the center of the far-right lane.

"At this time, DOT is protecting the airspace above the

immediate area and we can't get a close-up of the sinkhole. But from where we are, we can see thousands of cars stopped in both directions. People are starting to get out, probably trying to find out more about what is causing the hold-up. Hopefully, some will have TVs and will be able to see our live feed."

The reporter in the copter threw it back to the news desk where the senior anchor, a man in his late fifties, took over. His co-anchor, a blonde in her forties, was nodding her head as he spoke.

"We'll continue to show a live feed from Eagle Eight throughout the evening, but for those who have just tuned in, here's the latest from DOT.

"Around four forty-five this afternoon, a sinkhole opened up on the northbound shoulder of I-75 near mile marker 335. A state trooper notified DOT and we immediately shut down both sides of the highway between exits 329 and 341. Since then, we have dispatched our investigators and when we determine the sinkhole's size and depth, we will consider our next step.

"In the meantime, we have routed both northbound and southbound traffic onto service roads. Traffic on those roads is moving but very slowly. There's a lot of congestion, so if you can, avoid this area."

When the DOT spokesperson ended his report, the news anchor looked at his female co-anchor and asked, "Are there any updates from Eagle Eight?"

She smiled. "Yes Jim, there are. They are now above the sinkhole and we can see the damage it has done to the highway."

The screen filled with video from the copter showing the

gaping hole below it. The reporter in the air was saying, "This thing is pretty big. There's no way they can let anyone drive close to it."

He continued his reporting, showing the long line of cars on the south side going far into the distance.

In mid-sentence, the anchor interrupted the airborne reporter and said, "This just in from DOT. Cars stuck in the southbound lanes will soon be moving. DOT will keep that part of the highway closed, but with the help of state police, will be guiding the stopped traffic onto the shoulder until the next exit."

He looked at his co-host; she nodded and took over where he left off. "DOT says that with more than nine thousand cars backed up on the south side, it will take a few hours to get them all through the area. But at least they will be moving."

"Here's the bad news. Those stopped on the north side between the named exits will not be moving until DOT examines and fills in the hole. No estimate was given for how long that would take."

She closed her segment by saying, "It'll be a long night for those stuck on the north side of I-75."

As I watched the story unfold, I was thinking, '*Only in Florida*.' I-75 had been shut down due to accidents involving beer trucks, alligators, and now sinkholes. I wondered what would be next.

Seeing that I had plenty of time on my hands, I muted the TV and went back to my fridge. I'd stocked it with enough food for two people for a week. Even though I hadn't planned on spending the night on I-75, if I had to, I wouldn't starve.

I wasn't hungry just yet, so I headed to the couch and settled in for a nap.

It wasn't long before Bob joined me.

Chapter Nine

Sometime later, I woke to the sound of tapping on my side door. It wasn't a loud knock and no one was telling me to come out with my hands up, so I figured it probably wasn't the police.

But Bob wasn't so sure. In his mind, whoever was there had come to get him. So when he heard the tapping, he jumped up and headed to the back bedroom. About halfway there, he looked back at me as if to ask, "Aren't you coming?"

When it became apparent to him that I wasn't, he turned and took off. I couldn't see where he went, but I was pretty sure he had decided to hide in his pillow fort.

With Bob in his safe place, I walked over to the kitchen and looked out the small window over the sink. From there, I could see a young woman holding a child near my door. The woman looked to be in her mid-twenties, she was waif-thin, had short black hair and neck tattoos. She was wearing jeans and a Def Leppard tee. The child she was holding looked like it had been crying.

When she saw me looking at her, she pointed to the child and said, "We need your help."

I didn't see anyone else hiding in the bushes behind her, ready to jump me if I opened the door. In fact, there weren't any bushes to hide behind. Just a few feet of recently mowed grass leading up to the chain-link fence separating the highway from the fields beyond.

The woman looked relatively harmless so I opened the door to see what she needed. She looked tired, her eyes were red, and her hair uncombed. She smiled and said, "I hate to bother you, but I wonder if you have any juice. For my baby.

"We've been stuck out here for hours. Nothing to eat or drink. If you have apple or grape juice or even water that you could share, I'd be eternally grateful."

I had juice in the fridge. Water too. Even an unopened box of wine. What I didn't have was someone to talk to other than Bob and so far he hadn't said much during the trip.

I invited her in.

Her first question after stepping inside was, "Do you have a bathroom?"

I did and pointed to it in the back of the coach. She nodded and handed me the child, saying, "You hold her. I'll be right back."

The child, who had been crying when held by her mother, got quiet when she landed in my arms. She studied my face then pointed to the bathroom and squeaked out, "Mommy?"

It sounded like she was asking if I knew where her mommy had gone. Or maybe she was asking if the woman who had been holding her was really her mommy. Maybe she wasn't. Maybe she'd kidnapped the child and was on the run.

Chances were she hadn't.

She was just another one of the thousands of unlucky people stuck on the highway that day. The child was most likely hers.

When the child saw that her mommy wasn't coming back right away, she turned toward me. She stared at me for a few seconds then pointed over my shoulder and said, "TeeVee!"

I'd left it on with the volume down. Bart Simpson was now on the screen, running from Homer.

I was glad the sound was muted.

The child didn't seem to care whether she could hear the Simpsons or not. She just wanted to watch. To her, it was fascinating. Or comforting. Or maybe that's how her mother had raised her. In front of a TV.

When her mother came back from the bathroom, she took the child and thanked me profusely for inviting them in. She apologized for the way she looked, saying, "I'm Sierra. My baby's name is Tasha. We've been on the road for six days. We started in Seattle and are heading to Fort Myers. It's been a long trip."

Still holding the child, she pointed to the couch behind me and asked, "Mind if I sit?"

I didn't and she sat, putting the child on the couch beside her. She looked around then asked, "Are you here alone?"

"Yeah, just me and my cat."

She smiled again. I wasn't convinced it was real. "We used to have a cat. Had to leave him back in Seattle. With my ex. We'll get another one after we've settled in."

She pointed to the kitchen sink. "You have running water?"

I'd forgotten she'd asked about juice; she'd said she and her child were thirsty.

"Yes, there's water. And juice. Apple, orange, white grape. Whatever you want."

She patted her child on the head. "If it's not too much trouble, apple juice. In one cup, so we can share."

I grabbed a Tervis insulated plastic tumbler from the kitchen cabinet, filled it with apple juice and handed it to the woman. She took a long drink then helped her child sip from the cup.

When the glass was empty, she handed it back to me and stood. "Thanks so much for your help."

She picked up her child and headed for the door.

I could have invited her to stay or offered her something to eat. But I didn't. I just watched them leave. She opened the door, stepped out and started walking south.

I didn't check to see which car she got back into.

I should have.

Chapter Ten

About a half-hour after Sierra and her child had gone back to their car, I heard the whoop, whoop, whoop of a large helicopter. It was a sound I recognized from my time in the sandbox. It was a heavy lifter. The kind used to deliver tanks and artillery pieces to hot zones.

Looking up to confirm my suspicions, I was surprised by what I saw. Underneath the copter, a heavy-duty tow strap connected to a large canvas bag swinging slowly in the wind. I was sitting high enough up in the motorhome to see over the row of cars and watch what happened next.

The chopper lowered the bag and it dumped what looked like wet cement into what I assumed was the sinkhole. When the bag was empty, the copter went back the same direction it came from, its rotors again making the familiar whoop, whoop, whoop sound as it passed overhead.

Ten minutes later, it returned with a second load and dumped the contents of the bag in the same place. It reeled the bag in, turned and headed south as before.

Being pretty sure that the copter's runs were sinkhole related, I turned on the TV to see if there were any updates. Back on the same channel as before, the lead anchor was doing a voice-over of a video showing the copter dumping its contents into the sinkhole.

He was saying, "Well folks, it looks like it won't be long before they have that sinkhole taken care of. The DOT geophysicist who examined it said it was stable and had been caused by an irrigation line failure at a nearby agricultural facility.

"DOT filled the hole with a mixture of concrete and silica to create a plug. They said they will soon reopen one lane of northbound traffic letting those who have been stuck there finally leave."

This was good news. We'd soon be moving again.

I turned off the TV and went back to the bathroom to get ready for the road.

When I went in, I noticed the door to the medicine cabinet was slightly open. I knew I hadn't left it that way. If I had, everything in it would have spilled out onto the floor the first time we took a corner.

But there was nothing on the floor. The cabinet hadn't been open while we were moving. So either Bob or I had opened it; or someone else had.

I was pretty sure it wasn't Bob's doing. He's crafty but wouldn't have a reason to jump up on the sink and try to pry open the medicine cabinet. I knew I hadn't opened it either.

That left just one person. Sierra. The woman who had asked me to get juice for her child.

She had gone into the bathroom and stayed in there for at least five minutes. I didn't ask her about it at the time. It wasn't any of my business.

I opened the cabinet door and saw that the two bottles of prescription meds I had in there were gone. One was a thirty-day supply of painkillers and the other an anti-seizure drug.

She had taken both bottles, leaving me without my

medication.

I should have been upset. Not at her but at myself for keeping the drugs in an unlocked cabinet. That was my mistake. I should have locked the drugs away. But in my defense, I never planned on strangers spending time in my bathroom.

I checked to see what else might be missing; everything else seemed to be in order. I was relieved until I remembered that I kept my wallet upfront on the center console between the passenger and driver's seats. It would be in plain view of anyone in the RV.

I took a deep breath and headed up front fearing the worst.

If she'd taken my wallet, she'd have my credit cards, my driver's license and all the cash in it.

Chapter Eleven

My wallet was exactly where I left it and it appeared to be untouched. My cash and credit cards were still in it. My phone, which had been next to my wallet, hadn't been taken either. Both were where I had left them on the console over the engine.

That was the good news. The bad news was she had stolen my meds. The ones prescribed by my doctor to help with my recovery. The pain pills I wouldn't miss much. I had stopped taking them two weeks earlier. But I was still taking the anti-seizures and I wasn't sure what would happen when I stopped taking them.

Each of the pill bottles had a label with my name, my street address, the RX number and the phone number of the CVS that filled the prescription. Just about everything an identity thief would need.

She knew I was on the road and if she was so inclined, she could go to my home. The address was on the pill bottle. But if she went there intending to break in, she'd be disappointed. There was no home there. Only the cement slab I parked my motorhome on when I wasn't traveling. There was nothing there for her to steal.

But if she called CVS claiming to be me, being able to give them my name, home address and the RX number from the bottles, she might be able to get a refill on the meds. I needed to make sure that didn't happen.

I grabbed my phone, scanned through my recent call list and found the text from CVS telling me my prescription was ready. The message included the phone number of the store in case I had questions. I called it.

After waiting on hold for seven minutes, I was able to speak to Phil in the pharmacy department. I told him what had happened. That my meds had been stolen and I was worried the thief might try to get an early refill.

Phil said he understood and after I gave him my birth date, phone number, and CVS card number, he put an immediate hold on both prescriptions. They could not be refilled under any circumstances by anyone, including me.

I understood why they handled it that way. If they did it differently, drug addicts could claim their pills were stolen and get refills almost any time. Even if they had stolen the pill bottles themselves.

I wasn't a drug addict and didn't need a refill on the pain pills. But the seizure drug was a different story. I wasn't sure what would happen if I suddenly stopped taking them.

I asked the pharmacist what he thought and he said if my doctor had prescribed the pills, I should take them as indicated. He said to call the doctor and have him write a new prescription and they would fill it.

It was Saturday evening, almost closing time at the pharmacy. There was no chance I could reach my doctor and get him to write a new prescription on a weekend. I didn't need to explain this to Phil; I just thanked him for his help and ended the call.

I made a mental note to call my doctor on Monday and to get a lock for the medicine cabinet in my bathroom.

Cars in the lane to the left to me had started to inch

forward and I knew that as soon as that lane cleared, we would be next.

I moved up to the driver's seat from the couch and watched the parade of cars slowly passing by. I was looking for the woman who had been in my motorhome. If I saw her in a car, I'd get her plate number. I wanted to have it in case something came up with the missing drugs.

I checked the occupants of each car as it passed but didn't see her in any of them. The sun had set two hours earlier, and it was pretty dark. The street lights didn't help much; they just created a reflected glare on the windows of the cars as they went by.

If she'd been in one of them, I hadn't seen her. But maybe she was behind me, in the same lane I was in. If that were the case, my only chance of finding her would be to pull over and watch as cars went by.

I didn't want to do that. I just wanted to be on my way. But then I remembered she'd said she was heading to Fort Myers. If that were true, she'd be in the southbound lane, not the north one like I was. When traffic was stopped in both directions, she could have easily walked across the median to get to my motorhome.

Or maybe she was in the northbound lane all along and someone else was driving her car. She could have ducked down when they went by and I wouldn't have seen her.

Either way, I'd spent too much time worrying about her. She was gone, the pills were gone, and I probably wouldn't be seeing her again. I had to write it off as a mistake. One I wouldn't make again. No picking up strangers, at least until the meds in the bathroom were secured.

When the last car in the next lane over went by, a state

trooper at the head of the lane I was in started directing us over onto the far left lane. It was single file and slow, but at least we were moving.

As we got close to the sinkhole, just about every car slowed to take a photo of the army of emergency vehicles with flashing lights surrounding the newly poured concrete. I tried my best not to look but failed. Like everyone else, I wanted to see the hole that had held us up for nearly six hours.

After passing it by, the highway opened up to three lanes, moving fast going north. I stayed in the far right lane, knowing I'd soon be taking the exit to highway 301 after passing Ocala.

I figured that being that late in the day, the back road to Saint Augustine wouldn't be too busy.

I was wrong.

Chapter Twelve

Driving the back roads of Florida after dark is never a good idea because that's when the animals come out. The big ones like wild boars that can weigh up to three hundred pounds and travel in packs. And gators moving from one water source to another. And deer that often run out directly in front of you then freeze creating an unmissable target.

Hit any of these while rolling down the road at sixty plus and you're looking at some major damage. To both you and the critter you hit.

I wanted to avoid that, so my plan was to stop at the first Walmart I found and spend the night in their parking lot. I'd been up since six that morning and on the road twelve hours. Most of those had been spent waiting for traffic to clear. But they still added up.

The back road I was on didn't have any street lights. Plenty of woods and swamp on both sides. Great hiding places for the kind of wildlife that could ruin the rest of my night. Or put me back in the hospital.

That was something I wanted to avoid, so I was happy when I got to the Walmart Super Center in Palatka and saw several RVs parked in the lot. That meant the store allowed overnight parking, and it was something I needed to do.

I pulled in and parked close to a truck camper on a white Ford diesel dually, being sure to leave plenty of room between us. He wanted his privacy and I wanted mine.

After getting the motorhome closed up for the night and making sure Bob had food, water, and a clean litter box, I headed across the lot to Walmart's front doors. I was hungry and didn't want to fire up the generator which I would need to run the microwave to heat up a frozen dinner. I wanted something quick and easy and knew that Walmart had just the thing.

Inside, I headed to the deli at the back of the store. I knew it would be closed at that hour. They wouldn't be cutting meat or shoveling out chicken wings that late in the day, but there would be tubs of cold fried chicken and veggies in their coolers.

I grabbed an eight-ounce tub of cowboy beans, a tub of coleslaw, and a chicken breast. It would be a quick and easy meal, and if I ate the beans and slaw right out of the containers, there wouldn't be much to clean up.

After checking out, I headed back to the motorhome. Two other RVs had pulled in while I was in the store; an older one painted all black with a row of solar panels mounted on the side and next to it a fairly new Coachmen Mirada. They'd parked close to each other, side by side. They were probably traveling together. Maybe even heading to Saint Augustine like I was.

After I ate, I headed to bed. I usually sleep well when I'm on the road. Driving for hours, with the constant rocking and swaying of the motorhome, makes sleep easy when you stop for the evening. It works that way for both me and Bob.

But not that night. I didn't sleep much. And when I did, I kept having dreams about strangers coming into my RV.

In one of them, the wicked witch of the west had brought in some of her friends and made themselves home. When I confronted her, she said, "You don't live here anymore. Leave."

After waking up from that one, I got out of bed and rechecked the locks to make sure no one was coming in.

I had a few more interesting dreams after that one, most involving strangers either already inside the RV or outside trying to break in. All were unsettling. For both me and Bob.

The dreams could have been my subconscious trying to reconcile with the woman who had stolen my meds.

Or maybe it was the cowboy beans and coleslaw I ate right before I slept.

Either way, I hadn't got the sleep I needed for what was going to happen the next day.

When morning finally came, I pulled on shorts and a tee and headed back into Walmart. I was hungry and, like the night before, didn't feel like cooking in the RV. I wanted a quick bite of something filling, something that I didn't have to clean up after.

I just wanted to eat and get on the road.

Inside Walmart, I headed to the bakery section and grabbed a blueberry muffin and a cheese Danish. To wash them down and get a little caffeine in my system, I grabbed a cold bottle of Coke and headed to the self-check.

After paying and getting back to the RV, Bob was waiting for me at the door. He looked at the grocery bag I was carrying and said, "Meooow?"

I was pretty sure he was asking if I had gotten anything for him. I hadn't, but I did have treats in the top drawer near the kitchen sink. I pulled out the bag of treats and tossed two down the hallway. He immediately launched after them.

Chasing his food before he ate it was one of his favorite things.

While he was crunching on his treats, I sat at the table and ate the muffin followed by half of the cheese Danish. Both were pretty good. Or maybe I was too hungry to tell the difference between good and bad.

After eating, I raised all the blinds, secured the doors and cabinets and got ready to head to Saint Augustine. I'd programmed the GPS with Waldo's last known address the day before. It showed that it would take me at least two hours to get there. Back roads all the way.

When Bob heard me start the engine, he headed back to his pillow fort. He needed to catch up on the sleep he had missed out on the night before.

I did, too, but sleep would have to wait.

I needed to get to Saint Augustine and find Waldo.

Chapter Thirteen

Following the spoken directions from the GPS, it took me less than two hours to get to the address Waldo's mother had given to Marissa.

I was thinking that, being new to the area, Waldo would have gotten a place at a tourist court where they rented rooms by the week or month. Or maybe if he planned to stay longer, he'd rent an apartment. Either way, I had his address and the GPS took me to it.

When it said, "You have arrived at your destination," I wasn't too surprised to see that he had chosen to live in a place called the Shady Haven Trailer Park. According to the sign on the marquee, they rented furnished trailers by the week and offered discounted monthly rates. Utilities included.

Shady Haven was the kind of place that would be affordable, wouldn't require a long-term lease, and was turn-key as far as utilities and furniture were concerned. It would be an ideal place to hang your hat if you were new to the area and on a limited budget. Or if you were a transient just passing through.

I pulled into the entrance and parked near a small, white cinder block building. It had a sign that said it was the office.

Since the text with Waldo's address didn't include a trailer number, I wanted to see if the park manager could tell me which one was his.

When I reached the door of the office, there was a sign that said, "Ring buzzer for manager." To the left of the sign was a brown doorbell button. I pushed it and, somewhere in the distance, I heard a buzzer. Hopefully, the manager would hear it as well.

Five minutes later, a beige golf cart came rolling up from deep within the park. The driver, a woman who looked to be in her sixties, was wearing an ankle-length dress with buttons down the front. It was bright pink and could have been either a housecoat or a moo moo. I didn't know the difference and it really didn't matter.

She had a cigarette in one hand and on the seat beside her a clipboard.

She looked me over and then pointed to my RV. "That yours?"

I nodded. "Yes ma'am, it is."

"You looking for a place to park it?"

I shook my head. "No ma'am, I'm not. I'm looking for a friend of mine. Name's Waldo and he told me he was staying here. I just don't know which trailer he's in."

The woman again pointed to my motorhome and asked, "How long is that thing? Thirty, thirty-two, maybe longer?"

I didn't know why she was asking, but I wanted to stay on her good side, so I said, "It's thirty-two feet, bumper to bumper."

She nodded. "Got slides, right?"

"Yes ma'am, it does. Three of them."

She took a long drag on her cig then asked, "You traveling alone? Or you got people with you?"

"I'm alone, ma'am. It's just me. No one else."

She'd been asking questions about me and my motorhome and hadn't yet told me which trailer Waldo was in. I needed to find out, so I steered the conversation back to him. "So, my friend, Waldo, he said I could find him here. I know you probably have something better to do than stand out here in the sun, so if you can tell me which one he's in, I'll be on my way."

The woman took another long drag on her cigarette. She coughed once and said, "We got a Waldo here. Maybe more than one. But I can't rightly remember which trailer he's in."

She paused, took another drag, coughed again, and said, "We don't give out information about our guests to strangers. Most of them like it that way. But if you was staying here, that'd be different. You'd be a resident and I could probably help you out. We have a nice site back there that your RV would fit into. Full hookups.

"Course if you don't want to stay here, that's fine by me. But unless you are a paying guest, I can't tell you anything about Waldo.

"Now, if you was to pay in advance for a month, I could probably tell you how to find him."

She took a long pull on her cig and waited to see if I got the message.

I did. She wasn't going to tell me where anything was unless I paid her a month's rent in advance. Even if I didn't plan on staying a single day, it'd still cost me a month's rent. She had me over a barrel and she knew it.

I smiled, nodded toward my motorhome and said, "Now that I think about it, I do need a place to park it while I'm in town. I'm not sure how long I'll be here, but maybe I should go ahead and pay for a month. How much will that be?"

She dropped what remained of her cigarette to the ground, rubbed it out with her sandal and picked up the clipboard. She ran her finger down the page, stopped at a line number I couldn't see, and said, "I can put you in site seventy-one. It's near the back and you'll like the neighbors. The monthly rate is seven hundred. Paid in advance in cash."

The price wasn't bad. In fact, it was pretty good for a full hookup site in a Florida tourist town like Saint Augustine. I didn't try to bargain her down. I pointed to my RV and said, "I'll go get your money."

She nodded and I walked away. As usual, Bob met me at the door. He stretched out his front paws and tapped me on my shoe with his left one. He was showing he was glad I was back.

I didn't stay long though. I pulled seven hundred dollars from the safe I have hidden under the bed and went outside to pay the rent.

I handed the woman the cash, and after she carefully counted the bills, she handed me a sheet of paper with the heading, "Shady Haven Code of Conduct."

I scanned the page and saw the rules included "No open fires," "No unleashed pets" and "No shooting."

On the top of the page she had written, "Site seventy-one." She handed me a bright green card with the site number written on the top line and the date my next rent would be due below it. She said, "Put this on the driver's side of your windshield. It'll let us know you have paid and belong here."

She pointed to her golf cart. "I'll escort you back to your site. Follow me."

She hopped into her cart, or at least hopped the best way

a person can when wearing a full-length house robe, and waited for me to start my motorhome.

As soon as she heard my engine, she took off in her cart and I followed her to site seventy-one. When we got there, she sat in her cart and watched as I backed the motorhome into the site. After I had it positioned the way I wanted, I got out and went over to talk to her.

Before I could say anything, she said, "Waldo is in site seventy-three. Next door to you. Don't hurt him."

And with that, she drove off.

Chapter Fourteen

I didn't really know what Waldo looked like. I had the photo that had been texted to me, but didn't know when it was taken or if he'd grown a beard or changed his hair color since then.

All I knew, at least what I thought I knew, was he was living in the trailer next door to my RV, according to the park manager. It was possible she had lied or sent me to a trailer where a different Waldo lived.

I needed to find out.

Before heading over to his presumed trailer, I took a few minutes to hook up to shore power and turn on the air conditioner. I didn't want it to get too hot for Bob while I was gone. Not knowing how long I'd be staying in Shady Haven, I went ahead and ran the three slide rooms out. This would give me a lot more room inside and make it easier for Bob to get to his favorite places.

With Bob and the RV taken care of, I headed to the trailer next door where Waldo was supposed to be staying.

Like most of the trailers in the park, his was older, probably from the sixties, back when they were called mobile homes. They had wheels and were mobile in the sense that they could be delivered to a mobile home park. Usually, the wheels were removed soon after.

I couldn't tell whether they were still on Waldo's trailer or not. Like all the others in the park, his had faux brick skirting hiding whatever was underneath. I assumed the park's owners thought the skirting gave the place a bit of class. I guess it did.

Waldo's trailer was a single wide, like most of the others in the park. His was white with pastel-blue accents. There was a small deck on the front connected to a walkway that led to his front door, which was actually on the side of the trailer, meaning his front door was really his side door.

The trailer number, seventy-three, was painted on the street in front of the single parking space next to the deck. Having numbers displayed like this made it easy to find the right trailer. That was kind of important in a place like Shady Haven where there might be a hundred or more identical homes.

There wasn't a car parked in Waldo's driveway. It could have meant he wasn't home or that he didn't have a car. Either way, I was going to find out.

I went up the steps onto the deck, walked over to the side door, and knocked three times. Thirty seconds later, I knocked again. After two minutes, no one had come to the door.

I hadn't heard any movement inside, nor did I see anyone peeking out the windows. Being a Sunday morning, it was possible that Waldo had gone to church. Maybe all I needed to do was to wait for his return.

But I wasn't in the mood for waiting. I'd had my fill of that on the highway the previous day. I looked around to make sure no one was watching, then tried Waldo's door. It was locked.

Still up on his deck, I walked over to the nearest window and peeked in. I was surprised to see how nice the furnishings were. New couch and matching chair. Side tables with matching lamps, and a colorful woven rug between the couch and the front door. But no Waldo.

I tried to open the window, but it was locked. Not giving up, I went around to all the other windows and tried each. Like the first, they were locked.

I couldn't look into what I assumed was the bedroom window at the back of the trailer. It was raised higher than the others, keeping private whatever the occupants inside might be inclined to do on the bed.

If Waldo had been out the night before, he might be still sleeping or passed out if he partied a little too hard. I felt it was my duty to check on him, to make sure he didn't need medical attention.

I looked around the trailer trying to find something I could stand on so I could look into the bedroom window. Not seeing anything upfront or on the side, I walked to the back and saw a lone cinder block with a flower pot on top. The block was about twelve inches tall and six inches wide.

I figured if I stood it on its end and climbed up on it, I would have enough elevation to look into the bedroom window.

That's what I was doing when a male voice behind me asked, "What are you doing peeping into that window?"

I didn't answer right away. I wanted to see if Waldo was on his bed. That was a mistake.

Chapter Fifteen

Still trying to balance myself on the narrow cinder block, I turned to see who the voice behind me belonged to.

The man standing on the deck attached to the trailer next to Waldo's looked a lot like one of the drill sergeants who had been assigned to us during basic training.

He had the same kind of crew cut, same muscles and stance, and same demeanor. Standing there with his arms crossed, I half expected him to bark out an order. Something like, "Give me twenty push ups." I'd heard that just about every day in boot camp.

Except this wasn't boot camp. This was a trailer park, and the man wasn't my drill sergeant. Still, as a neighbor, he had a right to know why a peeping Tom was trying to look into Waldo's bedroom window.

When I didn't answer right away, he asked, "You some kind of prevert, trying to look in that window?"

I shook my head, a little off-balance as I was doing my best not to fall off the upended cinder block. With one hand against the trailer for support, I said, "No, I'm not a pervert. I'm just looking for Waldo. This is his trailer, right?"

Mister gravel voice didn't answer my question. Instead, he asked one of his own. "Why are you looking for him?"

I stepped down off the cinder block, walked over to the neighbor's trailer and held out my hand. "Name's Walker. Yours?"

He frowned, looked at my hand but didn't shake it. Instead, he said, "You didn't answer my question. Why are you looking for Waldo?"

Instead of answering, I asked, "When's the last time you saw him?"

He shook his head. "Nope, I'm not telling you anything until you tell me why you're looking for him."

Without thinking it through, I answered, "I'm trying to save his life."

Telling him that had been a mistake. Had I had thought about it before I opened my mouth, I would have known it would lead to more questions. But it was too late. I'd said too much too soon.

I waited, expecting the man to ask the logical follow-up. Like why did I think Waldo needed someone to save his life and why me?

But he didn't ask either of those questions. Instead, he said, "They call me Raif. You with those two other fellows who came looking for him?"

It was a question I didn't want to hear. If Mad Dog's guys already found Waldo, there wasn't much I could do about it except to pack up and go home. But maybe they hadn't found him yet. Maybe Raif knew where he was.

"No, I'm not with those guys. I'm here on my own."

He smiled. "So you say you're here to save Waldo, huh? I'm guessing by the way you're dressed you're telling the truth about not being with the other two. So, who you working for?"

I decided that telling him the truth was the best way to go.

"His mother. She sent me up here to find him. To keep him from getting hurt."

Raif nodded. "Waldo talked about her. Said she told him it was time to go out on his own. I guess that's why he came up here. To get a fresh start.

"But that doesn't explain why those two guys came to visit him. They rolled up in a black Escalade with dark-tinted windows. Stepped out wearing all black, black pants, black tees under black sports jackets. Reminded me of what Mafia enforcers are supposed to look like.

"So tell me, why would two guys like that be looking for Waldo? What'd he do?"

If Mad Dog's men were in town, hot on Waldo's trail, I needed to have someone on my side. Someone who could help me find him first. Someone like Raif.

I took a deep breath and said, "Waldo borrowed money from a man named Madicof. He told him he needed it to buy a business up here in Saint Augustine. He said it was an all-cash kind of place and he wouldn't have any problem paying him back.

"But he missed the first two payments and Madicof sent his guys up here to educate him. To show him why it was unhealthy not to make payments as agreed.

"That's why I'm here. To make sure I get to Waldo before Madicof's guys do. So, do you know where he is?"

Raif picked up a beer can that was on the deck railing. He took a sip, crushed the can and dropped it into a wire basket near the front of his deck. It was nearly full of similarly crushed cans.

He looked over at me, pointed at the basket and said, "We take recycling seriously around here. But those two goons, they didn't. They dumped their trash in Waldo's driveway. Beer cans and cigarette butts.

"When I saw them do that, I knew it wouldn't be me who told them anything about Waldo. When they asked about him, I said that as far as I knew, he had moved out a week earlier. He didn't tell me where he was going.

"They tried to get me to tell them more, but I didn't. I wasn't afraid of them. I've dealt with people like them before."

He reached into his pocket and pulled out a silver revolver. It looked like a thirty-eight. He flipped open the cylinder and spun it, showing me that it was loaded. "When I retired from the force, I kept this. Most of the time, it's inside. But when I see someone peeping into a bedroom window, I get the gun. You never know when you might need to protect yourself."

He paused, and I had two questions. The first was, "So Waldo moved? You're saying he doesn't live here anymore?"

Raif shook his head. "Before I answer that, why don't you and I take a little walk? Be a good chance to get to know each other a little better."

He looked over my shoulder and asked, "Where's your car? I didn't see you drive up in one."

I pointed behind me. "I came here in my RV this morning. Didn't plan to stay. But the manager wouldn't tell me which trailer Waldo was in unless I was a paying guest. So I gave her a month's rent and she sent me back here."

Raif laughed. "You're talking about the woman in the golf cart? She made you pay for a month? In cash. Am I right?"

I nodded. "Yeah, a month, in cash, upfront."

He shook his head. "You got played. That woman is not the manager. She's more like the assistant to the assistant park host. Her name is Ada and her real job is to drive around and make sure all the trash cans are empty and that vagrants haven't moved into any of the empty trailers.

"The real manager lives off-site and doesn't work on Sundays. When he's not here, Ada thinks she's in charge. She tries to be the one who checks in new guests and whenever she thinks she can get away with it, she'll charge them full price, get the money in cash, and move them to a spot in the back where the real manager won't see them.

"She'll pocket the cash and think no one's the wiser. But those of us who've been here a while know what's going on."

Raif didn't wait for me to ask why if everyone knew what was going on no one had reported her to the manager. Instead, he asked, "We going for a walk or not?"

After sitting in the driver's seat of the motorhome for too many hours the previous day, a walk sounded good, especially if it meant I might get some useful information that would help me find Waldo.

"Yeah, let's walk. Do I need to bring anything?"

He nodded. "Bring enough cash to buy a twelve pack. Let me put this gun away and I'll meet you in front of your RV."

He went inside and I went back to my motorhome to get my wallet. Bob met me at the door, stretching out to his full length to show me how big he was. He meowed loudly and started to walk toward the back of the motorhome. About halfway there, he stopped, looked over his shoulder and when he saw that I wasn't following, he meowed again. This time much louder.

I'd lived with him long enough to know what those loud

meows meant. He was saying, "Check my food bowl."

I followed him to the bathroom, where I kept his bowls and topped them off. Then I went back up front, grabbed my wallet and sunglasses and stepped outside.

Raif was waiting for me. He said, "See if you can keep up."

He took off walking at a fairly impressive pace for a man his age, and I did my best to stay close. I was hoping he'd want to talk while we walked, maybe he'd tell me more about Waldo.

But he didn't. He just walked. Like a man on a mission.

On my drive in earlier that morning, I had passed several convenience and liquor stores with signs saying they had cold beer. One was just across the street from Shady Haven. Nearby, there was an Irish pub. It, too, had a sign about cold beer. And if that weren't enough, there was a medical marijuana dispensary a few doors down.

I wasn't sure which of these places Raif was heading to, so I just followed. My plan was as soon as we got the beer, I'd start asking questions. The first would be, "What was the name of the taco stand that Waldo was buying?"

If he had told me and I had gone there on my own, things would have turned out differently. For both of us.

Chapter Sixteen

After not saying anything for the first ten minutes of our walk, Raif opened up and started asking me questions. He wanted to know how long I'd been on the road, whether I lived in my RV full time or not, and what I did for a living.

I figured he was asking because he wanted to be sure I wasn't with the bad guys, so I answered honestly. I told him I'd been living in the RV full time for over a year and had traveled all over Florida in it. As for a job, I told him I was semi-retired.

When he asked what "semi-retired" meant, I told him I'd lost my job in the corporate world and was living off my savings until I decided what to do next.

His next question was, "You were in the military, right? I'm guessing army. Maybe doing recon?"

I nodded. "Yeah, did two tours. How'd you know?"

"I can tell by the way you walk. The way you answer questions. The way you talk. Even the way you dress. They're all clues to who you are."

He continued. "I've been around enough army guys to see a pattern. I can usually tell which ones have seen action, which ones were the leaders, and which ones were the followers."

He didn't tell me which pattern I fit, and I didn't ask.

His next question was easier. "You're traveling alone, right? No one else with you?"

I wasn't sure why he wanted to know, but it seemed to be a question a lot of people asked, especially before they got into the RV with me.

"Yeah, it's just me. And my cat. Mango Bob."

Raif squinted. "You have a cat? Living in the RV with you? An ex-army guy with a cat? How's that working out?"

I thought about it for a moment before I answered, then said, "Living with him is a lot easier than living with some of the people I've known. As long as he has food, water, and a clean litter box, he's happy.

"I've been around people who never were happy. No matter where they were, how much they had, how great their life was, they weren't happy. Being around them made me miserable.

"So if it came to choosing, I'd stick with the cat."

Raif nodded. "I know what you mean. I've got a puppy living with me. Name's Eddie. He's a Yorkie but he thinks he's a big dog, like a shepherd or mastiff. He's not afraid of anything and sometimes that gets him in trouble.

"Me and Eddie, we usually walk twice a day. Early in the morning and again right before sunset. He'd be out walking with us right now except we've got to cross the highway and I don't want to chance it with him.

"He's a good dog. Don't want to lose him."

I felt the same way about Bob. I didn't want to lose him either. I'd come very close to never seeing him again after the accident. It was a miserable time for both of us.

Raif and I had been on the sidewalk going west from Shady Haven. We'd gone about a mile when we reached US 16. The sidewalk stopped at the intersection and I wondered which way we'd be going. Before I could ask, Raif pointed across the highway and said, "That way."

There was a crosswalk, but traffic was heavy, in both directions. Cars, trucks, and motorcycles. All going too fast. It would be too dangerous to try to cross until the light turned red. While we were waiting, Raif pointed to a gas station across the street; the Pump & Munch.

It struck me as a funny name, but it fit their business model. You could pump gas outside and then go inside to find things to munch on. Candy, donuts, and several varieties of jerky; typical convenience store fare. It wouldn't necessarily be good for you, but it would be cheap and you could wash it down with cold pop or beer from the coolers at the rear of the store.

When the crosswalk finally told us it was safe to go, we hurried across the road and into the Pump & Munch parking lot. Being a Sunday morning, business was slow. There were a few cars pumping gas, but it didn't look like anyone was going into the store.

When we got inside, we had the place pretty much to ourselves. The clerk behind the register, a man who might have been a Pakistani, greeted us by saying, "Raif, my good buddy. Always a pleasure to see you. What can I get for you today?"

Raif pointed to the coolers in the back. "You know why I'm here, Babar. Cold beer. I heard you might have some."

The clerk, whose name was apparently Babar, laughed and said, "Yes, cold beer is one of the things we always have. We stock it special for you."

I followed Raif as he walked to the back of the store. He opened one of the cooler doors and grabbed a twelve-pack of

Bud. He looked at me. "This work for you?"

I nodded.

With beer in hand, we headed to the front of the store. Raif put the cold twelve-pack on the counter and pointed to me. "Babar, this is my new friend, Walker. He's paying."

I nodded and reached for my wallet. But before I could get it out, a young kid, probably in his early twenties, wearing baggy pants and a dirty white T-shirt, walked in with a gun. He fired a round into the ceiling, then pointed the gun at the three of us and said, "Don't nobody do nothing stupid!"

I didn't say anything, but I was thinking the only person doing something stupid was the kid with the gun. Trying to rob a convenience store early on a Sunday morning, when they didn't have much money in the register, wasn't the smartest thing.

But apparently the kid hadn't thought it through. He wanted money, and maybe he figured because there wouldn't be many people in the store that early in the morning, he could get away with it.

He waved the gun in Babar's direction. "Empty the register. Put the cash in a bag."

Babar looked at Raif, and he nodded his head just slightly. I was thinking Raif was telling him to just do what the kid said. Don't make trouble. Just give him the money.

Babar got the message. He opened the register and started emptying the cash trays. While the gunman watched Babar with the money, Raif slowly reached up and pulled me a few inches away from the counter. The punk who was robbing the store saw him do it. He pointed the gun at Raif and said, "Don't try it, old man. This thing is loaded and I know how to use it."

Raif put both hands up in the air, palms facing the gunman, signaling he was in surrender mode. He wasn't going to do anything.

It didn't take long for Babar to get all the money from the register and stack it up on the counter. It didn't look like much. A few tens and twenties, but mostly fives and ones. Probably not more than three hundred dollars.

The gunman looked at the money, looked up at Babar and said, "Put it in a bag. But no funny stuff or you'll be the first to die."

Babar slowly reached under the counter and came up with a plastic bag. He picked up the money and started stuffing it in. When he was done, he set the bag on the counter and took a step back.

If the kid with the gun had been smart, he would have grabbed the money and headed for the door. But smart didn't seem to be in his wheelhouse. Instead of leaving, he turned his gun on me and said, "Hand over your wallet."

It was still in my pocket; I hadn't had time to get it out to pay for the beer. The thing was I wanted to keep it there. I didn't want to hand it over to the kid. Or anyone else. It had my cash, credit cards and driver's license in it, and I didn't want to be on the road without them.

So instead of reaching into my pocket, I shook my head and started to say, "Try to take it from me, see what happens."

Before I got the words out, he turned his attention to the gold chain with a small cross hanging from Raif's neck. He said, "I'm taking the chain, old man."

With the gun in his right hand, he walked over to Raif,

close enough to grab the cross. Like I said earlier, Raif had gray hair. He looked to be in his early sixties and his age showed in his face. From the gunman's perspective, he looked like an easy mark. An old man who wouldn't give him any trouble.

But he was wrong.

Chapter Seventeen

It was over quickly.

When the punk with the gun reached out to grab the gold chain, Raif surprised him with a snap punch to the solar plexus. The kid doubled over and, when he did, Raif grabbed his gun hand and bent it toward the ceiling until his wrist snapped.

Howling in pain, the kid dropped the gun and bent over to catch his breath. Raif could have left him alone at that point. The kid no longer had the gun and he didn't pose an immediate threat. His attempted robbery had gone south and instead of getting money, he had gotten a broken wrist and maybe a fractured rib.

But Raif didn't end it. He grabbed the kid by the back of his head and slammed his face down onto the counter, breaking his nose and knocking him out.

The kid slid to the floor, still breathing but just barely.

Raif poked him with his foot and, after hearing him groan, said, "Kid, you ain't going to die. Not yet. That might change when they get you down to the jailhouse."

He looked up at Babar and said, "Give me one of those zip ties you keep under the counter."

Babar reached under the counter and came up with a bright yellow zip tie about two feet long. After he handed it to Raif, he asked, "You want me to make the call?"

"Yeah, call them. Tell them there is an armed robbery in progress. They'll get here quicker."

While Babar was on the phone with 9-1-1, Raif zip tied the kid's hands behind his back. When he was done, he reached over the counter and grabbed two empty plastic bags. He used one as a glove to pick up the kid's gun, not wanting to get his own fingerprints on it. He dropped the gun into the second bag and tied off the top. He handed it to Babar and said, "You know the drill. Hold on to this until they arrive."

Raif took a deep breath and said, "Walker and I will be out back. When the police get here, tell them what happened and show the video from the security cam. If they need to talk to us, tell them where we are."

He pointed at me. "Pay the man for the beer before we get robbed again."

I pulled out a twenty, dropped it on the counter and said, "Keep the change."

Babar slid the twenty back. "No charge. It's on the house. For services rendered."

I left the bill on the counter and followed Raif out the front door. We could hear sirens in the distance, it sounded like they were getting closer.

Raif walked around to the back of the building and took a seat on a concrete bench under the branches of a gumbo limbo tree. He peeled the back off the twelve-pack and pulled out a beer.

He opened it, took a drink and looked at me. "What are you waiting for? Have a seat. Drink with me."

I wasn't sure drinking a few beers right before we talked to the police was a good idea. But after the long walk and the

74

excitement in the store, a cold beer sounded pretty good to me.

I sat down on the bench, grabbed a beer and took a sip. I wasn't much of a beer drinker. I'd never liked the taste, but on that day, I did. My throat was dry and the cold beer gave me the relief I needed. After a few more sips, I had the courage to ask Raif a question that I was pretty sure was going to upset him.

"Don't you think you were a little hard on the kid? After you'd broken his wrist and he dropped the gun, maybe you didn't need to slam his head down on the counter."

Raif nodded, took a long drink from his beer, and set it on the bench between us. He unbuttoned the top three buttons on his shirt and pulled it open so I could see his chest. He pointed at a coin-sized scar and said, "I've got three of these. Bullet holes. Got them when I was too soft on a kid like the one in there."

The first scar was inches from his heart. A little closer and he probably wouldn't have survived.

I nodded and said, "Tell me about it."

He sipped his beer and said, "This place we're sitting? It used to be Sanders grocery. A small family-owned business. Old man Sanders and his wife worked here. He made sure the shelves were stocked, she kept the books, and their son, Noah, ran the register when he wasn't in school.

"I was a detective at the time. Wearing street clothes, no vest and in an unmarked car. A call came in over the radio saying there was a robbery in progress at Sanders. I was only three miles out so I put the blues on and headed that way.

"When I pulled into the lot, a man, about the same age as the one we dealt with in there, came out of the store carrying a money bag in one hand and a gun in the other.

"I got out of my car, pulled my gun and told him to drop his and put up his hands. He didn't comply. Instead, he shook his head and shrugged. I told him a second time to drop his gun and raise his hands.

"That second time, it looked like he was going to comply. He dropped the money and started to raise his hands.

"I thought he was giving up. But I was wrong. He still had his gun, and with his hands raised to his chest, he pointed it at me and started firing. He kept shooting until the gun was empty.

"I was hit in three places. My right arm, my chest and just below my ear. The chest wound was the worst; I was losing blood and had a hard time breathing. I wanted to return fire, but my gun hand wouldn't work. The bullet to my arm had made it useless.

"After the kid saw that I couldn't shoot back, he walked over, pointed his gun at my head and pulled the trigger. I thought for sure I was a goner. But nothing happened. His gun was empty.

"Hearing sirens in the distance, the kid ran. Leaving me in the parking lot to die. He and I both thought I was a goner.

"But I wasn't. Backup arrived a few minutes later and I was still breathing. They took me to the hospital and I was rushed into surgery where they were able to remove two of the bullets. The third one, the one nearest my heart, had shattered my sternum. They would have to get it out later.

"The doctor said I died twice during surgery. Both times they were able to revive me. I don't remember dying. I'd lost a lot of blood and was out of it.

"I spent the next six weeks in the hospital, undergoing six more operations to try to remove bullet fragments near my heart. They got most of them but not all. I still have a few inside me.

"After the doctors were sure I would survive, they kept me another two months before they sent me home. The first month was mostly in a wheelchair. The second was physical therapy."

Raif took another pull from now nearly empty beer. "I didn't get the full report on the shooting until they released me.

"The surveillance video showed the kid walking into the store with the gun, a Glock 17. He pointed it a pregnant woman who was checking out and shot her point-blank. She was dead before she hit the floor.

"He turned the gun toward the register and demanded young Noah give him the money.

"He didn't hesitate. He grabbed a paper bag and filled it with cash. When he put it on the counter, the punk shot him dead.

"Hearing the shots from the back of the store, Mr. Sanders ran to the front. He barely had time to see the pregnant woman dead on the floor when he, too, was shot. He died twenty minutes later.

"Three bullets, three dead. The Glock 17 still had fourteen rounds in the clip. Those were the ones he fired at me. The ones that almost took my life like the lives he'd taken in the store.

"Internal Affairs did a full investigation and said that when I saw the kid raise his hands still holding his gun, I should have shot him. But I didn't. I hesitated because he was just a kid. At least that's what I thought.

"When they eventually caught him, they learned he'd been responsible for a string of robberies up and down Florida's east coast. He'd left nine bodies in his wake.

"He was twenty-six and had a rap sheet a mile long. But he'd never been sent to jail. Because he looked like an innocent kid, he was always given a break. Suspended sentences and probation.

"The nine people he killed might still be alive if someone had done to him what I did to that kid today. Maybe if someone had made him pay for his bad deeds, he would have gotten the message. Or at least sent to prison where he couldn't hurt innocent people."

Raif pulled another beer from the twelve-pack, popped the top and took a long drink. Then he looked at me and said, "That kid today? He came in with a loaded gun. He pointed at all three of us. He said he'd kill us if we tried to stop him.

"He wasn't wearing a mask, nothing to hide his face. He didn't care if we could identify him or not. He knew if we were dead when he left the store, we wouldn't be telling the police what he looked like.

"There were two things he didn't count on. One was me. I wasn't going to let some punk kid kill me just because I happened to be buying beer in the store he was going to rob.

"The other thing was the security cameras. They record everything in the store and out in the parking lot. If the kid had left us dead, the police could have watched the videos and would know what had happened."

Raif put his beer down. "No more beer for me. Need to be sharp when they come back here to question us."

I nodded and put my nearly full beer on the ground next to his.

Chapter Eighteen

We were still sitting on the concrete bench behind the store when a middle-aged man wearing black pants, a white shirt and thin black tie walked around to where we were sitting. He nodded at Raif and called him by name. "Raif, you doing okay?"

"Yeah, not bad. Considering."

The detective looked at me. "I don't think we've had the pleasure. I'm detective Martin Beck with the Saint Augustine PD. You have an ID?"

I nodded and pulled my driver's license from my wallet and handed it to him. He looked at it closely, spoke my name into his lapel microphone, and then handed it back to me.

Turning to Raif, he said, "You know how this works. I'm going to talk to your friend here, get his side of the story, then come back and talk to you. If you don't mind, lay off the beer until this is over."

The detective turned to me and said, "Follow me."

He didn't wait to see if I was going to. He just took off toward the store's parking lot. I followed, with a pretty good idea of what was coming next.

When we rounded the corner of the Pump & Munch, out of earshot of Raif, the detective pulled out a voice recorder and said, "Tell me what happened. From the time you entered the store until the police arrived. Don't leave anything out."

I didn't see any reason not to tell him the truth. I started with the kid coming in and firing a round into the ceiling, and ending with Raif and me sitting on the bench under the gumbo limbo behind the store.

When I was done, the detective nodded and said, "I have two questions.

"First, at any time were you in fear of your life?"

I answered immediately. "Yes, as soon as the kid fired the gun. He threatened to kill us all and it looked like he meant it. I wasn't sure we were going to get out of there alive."

The detective nodded. "Good answer. Now for the second question. Do you think that Raif used unnecessary force dealing with the gunman?"

I almost laughed. "So the guy comes in with a gun, threatens to kill us and somehow Raif, who is unarmed, is able to disarm the robber without any of us getting hurt. I think he deserves a medal. And no, I don't think he used excessive force."

That was the end of the questions. The detective thanked me for my time and we walked back to where Raif was sitting. He pointed at him. "Your turn."

They were gone for about twenty minutes. When they returned, neither was smiling. The detective gave me his card and said, "Call me if you remember anything else."

He didn't wait for a reply. He walked away.

When he was out of sight, I turned to Raif. "Are you in trouble? For how you handled the kid?"

He shook his head. "No, no trouble. At least not yet. They'll compare our stories with the security video and if everything checks out, there won't be a problem."

I was still sitting when he said, "I need to go back and check on Eddie. You coming?"

I stood and we walked back to Shady Haven. Neither of us said anything along the way, but when we got to my RV, Raif asked, "You hungry?"

It was about two in the afternoon; we'd missed lunch.

"Yeah, I could eat."

He nodded. "Good. Meet me at my place in thirty minutes. We'll take my car and go get some food."

He walked away, leaving me to think about what kind of day it had been so far. I'd driven a hundred miles, paid for a month's rent, met Raif, and survived an armed robbery. All that, and still no closer to finding Waldo.

When I stepped into the RV, Bob wasn't at the door waiting for me. I figured he was in the back, sleeping under the pillow fort I had built him before leaving that morning. When I went to check, all I could see was one paw sticking out under the pillows.

I said, "Bob, you okay?"

Hearing my voice, he crawled out from under the pillows. With blinky eyes, he said, "Murrph?"

He was either asking where I'd been or if it was feeding time. If I'd been a betting man, I'd put my money on the feeding time question.

I checked his food and water bowls, topped them both off, and headed to the couch. I was still wearing the same clothes I'd been in since leaving for Saint Augustine a day earlier. My plan was to rest for a few minutes, then shower and change, and be at Raif's door thirty minutes later.

It didn't work out that way.

Chapter Nineteen

Twenty-eight minutes after sitting down on the couch, I snorted myself awake. I'd fallen asleep and never gotten around to showering or changing clothes as planned. I guess it didn't matter. Raif probably wouldn't care.

I locked up the RV and walked past Waldo's place on the way to Raif's. No car in the driveway, no lights on in the trailer. It looked like Waldo hadn't made it back. Or maybe he had moved like Raif had told Mad Dog's collectors. It was one of the questions I needed answers to.

When I got to Raif's, he was sitting outside in one of the two wicker chairs on his deck, smoking a joint. He smiled, waved me over and asked, "You ready to eat?"

I nodded.

He reached into his pocket, pulled out a set of car keys and tossed them to me. "You're driving."

I was glad to get the keys. I didn't know how much or how long he'd been smoking, but I didn't trust him behind the wheel. Even though I was tired and didn't know my way around town, I was pretty sure it would be safer with me driving.

He finished off his doobie, dropped the remaining roach into the bucket of sand at his feet, and smiled. "Don't worry, it's legal. I've got a medical marijuana card. I buy it legally at the dispensary."

He pointed to the scar he'd shown me earlier. "My

medical retirement along with the three bullet holes was all I needed to get the card.

"I wasn't sure whether it'd help or not, but I was in pain and didn't want to get hooked on oxy. So I gave the green leaf a try. And by God, it actually helps ease the pain. Kind of mellows me out too. Sometimes I need that. Especially on days like today."

He stood and said, "Let's go. Car is on the other side.

He led the way to a late model Ford Taurus, white with dark-tinted windows. No badges or decals telling what the car was. No wheel covers, just steel rims painted white. It would have passed for a taxi if it had been painted yellow.

I unlocked the doors and we climbed in. Me on the driver's side and Raif on the passenger. The interior was stark. No leather seats, no fancy radio, no climate control. But it was clean, didn't smell bad and it would definitely be better than walking.

It started easily with a pleasant burble from the dual rear exhausts. I let it warm up for a minute then put it in reverse and we headed out.

When we reached the street leaving Shady Haven, Raif said, "Turn right."

Over the course of the next several minutes, he told me which lane to be in and where to turn until we reached our final destination. It was an older strip mall with a Wendy's burger joint out front. An auto parts store, a thrift shop, a sports bar named "Wish You Were Beer", and a self-service laundromat filled out the remaining store fronts.

Since it looked like the sports bar and Wendy's were the only two places that served food, I headed toward the bar. As I was lining up a parking spot, Raif said, "See the auto parts store? Head over there."

I did as he said, and when we got closer, he pointed to a brightly colored truck on the edge of the lot. "That's where we're going. Tina's Taco Palace."

I smiled. Maybe Raif had taken me to the place Waldo had bought. He'd told his mom he planned to buy a taco truck and maybe the Taco Palace was the place.

I pulled into one of the few empty parking spaces near the truck and turned off the car. I reached for the door, but Raif stopped me. "Before you go up there and start asking about Waldo, let's get our food and eat at one of the tables.

"When we're finished, you can talk to the girl working there. But not before we eat."

We got out of the car and as we walked toward the truck, the smell of tacos filled the air. There were two people in line in front of us, giving me time to read the menu. The food choices seemed to be limited to tacos and burritos. Your choice, beef or chicken.

Three soft tacos for five dollars. A dollar more if you wanted a soft drink. Raif knew what he wanted and ordered first. Three beef tacos with Verde sauce and a bottle of Jarritos mango soda. He pointed at me and said, "He's paying."

I stepped up to the counter and was surprised to see the person taking orders was not Waldo. It was a woman, about my age, five foot eight, medium build with dark red hair in a shag cut ending just below her ears. She was wearing an apron smeared with taco fixings and when she asked what I was having, she spoke with an unmistakable Irish accent.

Instead of ordering, I said, "You must be Tina."

She shook her head. "No, I'm not. There isn't a Tina."

Without smiling, she said, "There are people waiting behind you. Either order or get out of line."

I ordered.

"Give me the same thing as Raif."

She looked up from her order pad and said, "You sure you want the green sauce? You might be better off with the red."

I liked hearing her voice so I asked her to explain. She shook her head in disgust. "Either red or green. Red is mild, green is hot. Not for beginners."

I went with the red, paid for both mine and Raif's tacos, and headed to the picnic table where he was sitting. He saw me looking over my shoulder at the woman and said, "She's a real looker. And single too. Might be someone you'd want to get to know."

I wasn't so sure. She looked nice and had an interesting voice but didn't seem to be much of a people person. She was bothered that I had taken too much time to order. Maybe she was having a bad day. Or maybe she was one of those people who were never happy.

Maybe I'd find out when I asked her about Waldo

After we finished our food, Raif told me the woman's name was Erin and I should stay at the table while he had a word with her. He said it would be better if he spoke to her about Waldo before I did.

He got back in line and when it was his turn, he said something that made her smile; then he pointed back at me. I was surprised when she waved, so much so that, without thinking, I waved back. She watched me as Raif talked to her, and when he turned to leave, she smiled at me again. Maybe he had smoothed things over and she'd be willing to tell me where to find Waldo.

When Raif returned to the table, he said, "It's all set. You'll be taking her to dinner tonight. She wants you to pick her up here at eight this evening. You can use my car.

Take her wherever she wants to go and be nice. And Walker, take a shower and put on some clean clothes before you pick her up."

It was getting close to five and the dinner rush was on. The line for tacos was seven deep and building. I watched as Erin worked, hoping she'd look up and smile in my direction again. She didn't. She was too busy filling orders.

Raif stood and said, "Time to go. Other people need these tables and we're done. We're leaving."

He didn't wait for my reply. He walked away and I followed, thinking about Erin, wondering why she so readily agreed to meet with me later that evening.

I would soon find out.

Chapter Twenty

When we got back to Raif's place, he told me to keep the car keys. He said I could use it as long as I needed to, but I had to bring it back with a full tank of gas. That was something I could do.

Before we stepped out of his car, he popped the glove compartment and pulled out a semi-automatic pistol in a black holster. He shoved it in his pants and said, "I don't think you'll be needing this."

The pistol was the second time that day I'd seen Raif with a gun. I wondered how many more he had stashed away. As an ex-cop, he probably had several. Maybe even a few long guns too.

After getting out of the car, he headed up the steps to his trailer. His parting words were, "Take a shower, wear clean clothes and don't be late."

I smiled and said, "Sure thing, Dad."

He laughed as I walked back to my RV.

Bob was waiting for me at the door. He had a toy mouse pinned to the floor. He preferred real mice and especially live lizards, but when they weren't available, toy mice with gray fur were acceptable substitutes.

He flipped the mouse high in the air and caught it before it hit the floor. He chirped out something that probably meant, "See what I can do?" Then he batted the faux mouse down the hallway and into the bedroom.

It was clear he was in good spirits. So was I.

My dinner date with Erin was at eight. Three hours away. In that time, I planned to shower, shave and put on the least wrinkled clean shirt I could find. I didn't have many choices; most of my wardrobe had been lost in the fire when the RV had been hit.

With three hours to kill, I decided to take a few minutes and tidy up the inside of the motorhome. Nothing major, just a quick walk through picking up clothes off the floor, sweeping the litter that Bob tracked when he left his box and wiping down the counters.

I wasn't planning on having visitors, but you never know.

After getting the place presentable, I took a long shower, washed my hair, and shaved. I didn't want to add more wrinkles to the clothes I had planned to wear that evening, so I spent the next two hours walking around in my underwear.

When it got close to the time to leave, I got dressed, checked myself in the mirror, and told Bob I'd be back later. He rubbed up against my ankle, letting me know he expected me to come home at a decent hour.

After locking up the RV, I walked over to Raif's to pick up his car. He was out on his deck, smoking another joint. When he saw me, he waved and said, "You remember how to get there?"

"Yeah, I think so."

"Good. Let me see your phone."

I handed it to him and he punched in a number. A few seconds later, his phone rang. He ended the call, handed my phone back and said, "If anything comes up, give me a call."

It took me about ten minutes longer than I expected to get to the Taco Palace. I missed a turn on the way and ended up going over the bridge to Anastasia Island. Had I kept going south, my next stop would have been Daytona.

Fortunately, I was able to turn around and get back on track. I breathed a sigh of relief when I pulled into the Taco Palace five minutes early. Erin was still inside the truck, but it looked like she was closing for the night.

I got out of the car and took a seat at one of the picnic tables, wondering what Raif had said that helped her decide to let me take her to dinner. I'd have to ask him about it.

Ten minutes later, she closed the overhead panels and locked up the truck. She walked over to me, carrying a black gym bag.

I didn't ask her what was in it.

I should have.

Chapter Twenty-One

She smiled when she saw me and gave me an unexpected hug. Then she asked, "You have a shower at your place?"

I did and I wondered why she was asking. Maybe she thought I needed a shower, even though I had just taken one. Whatever her reason, I said, "Yeah, I have one. Why do you ask?"

She came up close, so close that I thought maybe she was going to give me a kiss. But she didn't, instead, she leaned in, pointed to her shirt and said, "Smell."

It was a strange request, but I didn't see any reason not to follow through, so I sniffed her shirt. It smelled like beef tacos. She had been stuck in the taco truck most of the day and it would be expected that she might smell like one. It didn't bother me. I was glad to be with her, taco smell or not. But she wasn't having it.

She said, "Take me to your place. I need a shower."

She walked over to Raif's car, put her gym bag in the backseat and sat down on the passenger side. Had I been quicker, I would have opened the door for her, but she was in before I had a chance.

When I got in on the driver's side, she said, "Raif told me you are staying in Shady Haven, a few doors up from his place. He also said if you got out of line, just tell him and he'd do something about it.

"Just so you know, I'm going to your place to take a

shower. Nothing else. So don't get your hopes up."

I couldn't help but smile. I was with a good-looking woman with a voice that could melt men's hearts. She wanted me to take her to my place. I couldn't think of any way the day could have gotten better.

When I pulled out the parking lot, I almost went the wrong way. My mind was on the woman sitting next to me, not on the road I needed to take to get back to my RV.

Seeing that I'd almost missed the first turn, Erin gave me directions and we arrived at my place eight minutes later. I got out of the car first, and, like a gentleman, opened her door for her.

She held out her hand, and I took it as she stepped out of the car. It was soft and warm and I felt good holding it. But it didn't last long. She let go, opened the back door of the car and pulled out her bag.

I watched as she did, again wondering what might be in it. Like the time before, I didn't ask, I just watched her.

We were still standing outside of my motorhome when she asked, "Are you going to invite me in or are we going to stand out here all night?"

I invited her in.

As usual, Bob met me at the door. When he saw the red-headed stranger, he looked at her, meowed softly and, instead of running away like I thought he would, he rubbed up against her ankles. He followed her and meowed softly as she walked over to the couch. I'd never seen him act that way around strangers. Usually, he'd run and hide until he was sure the new people weren't a danger.

But not this time. It was almost like she was covered in catnip and he couldn't get enough of her. I kind of felt the same way, minus the catnip.

She stood in front of the couch with Bob at her feet and said, "This is nicer than I'd thought it'd be. Lots of room to move around. I like it."

Still holding her little black bag, she asked, "Where's the shower?"

I pointed down the hall. "The door on the left, just before you get to the bedroom. There's a clean towel. If you need anything else, just let me know."

She nodded, pulled out her phone and punched in a number. When the call connected, she said, "I'm here. If there is any trouble, you know where to find me."

Before I could ask who she'd called, she punched in another number and said, "This is Erin. I need a to-go order. A large veggie pizza and two house salads. My friend Walker will be there in ten minutes to pick it up."

She ended the call and turned to me. "If you don't mind, while I'm in the shower, could you go over to the Mellow Mushroom and pick up our dinner?"

The question of where we were eating had been answered. It would be takeout. That sounded pretty good to me. The only problem was I had never heard of the Mellow Mushroom and had no idea where it was.

She was waiting for my answer, so I said, "Just tell me how to get there."

She smiled and said, "Turn right out of Shady Haven, go three miles, and the Mellow Mushroom will be on your right. The food will be ready when you get there."

I nodded and headed for the door, but she stopped me with a question. "You have any wine in here?"

"Yeah, Black Box Chardonnay. In the fridge. Will that do?"

"Perfect. Now go get the food. I should be out of the shower when you get back. But if I'm not, no peeking."

Chapter Twenty-Two

It took me less than twenty minutes to get to the Mellow Mushroom, pay for our food, and get back to the RV. Erin was out of the shower and sitting on the couch, Bob at her side. She had changed into black shorts and a white tee shirt. She had one of my towels wrapped around her head. Presumably to help dry her hair.

I put the pizza and the two salads on the kitchen table, went to the fridge and got the box of wine. I poured two glasses and said, "Dinner is ready."

Erin joined me, and we started in on the salads. Five minutes later, we attacked the pizza. While we were eating, I tried to make small talk but wasn't doing a very good job.

One of the questions I came up with was, "Are you a vegan?"

In my mind, it sounded like a reasonable thing to ask. She had ordered a veggie pizza and veggie salads. There was no meat on the table.

She laughed at the question. "No, I'm not. It's just that I've been cooking meat all day, and I needed a break. So it was salads and veggie pizza.

"Give me a day or two and I'll be back on the meat bandwagon."

After I poured her third glass of wine she said, "I'm celebrating."

It was clear she wanted me to ask why, so I did. "Why?

Being out with me? Is that it?"

She laughed. "No, that's not it. In fact, it should be you celebrating the opportunity to be with me this evening. I'm celebrating something else. A big change in my life."

I waited for her to tell me more, but she didn't. I figured she wanted me to again ask about it, so I did. "Okay, tell me more about this big change in your life."

She smiled. "As of today, I'm officially homeless and no longer work at Tina's Taco Palace. The sale finally went through."

My first thought was Waldo had bought the business, the one he had borrowed the money for. I'd needed to ask Erin if he was the buyer. But I wanted to wait before I mentioned his name. I was enjoying spending the evening with her and didn't want to mess things up.

"So, you sold your taco truck. Did you get what you wanted for it?"

She nodded. "I did. In fact, I got more than I was asking. I'm pretty happy about it."

"But what about the other thing? You said you're now homeless? Why is that?"

She took a sip of wine and said, "It's a long story. After we eat, I'll tell you all about it."

Over the next half hour, we ate pizza, drank wine, and generally enjoyed each other's company, at least I enjoyed hers. I wasn't so sure her joyous nature was about being with me. It could have been, but more likely it was because she'd just sold her business. That would make almost anyone happy.

As we were finishing our meal, and after three glasses of

wine each, I said, "I love your accent. Irish, isn't it?"

"Yes it is, and you're probably wondering how an Irish girl like me ended up in Florida selling tacos out of a truck."

I nodded. "Yeah, I was wondering about that. I'm sure it's an interesting story. If you feel like sharing it with me, I'd love to hear it."

She pointed to the couch. Bob was curled up on it, pretending to be asleep, but I knew better. He was watching and listening to Erin. When he heard her say, "Let's move over there," he stood, stretched and said, "Murrph." As in, "Come sit by me. I'll let you rub my belly."

I filled Erin's glass and joined her on the couch. Bob didn't hesitate; he curled up in her lap.

With wine glass in one hand and the other petting Bob, she said, "My mother was living in Colorado when I was born. After her divorce, she moved us back to Dublin. We were there for almost twenty years then moved back to the States when her brother was hurt.

"He lives in Saint Augustine, and that's how we ended up here. While Mom tended to him, I found a job in a real estate office filing paperwork. They put me in a cubicle with a small desk and no window.

"Even though the job paid well, I hated it. I hated being trapped indoors for most of the day. My only escape was the forty-five minutes I got for lunch. It wasn't enough time to go far, so I started eating at the nearest place. Tina's Taco Palace.

"We didn't have tacos and burritos in Dublin, at least not the kind they make here, so it was a new experience for me. After eating at Tina's every day for three months and watching the customers come and go, I decided that dishing out tacos would be more fun than working indoors hidden away in a cubicle.

"I asked Miguel, the owner of the truck, if he'd give me a job. But he said he didn't think a red-headed Irish girl would last long serving up tacos in a truck without air conditioning. He said it was hot work and I'd be on my feet all day.

"I didn't get the job. But I didn't give up. About once a week, I'd ask Miguel if he was ready to hire me. It was a running joke between us. I'd always ask, and he'd always say, 'No.'

"But one day, instead of me asking him about the job, he asked if I still wanted to work there.

"Miguel explained he was having a problem with immigration and he needed to leave the country. He said his wife and three children had already gone back to Mexico, and he wanted to join them.

"He needed to cash out quickly and offered to sell me the truck. The price was more than fair but more than I had. I could pay him half but no more.

"He had seen the Toyota truck I'd been driving and said if I didn't owe anything on it, he'd take it in trade. I could pay half in cash, and the rest would be covered by the value of the truck.

"It sounded like a great deal, so I agreed. Two days later, I was the owner of Tina's Taco Palace.

"I gave my two weeks' notice at the real estate office, explaining that I had bought the taco truck. My manager was surprised but not all that upset. He liked the tacos he got there and was happy someone would be taking over the business.

"After buying the truck, Miguel spent two days showing me how everything worked. He showed me how to make tacos and burritos and where to get fresh ingredients every morning. I worked by his side, trying to take everything in. I wanted him to stay longer, but he said his time was up, and he needed to get back to Mexico.

"So after he was gone, I got my wish. I was selling tacos in a truck. By myself, with no one around to guide me.

"I did hire a schoolgirl to work with me during the evening shift and on Saturdays. Her being around on our busiest days gave me a bit of breathing room.

"But she got days off and I didn't. For me, it was a full-time job. Starting early in the morning when I'd go out and buy supplies and ending ten hours later after cleaning up the truck at the end of the day.

"The hours were long, and it was hot in the truck, but I liked it a lot better than working in an office. I was outdoors, met a lot of people, and didn't have to answer to anyone. If I wanted to take a day off, I could. I never did though. There were too many people who depended on the truck being open for their lunch and dinner meals for me to take off."

She paused, took another sip of wine, and looked down at Bob who was still in her lap.

"So what is it with this cat? He's been following me around and trying to get in my lap ever since I got here. He even followed me into the shower. Does he do that with all your lady friends?"

I looked down at Bob. "We don't get many visitors here in the RV. And when we do, he usually hides. But with you it's a different story. For some reason, he adores you. Maybe it's your accent."

She shook her head. "It's not the accent. It's the smell of tacos. He got a whiff of me and thought I was bringing him food. Poor thing is probably hungry. He's probably starved for affection too."

I laughed. "Erin, he gets plenty of food. That's why he weighs almost twenty pounds. He never goes hungry around here. Eats whenever he wants. And he gets all the pets he wants."

She looked down at him and, in a baby voice, said, "You want to come home with me, Bob? I promise to feed you better than Walker does."

He answered, "Murrrph." He'd follow her anywhere.

Chapter Twenty-Three

"Erin, tell me why you're homeless."

She finished off her fourth glass of wine and said, "You first. Tell me how you ended up living in this motorhome. Maybe then I'll tell you about me being homeless."

I nodded. "Okay, it's a deal. I'll go first.

"I was married and working as an IT manager for a big company. They downsized and I was laid off. My wife filed for divorce the same day. Soon after, I had no job, no wife, and no place to live.

"I needed a place to stay so I bought an RV. I've been living in one ever since. End of story."

Erin shook her head. "I don't think that's the full story. I think you left out some important details. Like did you and your wife have any kids? And why did she divorce you? Were you mean to her?"

I shook my head. "No Erin, I wasn't mean to her. Far from it. In fact, I thought we had the perfect marriage. I was happy and thought she was too. At least up until the day she surprised me with divorce papers.

"When I asked her why she wanted out, she said she was doing me a favor. She was setting me free.

"At the time, I didn't want to be free. I wanted to be married to her. But, apparently, she no longer wanted to be married to me. So she filed and I signed. We didn't have any kids and we split everything down the middle. No long, drawn-out fight over who got what. My attorney said it was the easiest divorce he'd ever handled. He told me I'd be a fool to fight it, so I didn't. I signed the papers and she sent me on my way.

"Like I said, I never saw it coming. I thought she was the love of my life. I guess I was wrong."

I took a deep breath and said, "No more about me. You're supposed to be celebrating tonight, not listening to my sob story. Tell me something about you. Something I don't know that'll make me smile."

She nodded. "Okay, since you asked, I will."

She pointed to her wine glass. "We Irish girls are supposed to be able to hold our liquor. But not me, not tonight."

She was slurring some of her words when she said, "You're the kind of guy a drunk girl could get into a lot of trouble with. You probably know that, don't you? That's why you've been keeping my glass full. To get me into trouble."

She lifted Bob up off her lap and set him in mine. She pointed to the back of the motorhome. "The bathroom is back there, right?"

"Yeah."

She was about halfway there when Bob joined her. This time, he didn't wait to be asked. He went into the bathroom with her. I could hear him meowing and chirping and her talking to him over the sound of the bathroom vent fan.

When she came back out, Bob was at her heels. I was still sitting on the couch and expected her to sit down beside me. But she didn't. Instead, she pointed to the clock over the kitchen sink and said, "It's getting late. I need to be going."

Both Bob and I wanted her to stay. We didn't want her to go. "It's not late. You don't have to worry about getting up and going to work tomorrow. You're celebrating. You can stay up as long as you want."

She reached out, took my hand and said, "Walker, if you're still here in the morning, we'll get breakfast. Around eight, okay?"

I nodded. "Yeah, breakfast sounds good."

She headed for the door, and I said, "Wait, you don't have a car. I'll need to drive you."

She shook her head. "No, you've had too much to drink. Neither of us should be driving anywhere. I can walk."

There was no way I was going to let her walk home in the dark in Florida. Too many things could go wrong.

I grabbed the car keys off the counter and said, "You're not walking, it won't be safe. I'll drive you."

She shook her head, leaned in and kissed me on the cheek. "Walker, you're sweet. Worried about me getting home on my own. But it's not a problem. I'm staying with my uncle. His place is just two doors down."

"Your uncle lives here? In Shady Haven? Have I met him?"

She nodded. "You mean he didn't tell you? Raif didn't tell you he was my uncle and I was staying at his place?"

He had never mentioned it to me. I asked her to make sure we were talking about the same person. "Are we talking about Raif? The ex-cop who lives two doors down? He's your uncle?"

She nodded. "Yes, he's my uncle, on my mother's side, and he's the reason we moved back to the States. To be with him while he was in the hospital."

"So that's where you'll be spending the night? At Raif's?"

"Yes, dear. I'll be sleeping just two doors down. If you're worried I might be in danger on my walk there, feel free to go with me. Just don't expect a goodnight kiss at Raif's door. He's a little protective of me."

I could understand that. He'd set his niece up with me, a complete stranger, and probably knew she had come to my RV. He would likely be up, waiting to see if she called for help or came home crying about something I'd done.

Remembering how he had dealt with the kid in the convenience store, I didn't want to give him any reason to do the same to me.

"Erin, I've enjoyed your company and it'd be my pleasure to walk you home."

She smiled, grabbed my hand, and we headed out.

Chapter Twenty-Four

It was a short walk to Raif's and Erin didn't seem to be in a hurry to get there. She stopped several times to look at the stars or maybe to regain her balance. It was clear the wine had an effect on her.

As we walked by Waldo's trailer, I noticed the lights were still out and there was no car in the driveway. It didn't look like anyone was home.

Maybe he, too, was out celebrating. His purchase of the taco truck would have given him reason to. But maybe, instead of celebrating, he was hiding from the two beefy guys who had come looking for him.

Erin stopped in front of his trailer and slurred out the word, "Bastūn!"

I didn't know much Irish slang, but I was pretty sure "bastūn" wasn't a compliment. Still standing and pointing at his trailer, she leaned into me and whispered, "He owes me money. Will you help me collect?"

I nodded. "I will, I'll help you find Waldo and get your money."

She stumbled into me, put both hands on my chest and said, "I like you, Walker. Do you like me?"

I almost laughed at the question. I'd heard variations of it before, mostly from women who'd had too much to drink. I suspected that tears would soon follow.

With my arm around her shoulder, we started walking

again. Surprisingly, we made it to Raif's trailer without any trouble.

He was outside on his deck sitting in the same chair he had been sitting in earlier. When he saw how Erin was wobbling, he came down off the deck to help me get her to the door. Just as he got close, she puckered her lips and leaned over to kiss me. In doing so, she lost her balance and had Raif not been there to catch her, she would have fallen flat on her face.

He shook his head, turned to me and said, "I'm going to put her to bed. Wait out here until I get back."

He led her up the stairs and to his front door. On the way I heard her whisper, "I like him. Please don't hurt this one."

I didn't hear his reply, but I was hopeful that after I told him nothing had happened between us, he wouldn't be too upset.

A few minutes later, he came back out, grinning ear to ear. He looked at me, shook his head and said, "You got her drunk. Then you brought her here. What were you thinking?"

He sat in the chair he'd been in earlier, pointed to the one beside it and said, "Have a seat. Let's talk."

Even though I probably wasn't sober enough to drive, I was sober enough to talk. I sat down beside Raif and said, "It's a nice evening. Feels good to be outside."

I was trying to get the conversation off to a good start. Talking about the weather usually did the trick. But not this time. Raif had other things on his mind.

He turned to me and said, "Two things you'll want to know about that woman.

"The first is if you make her mad, you'll get to see her Irish temper. You'll hear words you've never heard before and never expected to come out of that girl's mouth. Best case, never make her mad. And if you do, don't argue and don't run. Just stand and take it like a man.

"The second thing is, if you let her, she'll break your heart. It's easy to fall for her, easy to think you're in love. But not so easy if you find out she doesn't feel the same way.

"I'm not saying that's the way it'll go with you two, but it might, so be careful."

I nodded and said, "Nothing happened between us. Back at my place all we did was eat dinner and talk. Nothing else."

He reached over and put his hand on my shoulder. "Son, you think I'm blind? She's drunk as a skunk. So you did more than just talk. But I'm not blaming you. In fact, I probably ought to thank you.

"She was going to celebrate tonight with someone, and I'm just glad it was with you instead of a stranger who might have taken advantage of her. That's why I set you two up.

"When I learned you were looking for Waldo, the same as she was, and that you were staying just two doors down from me, I figured you were the safest person to be with her while she celebrated. So when we were at the taco truck, I put my plan in motion. I told her you wanted to take her to dinner but were too shy to ask such a pretty girl.

"I knew she was looking for someone to celebrate with and you were the perfect choice. Someone I could keep my eyes on.

"So yeah, you got her drunk. I don't begrudge you for that. She probably needed to get drunk. It's been three years since she didn't have to worry about getting up early the next day. Letting off a little steam will be good for her.

"But like I said, be careful. She'll break your heart."

He changed the subject. "Did you two talk about Waldo?"

I shook my head. "No, it never came up. I didn't even know she was looking for him until we walked by his trailer. She called him a word I'd never heard before. A bastūn."

Raif smiled. "Yeah, she doesn't think much of him."

"Didn't he buy her truck?"

Raif took a deep breath and said, "Ask her. When she's sober, she'll tell you all about it."

He was right. She would.

Chapter Twenty-Five

The next morning, Erin showed up at my door just after eight. She was all smiles and said, "Come on, let's go get breakfast. I'm starving."

Either she didn't have a hangover or she was hiding it pretty well. I wasn't. I had a pounding headache and my eyes hurt. But I wasn't going to tell her. Instead, I said, "We can eat here. I've got eggs and juice in the fridge."

She wasn't having it. "I want pancakes and I don't want to wait for you to make them. So let's go. You're driving."

I still had Raif's keys from the night before and he'd said I could use his car as long as I brought it back with a full tank of gas. I grabbed the keys and my wallet and headed for the door.

Ten minutes later, we were pulling into a McDonald's parking lot. It was Erin's decision. She had said they had the best pancakes and we wouldn't have to wait long to get them. She was right, at least on the second count. We were at a table eating hotcakes covered in syrup four minutes after placing our order.

Erin went through her first three quickly and went back for more. I passed on the second helping. Three pancakes from McDonald's were enough for me. She had ordered orange juice and I had gotten a medium Coke, hoping the caffeine would help with my headache.

It didn't.

It was still pounding when Erin came back to the table. She offered to share her pancakes with me, but I declined. I wasn't sure my stomach could handle the extra food so I sat there and watched as she ate.

In my eyes, she was a beautiful woman. Dark red hair, blue eyes, fair skin. Medium build, and almost giddy about not having to go into the back of the taco truck. It was nice to be around her when she was happy and her smiling face was helping me feel better. Or maybe it was the Coke.

I wanted to hear more of her voice, so I asked, "Yesterday, you said there was no Tina. So why is the place called Tina's Taco Palace?"

She looked up from her food, her eyes twinkling. "A guy named Tony was the original owner. He bought the truck and outfitted it for food prep. His plan was to park it near his buddy's bar and sell pizza and calzones.

"He was a large man. His street name was Fat Tony. Everybody in the neighborhood knew him and he thought that calling the truck 'Fat Tony's' would bring in customers.

"But it didn't. Only those that knew him were brave enough to venture into the neighborhood where he parked the truck. And tourists weren't very interested in eating at a place with 'fat' in the name.

"Tony decided a name change was in order, so he changed it to 'Tony's Place.' He figured it was a good name for an Italian pizza truck.

"The name change helped a little, but he didn't get many repeat customers. The problem was the food. It was greasy, took time to prepare, and hard to eat without making a mess.

"Eventually Fat Tony got tired of trying to make a profit and sold the truck to Miguel, who was looking to get into the business. Tony had two conditions. Miguel had to move the truck to a new neighborhood, far from where it had been parked. And he couldn't use Fat Tony in the name.

"Miguel had already decided to move the truck. A friend of his owned the auto parts store and said he could park the truck there.

"Miguel wanted to sell the kind of food he was familiar with. Street tacos and burritos. And he wanted the name to reflect those offerings.

"So he contacted a friend and asked him to paint a sign for the truck with the words 'Tony's Taco Place' on it. And to make sure the sign had the right name, Miguel wrote it on a napkin and gave it to his friend. They agreed on a price, and the sign was painted.

"But when the friend showed up with it, there was a problem. He had made a mistake. He had misread Miguel's handwriting and ended up painting 'Tina's Taco Palace', instead of 'Tony's Taco Place'.

But Miguel wasn't upset. He actually liked the new name. He thought calling the truck a palace made it sound classy. And using a woman's name, Tina, made it even more appealing.

"So there never was a Tina. It was just a misunderstanding between Miguel and the painter.

"Not long after he had the sign mounted and opened the truck for business, customers started coming. And they kept coming back. The food was good, the price was fair, and people liked the tacos.

"It wasn't long before the truck was quite profitable. It was hard work, but Miguel didn't mind. He was proud he owned a successful business. It was the American Dream.

"If he hadn't had to leave the country, he'd probably still be running it.

"When I bought it, I didn't see any reason to change the name. The place was well known as Tina's and had a good reputation. The person I sold it to isn't planning on changing the name either. It'll still be Tina's Taco Palace but with someone else making the food instead of me."

She smiled when she finished the story. It was clear she was happy to be eating hotcakes at McDonald's and not thinking about having to make tacos the rest of the day.

Since she was in a talkative mood, I asked about the new owner. I was expecting to hear how Waldo had bought the business from her and why she thought he still owed her money.

But I was wrong. What she told me changed the way I thought of her. And Waldo.

Chapter Twenty-Six

We were still at McDonald's. Sitting in a booth near the front of the store. The morning rush was over, and there were only a few customers left inside.

Since we weren't keeping others from finding a place to sit, we stayed a bit longer. Erin had finished her pancakes and seemed to be in a good mood. The pancakes and extra syrup had energized her.

I figured it was a good time to ask the question both of us knew was coming. I started by saying, "Waldo? So he bought the Taco Palace from you?"

She shook her head and frowned. "No, he didn't. He said he would, even showed me the money, but then, on the day we were supposed to sign the papers, he was a no show. He sent me a text that said, 'Sorry, I've changed my mind.'

"I never planned to sell the business in the first place. I was working the lunch shift, and this guy shows up and says he wants to buy the taco truck. I told him it wasn't for sale, but he said, 'Everything is for sale. Just tell me your price.'

"Up until that moment, I had no thoughts of selling. I was making decent money with the truck, and other than the fact that I had no social life and was working too many hours, I was happy.

"But when Waldo challenged me to come up with a price, I decided it would be nice to have my freedom back, if I could get what the truck was worth to me.

"When he wouldn't take no for an answer and wouldn't leave, I gave in. I calculated what my net profit would be for the next twenty-four months, added fifteen thousand to that, and gave him the number.

"I expected him to walk away. He could have bought a new truck and outfitted it for what I was asking. But maybe he didn't know that. Or maybe he didn't care. Whatever the reason, he didn't even try to negotiate a lower price. He just stuck out his hand and said, 'I'll take it.'

"He went to his car, a crusty old Celica, and came back with a black bag. It was filled with cash, mostly hundred-dollar bills. He said they could all be mine. All I needed to do was to get the title and occupancy license transferred into his name and he'd pay me what I was asking.

"It sounded too good to be true. When I woke up that morning, I hadn't planned to sell the truck. But by the end of the day, it looked like I was going to get paid more than I thought it was worth, in cash.

"Waldo only had one condition for the sale. He wanted me to work in the truck with him for two days, to show him the ropes. He needed to know how everything worked.

"It was a reasonable request and I agreed. He told me he was new in town and asked if I knew a place he might be able to rent for a month or two. I should have kept my mouth shut, but I didn't. I told him about Shady Haven.

"The next morning, he showed up right on time and seemed eager to work. I showed him everything. How to order fresh ingredients and who to order from. How to prep for the day's sales. How to run the register and how to keep things clean. At the end of the day, I showed him how to close down for the evening and where to hide the lock box with the daily cash proceeds.

"He stayed in the truck with me most of the day, only taking bathroom breaks and time out to eat. There didn't seem to be a problem and he acted like he enjoyed the work. We had a big crowd that day, so he stayed busy.

"The next morning, he showed up an hour late. He didn't seem nearly as eager to work as he had the day before. I figured that maybe being on his feet selling tacos for ten hours that first day had worn him out. I know that the first few days after I took over the truck, it wore me out too.

"So anyway, he worked with me most of that day, and when we closed for the night, he told me to have the papers ready the next day and we'd do the deal in the morning.

"I went to Uncle Raif's place that night, and when I told him I was selling the taco truck, he was surprised but happy for me. He knew I was putting in long hours, and maybe I needed a break.

"That evening, when we went for a walk, I noticed Waldo's car was parked in the driveway next to Raif's. The lights were on in the trailer, and we could hear someone moving around inside. We didn't stop then, but on our way back, Waldo was sitting out on his deck.

"I introduced him to Raif and they made small talk for a few minutes. No mention of the food truck deal from either one of them. Just complaints about the weather and the traffic.

"Later on that evening, Raif cautioned me. He said I shouldn't rush into the deal until I found out more about Waldo and how he got the bag of cash he had shown me. I didn't listen. I was thinking about how nice it would be not to spend most of my day slinging tacos.

"The next morning, I dug out the title and the Florida Dispensary license, and headed to Tina's one last time. Or at least that's what I thought.

"Waldo wasn't there when I arrived. But he, or someone else, had been in the truck. The proceeds from the previous day's sales were gone. Someone had discovered where I hid the lock box and cleaned it out.

"I was worried that when Waldo showed up and learned that the truck had been robbed, he would back out of the deal.

"As it turned out, I shouldn't have worried. Waldo never showed up that day. Or any day since."

She paused and pointed to the drink counter. "You mind getting me a Coke? I think I need the caffeine."

I didn't mind. In fact, another Coke sounded good to me as well.

I went to the counter, ordered two medium Cokes, and brought them back to the table where Erin and I had been sitting. But she wasn't there. She was gone.

Chapter Twenty-Seven

I still had the car keys in my pocket and was pretty sure Erin hadn't left without me. If she had, she was on foot. It would be a long walk back to Shady Haven.

Most likely, she had gone to the ladies room and all I needed to do was to wait for her return. Five minutes later, she was back. Big smile on her face when she saw me. "You didn't think I bailed on you, did ya?"

"No, that thought never crossed my mind. What about you? Did you think you might come back to the table and I'd be gone?"

She shook her head and her eyes flashed a warning. "If you ever leave without letting me know, you'll regret it. When I catch up to you, I'll make you pay."

She didn't sound like she was joking. In fact, it sounded like a warning to never cross her; something I wasn't planning to do.

After she sat and took a sip of her Coke, I asked, "So if Waldo didn't buy your truck, and you were celebrating last night because it was sold, who did? Who bought it?"

She smiled. "Funny story. Somehow word got around that I might be interested in selling Tina's. One of the people who heard about it was the owner of Benito's Burritos. They have a place on A1A and do a lot of business there.

"Anyway, the day after Waldo bailed on me, Benito visited and offered to buy Tina's. He said he was looking to expand, and having a taco truck would be a good fit. He already had people who could work it and he'd rather own it than have it as his competition.

"He didn't know the amount Waldo and I had agreed on. So I added ten thousand and told him that was the price.

"I was surprised when he said, 'That'll work for me.'

With him, it was an easy transfer. He was already in the business and had a staff that I didn't need to train. His people already knew how to make burritos, tacos, and a lot more. And he already had suppliers lined up that he would need to keep the truck operating.

"There was no drama. He paid me and we closed the deal yesterday morning."

"And you're happy? About no longer owning your own business?"

She shook her head. "I don't know whether I'm happy about it or not. I'll miss my regular customers and I'll miss seeing money in the box at the end of the day. But when I deposited Benito's check, my bank account sure was happy."

She took a deep breath and said, "Now all I need to do is find Waldo and get the money he took from me. It had to be him. No one else knew I had a cash box or where it was hidden. It had a little over a thousand dollars in it, and he took it."

Her eyes flashed again. "It's not so much the money. It's the thought that he stole from me and thinks he can get away with it. It's not going to happen. I'm going to find him, and when I do, he'll pay in blood."

Not knowing what to say about what she was going to do when she found him, I just nodded. I didn't want anyone hurting Waldo. But if he owed her money, I wanted him to get right with her before I took him home.

We'd been at McDonald's for almost an hour. Sitting underneath bright fluorescent lights. I'd been feeling pretty good since the first Coke. No indications that anything was about to go wrong. But just as we were getting ready to leave, I could feel it coming.

It'd been two days since I'd last taken my anti-seizure med and it was probably two days too long. I could feel the change wash over me. First thing to go was my eyes. My vision narrowed then blurred. Soon I wasn't able to focus on anything in the room. Not even Erin.

I tried my best to act like nothing was going on, but Erin noticed. She asked, "You feeling okay?"

"Yeah. It's just that my eyes hurt. Probably from drinking too much last night. I'll keep them closed, and they'll clear up in a few minutes."

I pulled the car keys out of my pocket and slid them over to her. "I need to get back to my place and make a call. You mind driving?"

She took the keys. "You sure you're okay? You're starting to look a little pale."

I nodded. "It's just my eyes. If I keep them closed for a few minutes, I'll be fine."

When she stood to leave, I could barely see her. But not wanting to be left behind, I stood and put my hand on her shoulder. Like the blind person I was at that moment, I let her walk me to the car.

We had parked close to the entrance, so it wasn't much of a walk. Erin led me to the passenger door and opened it for me. As I got in, she repeated the question she'd asked earlier. "Are you sure you are okay? If you're getting ready to stroke out, let me know and I'll get you to the hospital."

"It's just my eyes. That's all. They'll clear up in a few minutes."

She closed my door and climbed in on the driver's side. I heard the engine start and felt the car move as she put it in reverse to pull out of our parking space. Then I felt the clunk of the transmission going into drive.

For the next few minutes, neither of us said anything. I kept my eyes mostly shut, only opening them to see if my vision had cleared up. It hadn't.

Erin finally broke the silence. "You know about this car, don't you?"

I shook my head. "No, the only thing I know is Raif said I could use it as long as I needed it if I brought it back with a full tank of gas. Is there something I'm missing?"

She reached out and patted me on the shoulder. "Raif doesn't let many people drive his car. The fact that he gave you the keys means that, for some reason, he trusts you.

"To him, this car is pretty special. It was the one he was driving when he was shot. It's still got two bullets rattling around in the driver's door. Those bullets might have killed him if it weren't for the car.

"But that's not the only reason the car is special. On the outside, it might look like a Plain Jane Ford Taurus. But it's not. It's a special order Police Interceptor. It has a twin-turbo Eco boost motor pumping out three hundred sixty-five horses and three hundred fifty pound feet of torque.

"It's got a beefed-up heavy-duty suspension, all-wheel drive, and over-sized brakes. The frame has extra supports to help the car survive a crash. All this is from the factory.

"It was tuned for sustained high-speed pursuits. Top speed is one-thirty and they say it can do that for an hour without any problem.

"Ford didn't offer these cars to the public. They were police only. Raif was a detective at the time, so he had no problem ordering the car the way he wanted it.

"He hadn't put many miles on it before he was shot, but when he recovered, he wanted the car. He said they may have retired him from the force, but he was keeping the car. And he did.

"It was, and still is, a very special thing in his life. Keep that in mind next time you drive it."

I'd been sitting in the passenger seat with my eyes closed, listening to Erin tell me about the car. It was an interesting story about an interesting car. I'd not heard of the Police Interceptor model but thought I might look into one when I got back to my home base. But for the moment, my focus, or lack of it, was on my eyes. I wanted the vision problem to go away.

I still had them closed when Erin said, "We're here. You need help getting out?"

I opened my eyes and was happy to see that most of my vision had returned. My peripheral was still not right, but I could see well enough to get out of the car and walk to the RV.

I opened the door and waited for Erin to join me. When she didn't, I asked, "Aren't you coming in? Bob will be really disappointed if you don't. I just need to make a quick phone call; then we can start looking for Waldo."

She hesitated like she was thinking it over but finally said, "I'll come in to see Bob. But after that, we need to look for

Waldo. I want to get my money back."

Chapter Twenty-Eight

Bob was waiting at the door. He meowed loudly as if to say, "I'm hungry, feed me."

I was pretty sure his bowl still had food in it, but I wasn't going to let him go hungry, so I went back to check. He normally follows when I do this, but this time he didn't. His bowl was nearly full, so it wasn't the food he wanted. I checked his water and litter box, both were fine.

When I headed back up front, I could see why he hadn't followed me. He was more interested in having Erin pet him than worry about his food, water or litter. She was sitting on the couch; he was in her lap, purring loudly. They both looked contented and I didn't want to break the spell, so I left them alone.

I grabbed my phone, went to the bedroom and closed the door. I called the doctor's office, and after being put on hold and waiting five minutes, I finally reached his nurse. I explained the situation; that my meds had been stolen and I needed new prescriptions.

She looked me up in her records and then put me on hold again. A few minutes later, she came back on the line and said, "Mr. Walker, your doctor said he could write you a prescription for the anti-seizure drug but not the pain meds. Will that work for you?"

I told her it would and asked to have the prescription sent to the CVS pharmacy next to McDonald's in Saint

Augustine. She said they would, and I'd get a text when it was ready.

I ended the call and went back up front. Bob was still on the couch, but Erin was gone. I hadn't heard her leave, but since there weren't many places in the RV to hide and I couldn't find her inside, she had to be gone.

I gave Bob a pet and went out to see if I could find her. It didn't take long because she was leaning against the front fender of Raif's car, talking on her phone. When she saw me, she smiled and pointed up with her index finger. I took it to mean she would be with me in a minute.

When her call ended three minutes later, she asked, "Where do we find Waldo? You have any ideas?"

I did, and I shared them with her.

"We start at his trailer. Maybe he came back. Or maybe there's something inside that will tell us where he went."

We went next door; Waldo's car was still gone and there were no lights on inside. But it looked like his front door was slightly ajar. I wanted to check to see why, but Erin said no. She wanted me to stay outside and be her lookout. If I saw Waldo coming back, my job was to let her know so she could get out without him seeing her.

She went up his steps and gently pushed on the front door. The door swung open, giving Erin a clear view inside. She looked in and then turned back to me. I could tell something was wrong, so I left my lookout post and went to join her.

When I reached her, she was still standing outside his door. She said, "Take a look. Tell me what you think."

I stepped over the threshold to get a better view, and what I saw suggested someone else had been in the trailer, looking for something.

Every drawer had been opened, with its contents dumped on the floor. Same with the kitchen cabinets. They were all open and whatever had been in them was on the floor below. The couch had been turned over, its cushions ripped open. It looked like nothing had been left untouched.

Erin turned to me and whispered, "Let's go in. But don't touch anything."

She stepped past me and went in first. I followed.

Inside, she gingerly made her way to the back bedroom. It, too, had been tossed. The few clothes that had been in the closet were now on the floor. The bedside table lamp had been shattered, broken beyond repair. The mattress had been stripped, turned over, and cut open.

It was clear someone had been searching for something. It wasn't clear whether they had found it or not.

Erin backed out of the bedroom and we left the trailer the same way we had gone in, being careful not to touch anything. We didn't want to leave our prints inside, in case the police came to investigate.

Back outside, Erin turned to me and said, "Tell me who else is looking for him and why."

It was a question I knew the answer to. I could have lied and said I didn't know. But I didn't. I told her the truth. I gave her the short version. "Waldo borrowed money from people he shouldn't have. He didn't pay it back like he promised, and now they are looking for him. They're probably the ones who trashed his trailer.

"We need to find him before they do. If we don't, you'll never get your money back."

She nodded as if she understood. Then she pointed at Raif's trailer. "We should check on him. See if he is okay; make sure that whoever tossed Waldo's place didn't do the same to his."

Chapter Twenty-Nine

Raif wasn't sitting outside on his deck like he had been the last three times I'd been to his place. But there was a car parked in his driveway. A baby-blue Subaru Outback. I'd not seen it there before.

Erin walked over to Raif's front door and knocked. I knew she had a key and could have let herself in, but seeing that Raif had company, she thought it better if she let them know she was outside.

After hearing the knock, a woman wearing one of Raif's shirts and not much else came to the door. She saw Erin and said, "Oh, it's you."

Erin smiled and said, "Fay."

She said it in a way that made me think that maybe she and Fay weren't the best of friends.

She took a deep breath and asked, "Is Raif okay?"

Fay smiled. "I think he's better than okay. He sure was this morning. He's in the shower right now. You need to talk to him?"

Erin shook her head. "It can wait. But let me ask you a question. Did either of you hear or see anyone next door? It looks like someone broke in and wrecked the place."

Fay leaned out to look at the trailer next door, giving me an intimate view of her long, tanned legs. For a woman in her late fifties, she looked to be in good shape.

She saw me checking her out and winked. Then she turned back to Erin. "We didn't hear anything. We were kind of busy, if you know what I mean."

Erin smiled. "Well good for you. I'm glad to hear everything still works at your age."

She pointed back to me and said, "That's Walker. Tell Raif I'll be staying with him for the next few days. If he needs to talk to me, he can find me there."

Fay gave me the once over, and said, "You two have fun. I know Raif and I will."

Erin left the deck, walked over to me, grabbed my hand, and guided us back toward my RV. As soon as she was sure Fay couldn't hear her, she said, "Remember when I told you I was homeless? She's the reason. She's been bugging Raif about moving in with him. I guess she's gone and done it.

"Raif told me all three of us could live in his trailer and Fay wouldn't mind. To me, it didn't matter whether she minded or not. I wasn't going to live under the same roof with her.

"I'm happy he has found someone, even if it's Fay. But I don't want to be the third wheel and I don't want to hear them at night, in the morning, or whenever else they go at it.

"So, as of today, I'm officially moving out. And since I haven't found another place yet, I'm homeless. Unless you let me bunk in with you for a few days."

I didn't hesitate with my answer. "I'm sure Bob would love to have you around. And I could probably learn to put up with you."

She crossed her arms and said, "You think you could learn to put up with me? Is that what you said? You're kidding, right? I'd be doing you a big favor if I stayed with

132

you. You need someone like me around to keep you out of trouble. So say, 'Yes, please come stay with Bob and me.'"

And that's what I did. "Erin, nothing would make me happier than if you were to spend a few days with us. It would be the highlight of my life."

She smiled. "You bet it would. It'll be something you won't soon forget."

She grabbed my hand and led me to my front door mumbling, "If Fay thinks she's the only one around here who knows how to have a good time, she's wrong."

I didn't dare ask her what she meant. But I definitely was looking forward to finding out.

Back inside my RV, Erin looked around and asked, "Does the couch fold out into a bed?"

I nodded. "It does. You'll be comfortable there."

She grinned. "I'm sure one of us will be. Not so sure it'll be me though."

She walked to the back bedroom, where I'd be sleeping, and found Bob on the bed. She asked him if it would be okay if she joined him, and he said, "Murrrph." Yes, he would like it very much if she got into bed with him.

She lay down beside him and after a minute said, "Walker, why don't you come join us? I need to ask you something."

I wasn't sure what she was going to ask, but if she were going to ask it while we were lying on my bed, I definitely wanted to find out what it was. I pulled off my shoes, walked back to the bed and got in beside her.

It wasn't the first mistake I had made that day. And it wouldn't be the last.

133

Chapter Thirty

I had just gotten comfortable beside Erin when she rolled over to face me and asked, "What are we going to do next?"

I didn't answer right away. I could think of several pleasurable things we could do, but I wasn't totally sure that's what she had in mind. I thought about it and said, "We can do whatever you want. You're the guest here. Tell me what you want me to do. Where to start."

She laughed. "No, Walker, I'm not asking about that. And if the time ever comes, I won't need to ask, you'll know.

"I'm asking about Waldo. Where do we go from here?"

I was somewhat disappointed that after she asked me to get in bed with her, she wanted to talk about Waldo, and apparently nothing else.

I thought about her question for a moment, then said, "You were the last person who we know spent time with him. That means two things.

"First, it means you may have heard him say something that might help us find him.

"And, second, the goons looking for him will probably come looking for you after they figure out you owned the taco stand he wanted to buy.

"They'll think you know where he is. That means trouble. For you. And maybe even Raif if they can't find you.

"So what we need to do is make sure they can't find you.

Or me—because if they ask the park manager about Waldo, she might mention that I, too, was looking for him.

"If she tells them I'm in the park in my RV, they'll come looking for me. If they find you here, it'll look bad. They'll think we both know where he is. And they'll do whatever it takes to get it out of us.

"So we need to move. To someplace they won't find us."

Erin nodded in agreement. "You're right. We don't need to be here if they come looking for either of us."

She rolled out of bed, stood and said, "I'm going over to Raif's; let him know what's going on. You get the motorhome ready to move. I won't be gone long."

I would have liked to stay in bed a bit longer with her. After my early morning's blurred vision episode, a little quiet time giving my eyes a rest was something I was looking forward to.

But it wasn't in the cards. I needed to get the motorhome ready to roll.

I reluctantly got up out of bed, walked to the front of the RV, and brought the two front slides in. Then I went back to the bedroom, picked up Bob, and brought the rear slide in. He didn't like it when the walls were in motion and couldn't figure out which direction they'd be going. I always worried he might panic and run into the path of one of the moving walls. So I always made sure I was either holding him or he was locked in the bathroom when the slides were going in or out.

After getting them in, I put Bob back on the bed and went outside to unhook from shore power. Before going to the power pole at the rear of the RV, I checked to make sure the guys in the black SUV hadn't parked nearby and were watching me.

They weren't. I took care of the hookups and headed back inside. I walked from front to back picking up anything that might slide off a counter or break while I was driving. Then I locked all the cabinet doors and made sure we were ready to travel.

A few minutes later, Erin came back, carrying a small, black overnight bag. Apparently, she had two of them. The one she had brought with her the night before and the one she had just brought from Raif's. She dropped the bag on the couch and said, "I filled him in and he agrees we should move, at least temporarily. He suggested we go to Anastasia State Park. They are usually full up this time of year, but I called and they had two sites available. One in the sun and one in the shade. The one in the shade was only available for a day, but the one in the sun was open for the next four days. I told them we'd take it and would be there within the hour.

"Raif said to keep his car as long as we needed it. If he wanted to go anywhere, Fay would take him."

She looked around the motorhome and said, "If you're ready to leave, we should go. I'll drive Raif's car and you can follow me to the park."

Twelve minutes later, after leaving Saint Augustine and crossing the Bridge of Lions to A1A south, we took a left onto Anastasia State Park road and followed it to the check-in station. I parked the motorhome in the RV lot and went inside to see about a site. I told the ranger behind the counter that Erin had just called, and they were holding a site for us.

I gave him my name, showed my Florida driver's license and the RV's plate number. He entered the details into his computer, told me how much it would be, and I paid using a credit card. He ran it through his machine and had me sign the charge ticket. Then he gave me a receipt and a bright yellow card with our site number written on it, along with the date we would be leaving.

Before I left the office, he explained the park rules. They were the same as the other Florida state parks where I'd camped. After he asked if I had any questions, he gave me a park map with the route to our site highlighted in yellow.

I thanked him for his assistance and went back out to the RV. Erin had parked Raif's car nearby, and I went over to show her where we would be staying. She looked at the map and said, "Let me go first, it'll be easier that way."

I knew what she was saying. It would be easier for her to find the site in a car than it would be for me in the motorhome, mainly because I was taller, wider, and had to go slower. I had to watch for low-hanging branches, narrow turns, and hidden drives.

She took off, and I followed, trying my best to keep up. After a series of turns taking us down narrow shell-covered roads with thick tropical foliage on both sides, we reached our site. Number one hundred seven, in the Coquina campground.

The site, like all that we had passed, was narrow and paved only in crushed shell. But it looked fairly level and was far enough away from Shady Haven that we wouldn't have to worry about the guys in black finding us.

After three tries, I finally got the motorhome backed into the narrow site, close enough to the power pole with enough space on each side to run the slide rooms out without hitting anything.

The site was deep enough for Erin to park Raif's car in front of the RV without sticking out onto the road. After she had it parked, she came over to me and said, "It took you three tries to get it parked. I thought you being a full-time RV'er, you'd be better at parking it."

I nodded. "Yeah, I thought I'd be better at it too. But on these narrow park roads with tight turns, you can't just blindly back into a site. You have to watch out for low-hanging branches, picnic tables and the power pole.

"So yeah, sometimes it takes me three tries to get into a site. Next time I'll let you do it. See how many tries it takes you."

Erin was smiling when she said, "It's a deal. I'll do it next time."

She took a deep breath and asked, "Now that we're here, what's next?"

Chapter Thirty-One

"Okay, we know that the two guys looking for Waldo think he's still in Saint Augustine. If they'd found him, they probably wouldn't have tossed his trailer a few hours ago."

We were back inside the motorhome. After getting it parked, I hooked up to shore power, and with Erin holding Bob, I ran out the three slide rooms. This would give us enough room to move around without bumping into each other.

With the slides out and the power on, we sat at the kitchen table and listed the things we knew for sure about Waldo's whereabouts.

The list wasn't long. Just two items so far and we weren't really sure about those two.

"Can't you call his mother? Ask her if he's still up here? If she says he is, ask if she knows where we can find him?"

It was a good question. One that would have been easy to answer if I had his mother's phone number. But I didn't. My only contact was Marissa Chesnokov and she had asked me to be careful when I called her. She didn't want her husband to know about the search.

I did have the number of her burner phone, and being nearly midday, I figured maybe she would answer if I called.

After five rings, she picked up. "Walker, do you have good news for me?"

I didn't, but I didn't have bad news either. We thought

Waldo was still alive, we just didn't know where.

"We haven't found him yet, but the two guys Mad Dog sent up here looking for him haven't found him either.

"He didn't buy the taco truck and he's moved from the address you sent me. So we need your help."

I paused, long enough for her to ask, "You said 'we'. I thought we agreed you were going to do this alone. Who's helping you?"

I looked over at Erin and smiled. I couldn't help it, she made me feel good. I answered Marissa's question.

"The owner of the taco shop. She's helping me. She's the last one that spoke to Waldo and she knows more about Saint Augustine than I do. I haven't told her about you. But I don't think there'll be a problem."

I waited to hear what Marissa would say, expecting it wouldn't be anything good. But I was wrong. Instead of scolding me, she asked, "It's a woman that's helping you? Let me guess, she's about your age? And pretty? And hopefully single?"

I nodded, even though she couldn't see me nod, and said, "Yes, she's a woman and, yes, she's pretty. And smart and she's with me right now. Would you like to talk to her?"

"No Walker, I don't need to talk to her. I trust your instincts on this. If you say she's helping you, that's all I need to know. But don't tell her who you're working for, understood?"

Again I nodded, a habit I needed to break, at least while on the phone. "Don't worry, we're being discreet. But like I said, we've run into a dead end and need your help. We need you to call Waldo's mother and ask if she's heard from him lately. If she has, try to find out if he's still in Saint Augustine.

If he's still here, it would help if we knew where he was staying. If he has a new phone number, get it. We'll want to call him."

Marissa said she'd try and would text me with whatever she found out about Waldo's new digs.

After I ended the call, Erin asked, "Was that Waldo's mother?"

I shook my head. "No, a close friend of hers. She said she'd speak to his mother and text us with anything new."

Erin grinned. "So who's this woman you told her about? You said she was pretty and smart. Anyone I know?"

I smiled and said, "I don't know if you know her or not, but I'll introduce you next time I see her. But right now, we need to leave. There's something I need to do."

Erin didn't ask why or where we were going. She just picked up the car keys and said, "I'm driving."

That was fine with me. I didn't know Saint Augustine well, and she did. Earlier, I'd gotten a text from CVS telling me my prescription was ready for pick-up at the store on A1A South. According to Google Maps, it was a short drive from the park.

After passing by the ranger station on our way out, Erin asked, "Where are we going? I need to know which way to turn when we get to the highway."

"Turn left, we're going to CVS."

She nodded, and when we reached A1A, she turned left and headed south. Three minutes later, we pulled into the CVS parking lot. I went inside, picked up my prescription and a bottle of water and came back out, carrying a white CVS bag with drug information stapled to it. There was no way Erin didn't see what I was carrying.

When I got back into the car, she nodded toward the bag and asked, "Are you contagious? Anything I need to worry about?"

I shook my head. "No, the pills are for my eyes. I had a concussion and my doctor said to take one of these every day. My prescription ran out and I needed it refilled. That's why we're here."

I pulled the bottle out of the bag, screwed off the top, and shook out a single pill into my open palm. It was small but had proven to be effective. I put it in my mouth, chased it down with a swig of water, and put the bottle back in the bag.

When I was done, Erin asked, "All better now?"

I nodded. "Yeah."

We were still sitting in the parking lot of CVS. The air conditioner in Raif's car had no problem keeping it cool inside, even on the low fan setting. Maybe a beefed up AC was one of the other standard features on the police interceptor. It made sense that it would be, police spend a lot of time sitting in a car and a good air conditioner, especially in Florida, was a must-have.

I tapped the dash with my right hand and said, "I like this car. I want one. Think Raif could help me get one like it?"

Erin nodded. "He could if you really wanted one, but after a few days riding around in this one, you might change your mind.

She paused, then asked, "You getting hungry?"

"Yeah, what do you have in mind?"

"Burritos. From Benito's. They're just down the road.

Thought maybe we ought to stop in and talk to Benito. Let him know about the two guys looking for Waldo. About how they might stop by the Taco Palace asking about him."

She was right. We probably needed to let the new owner of the taco truck know about the guys looking for Waldo. His people working there wouldn't know who Waldo was or how to find him. But they might give them Erin's contact info. That wouldn't be good.

Erin pulled out of the CVS and, six minutes later, we parked in front of a brightly colored building that looked like it had once been a gas station. The building itself was clean, the roof was new, the signage on the outside professionally done, and it looked like a safe place to eat burritos and tacos.

Erin led the way and we were soon inside placing our orders. We both ordered the same thing. Tijuana Cart Tacos. Three for six-fifty. She ordered an orange mango drink to go with hers, and I stuck with bottled water.

While we waited for our food, Erin went to the small office in the back and spoke with Benito. A few minutes later, she came back to my table and gave me a thumbs up. The meeting had gone well.

The tacos were good, in fact, the best I'd ever had, but I didn't tell Erin that. The tacos she had been making were also good. Not quite as good as Benito's but still better than what you get at most places.

After we finished eating, she asked the same question she'd asked back in the RV. "What do we do next?"

I thought before I answered, and the best I could come up with was, "We go back to the RV and try to figure this out."

Chapter Thirty-Two

On the way back to the motorhome, I sat in the passenger seat and watched Erin and listened to her voice as she drove. That's when I decided that maybe she was right about Raif's car. It wasn't the car that I liked so much it was riding around in it with her.

There was no way I was going to share this thought, so I just admired the view and kept my mouth shut.

When we got back to the motorhome, Bob was waiting for us at the door. I went in first, and he ran over to greet me. He rubbed up against my ankle, but as soon as he saw Erin behind me, he chirped and ran over to her.

Seeing Bob heading her way, she bent over and called his name. "Bob, you're such a good-looking kitty. I need one just like you."

I don't know how much he understood, but his ears perked up when he heard her say his name. From then on, he was her shadow. He stayed at her feet and followed her as she walked to the back bedroom. There, she kicked off her shoes and sat down on the bed. Bob sat beside her.

I was still up front when she called out, "Walker, Bob and I have decided to take a little nap. You should join us."

We had just eaten lunch and a nap sounded like a good idea. Especially with Erin lying beside me. I didn't hesitate. I went back and joined them on the bed.

The low hum of the overhead fan along with the muted

sounds of traffic out on A1A was all that it took for me to doze off.

Sometime later, I woke to Bob's claws digging into my chest. He was snuggled in between me and Erin and was making donuts, pushing his feet in and out, using me as his backboard. His deep purring told me he was a very contented kitty.

I needed to get up and pee but didn't want to disturb either Bob or Erin, so I just lay there, trying my best not to think about waterfalls and fire hydrants. But it didn't work. I needed to get up and take the short walk to the bathroom.

When I rolled over to get out of bed, Erin reached out and touched my shoulder. "Me first. It'll just take a minute." Then she got up and went to the bathroom.

Four minutes later, when she returned, I didn't have time to make small talk. I needed to pee, and I'd almost waited too long. I quickly got up out of bed, headed to the bathroom and took care of business.

After washing up, I went back to the bed, planning on resuming my nap with Erin at my side. But it wasn't to be. Both she and Bob were gone. Not wanting to nap alone, I headed up front and found them both on the couch. Bob was in Erin's lap, and she was gently stroking his back.

When she saw me, she said, "Bob and I decided it was time to get up. Glad to see you are joining us."

She patted the couch and said, "Come, sit by me."

After I'd sat, she said, "You know, I don't really need to find Waldo. I'd like to get my money back, but I don't want you or Raif to get hurt. So if you decide you don't want to look for him anymore, that's fine by me.

"But if you want to keep looking, that works for me too.

148

We just have to be careful. And we need something to go on. Something that'll point us in the right direction."

I nodded. "You're right. If we're going to keep looking for him, we need a lead. But if it gets dangerous and you decide to bail, I'll understand. I don't want you to get hurt. I'm not trying to get rid of you. In fact, I kind of like having you around. You know all the best places to eat."

She smiled and said, "Okay, it's settled. We'll keep looking for him. Where do we start?"

Before I could answer, my phone buzzed with an incoming text. I clicked accept and read the message. It said, "W still in SA. Told M he was getting in on the ground floor. Didn't say what. Will text with more if I get it."

I read the message out loud to Erin. She listened and said, "Read it again. This time, slower."

I reread it, and Erin stopped me after the first word. She said, "W obviously means Waldo. Continue."

As I read the rest of the message, she nodded as she heard each word. When I got to "M", she said, "That probably means his mother. Continue."

I read the rest without being interrupted. When I was finished, Erin said, "So, it sounds like he called his mother and told her he's still in Saint Augustine. He thinks he's getting in on the ground floor of something. But we don't know what.

"All we need to do is figure out what he's talking about. You have any thoughts on that?"

I did.

Chapter Thirty-Three

"So you were the last person we know who spent any time talking with Waldo. You were with him for two days showing him how to run the Taco Palace.

"You couldn't have been busy serving customers all the time, and when it was slow, you two must have talked about things other than food.

"What do you remember?"

Erin thought for a moment, then said, "He told me he wanted to tour the old fort downtown, Castillo de San Marcos.

"He also said he wanted to visit the Pirate Museum. It's across the street from the fort."

She closed her eyes for a moment then opened them and said, "The Fountain of Youth. He wanted to visit the Fountain of Youth. Said he wanted to drink the water.

"That's all I remember. The fort, the museum, and the fountain. The same places most tourists want to see."

"Okay. So, we know he's interested in tourist attractions. Maybe that's the kind of business he thinks he's getting in on the ground floor of. Or maybe, like every new visitor to Saint Augustine, he wants to see the attractions.

"There has to be more than that. Did he talk about his car or his hobbies or favorite songs or movies?"

Erin frowned then said, "He wasn't much of a talker. He

grunted a lot. And he complained about the heat. Said it was hot in the taco truck. Said that when he bought it, the first thing he'd do was add air conditioning."

I nodded. "What else do you remember? What about his car? Did you see what he was driving?"

She laughed. "Yeah, I saw it. An old Camry. Faded silver with paint peeling off the hood and roof. It looked like it had been through a hail storm. Had lots of golf ball-sized dents.

"He said he didn't care too much about cars. As long as it got him where he wanted to go, he would drive anything.

"Video games. That's what he mostly talked about. And when he did, I tuned him out. I didn't have time to play games and wasn't interested in what he was saying about them.

"I do remember him telling me about his computer setup. How it had lots of rams and gigs and was super-fast. He said as soon as he moved into a place with internet, he would be setting it up."

She paused, and I said, "Erin, you're doing good. Starting to remember the little details. Any of those could be important. What else did you talk about?"

She rubbed her chin. "He asked me what I was going to do after I sold the business. He seemed really interested in my answer."

She waited for me to ask the question she knew I was going to. "So what did you tell him? What were you planning to do after you sold him the truck?"

She shook her head and said, "Up until he asked, I hadn't really thought about it. I was too busy keeping the business open to worry about what I was going to do next. But I think I told him I wanted to own something like Shady Haven. A place where people paid you to park.

"He wanted to know more, so I told him that Shady Haven had over a hundred trailer and RV sites and most rented for seven hundred a month. I remember him saying that it didn't seem too profitable. Just making seven thousand a month renting trailer sites.

"That's when I realized he wasn't too good at math. A hundred sites times seven hundred would be seventy thousand a month, not seven thousand. I didn't bother to correct his mistake. But I think he finally figured it out because later on he said, 'I guess something like that could work. Not much labor involved. And people pay you to sit in an office and collect rent. Sounds good to me.'"

I nodded. "Did he ask you any more questions about Shady Haven? Maybe about how much money it would take to buy a place like that?"

"No, we got busy after that, taking care of the lunch rush. In fact, we stayed pretty busy until closing time. He didn't say much the rest of the day. He just complained about the heat and grunted every time we got an order."

I thought about what she had said. "Let me guess. He asked the question about what kind of business you wanted to do next on the second day he worked with you. Am I right?"

Erin squinted, trying to remember. "Yeah, I'm pretty sure it was the second day. The last day we worked together. The last day that I saw him."

I smiled. "Okay, maybe we're getting somewhere. We know he said he's getting in on the ground floor of something. And we know he's interested in tourist attractions and video games. He said he wants to work where it's air-conditioned. That rules out just about everything outdoors, including food trucks.

"There are lots of tourist attractions in town, and many are inside with air conditioning. Maybe he's thinking along those lines. Finding a tourist attraction he could buy."

Erin nodded. "That's not all. We know he doesn't like hard work. He'd rather be indoors sitting in front of a computer, playing video games."

She took a breath and said, "Maybe that's it. Maybe he's found a business for sale where people pay to play video games."

I nodded. "Yeah, based on what we know, that might be the kind of business he'd want to own. But how do we find out if any are for sale or are getting ready to open?"

Erin smiled and asked, "You have a computer here?"

"Yes."

"Good. Get it out. We'll check Craigslist, see if there are businesses in the for sale section that might fit the bill. We'll do the same on Facebook Marketplace.

"If we don't find anything, we can go back to his trailer. Now that we know what we're looking for, we might get lucky. Maybe we'll find a newspaper with something circled in the classifieds."

I wasn't sure we'd be that lucky and I didn't think going back to Waldo's was such a good idea. The thugs looking for him could be watching the place. If we showed up, they might ask us questions we didn't want to answer. I didn't share my concerns with Erin. I was hoping we'd find a few leads on Craigslist and wouldn't need to go back to the trailer.

154

I went to the closet in my bedroom, grabbed my laptop and brought it back up front. Four minutes later, we were sitting at the kitchen table scanning the businesses for sale listings on Craigslist.

Chapter Thirty-Four

"How about this one?"

I pointed to the listing for an affiliate marketing program. I knew it was a scam and figured Erin did too. She didn't disappoint. She said, "Waldo's not that dumb. He's close but not there yet."

Scanning down the list, we saw several vending machines for sale, supposedly turnkey. All you had to do was buy the machines, convince businesses to let you put them in their buildings, then buy inventory and restock the machines.

It sounded iffy. Too much work. Not the kind of business that would appeal to Waldo.

There were three food trucks for sale, none of them operational. We figured that after his two days working with Erin in her hot truck, he probably knew he wasn't cut out for that kind of work.

There were a few other businesses for sale—a barbershop, a tattoo shop, and a sign-printing business. These could be profitable if run by the right person. But that person wouldn't be Waldo. From what we knew about him, he didn't have the skills needed to cut hair or operate a tattoo gun.

We checked the first two hundred and twenty listings and nothing jumped out at us.

Disappointed with what we hadn't found on Craigslist, but not ready to give up on the search, I suggested we look at eBay. Erin had a better idea. She said, "Stay on Craigslist. Check the video game section. Maybe we'll find something there."

Her suggestion made sense. Waldo had said he was big into video games. If he found a business that had something to do with computers and games, and he felt he could get in on the ground floor, it might be just the thing.

I clicked over to the gaming category, and we started scanning the listings; the same as we had done with the businesses for sale.

Most were for old game cartridges being sold. A few game controllers, some old Nintendo systems, and PS2 games. None of which we thought he'd be interested in.

But there was one listing that seemed promising. A complete video gaming parlor. A place where people could go and play video games. The inventory included twenty-two inter-connected high-speed computers, a router, a wireless network, and a payment gateway.

The description said that the items were from a profitable walk-in gaming parlor and the sale included everything needed to restart the business. The kicker in the description was the words, "Ground floor opportunity for the right person."

We agreed it was the kind of business Waldo might be attracted to. But we didn't know if the equipment was still for sale. The listing didn't include a phone number. Just a blind email address through Craigslist. The seller didn't want the world to see his phone number or actual email address.

Having posted several items on Craigslist, I knew why he had done it that way. Every time I put something up there for sale, I'd get a lot of junk email and phone calls from people trying to scam me. They'd usually say they were sending a money order for the full price. After it arrived, they promised one of their friends would come by and pick up the item.

Of course, the money order would be fake and if you let the 'friend' take the item before the bank alerted you to the fraud, you'd end up empty-handed. No money and no item.

People who frequently used Craigslist to sell items knew better than to show their contact info in the ad. Using Craigslist's blind email forwarding service was the best way to keep the scammers at bay.

We weren't scammers, but we did want to know if the gaming equipment had been sold, and, if so, to whom. The only way to find out was to use the Craigslist contact form to send an email to the seller.

I typed out a message and had Erin review it before I sent it. It said, "I might be interested in your gaming parlor equipment. Is it still for sale? If so, when and where can it be seen? We are in Saint Augustine and can meet you anytime."

I included Erin's phone number and signed it with her name, figuring anyone selling a video gaming parlor would probably reply to a message from a woman faster than they would from a man.

After she changed two words in the message, I clicked "send".

We didn't expect a reply right away. Most sellers wouldn't be spending their time sitting in front of their computer waiting for the next email from Craigslist. Most would check their inboxes once or twice a day and then reply whenever they felt like it.

It might take time for the seller to get back to us, but at

least it was a promising lead. The first we'd had.

We scanned another hundred listings and didn't find anything we thought Waldo would be interested in. But we weren't going to give up. At least not yet.

"Think we should still check eBay?"

Erin nodded. "Yeah, we should. Waldo probably looked there as well. I sure would have."

I entered eBay's URL, and we were soon on the site. I clicked on the "business for sale" category, and we started scanning the ads. The first few pages were full of turnkey adult video and cam girl websites, travel and dating websites, and wholesale perfumes.

Nothing we thought would appeal to Waldo, except maybe the adult video and webcam businesses. But I suspected if he was interested in cam girls, he'd visit them in the privacy of his bedroom.

Finding nothing in the general business category, I narrowed the search to retail businesses in the Saint Augustine area. This produced fewer but far more interesting results.

Among the businesses for sale were a pawn shop, a vape store, a tire store and something called the Monkey Train. We ruled out the pawnshop and tire store; both were priced well above what Waldo could afford. The vape store was in his price range, but we weren't sure it would be something he'd be interested in.

The Monkey Train was a different story. It checked a few of Waldo's boxes. It was a tourist attraction consisting of three cartoon train cars being pulled by a battery-powered golf cart that looked like a train engine. It currently operated indoors (in a mall) and was an all-cash business. There were no fixed hours, which meant the operator could sleep in and close down whenever they wanted to. It sounded exactly what Waldo would be interested in.

I clicked the link to learn more and everything looked good until I reached the final line in the description. It said, "Currently located in Colorado Springs, Colorado."

For most people, including Waldo if he had any sense, the distant location and the cost of transporting the train to Florida would be a deal killer.

We continued to scan the ads, page after page, until Erin said, "There's something. A clothing optional RV park. Click the link. I want to see what it says."

Chapter Thirty-Five

Erin asked me to read the listing out loud. I did, using my best announcer voice.

30 Site Clothing Optional RV Resort with 11.5+/- acres in St. Johns County, Florida

Includes:

- Office/Restaurant building
- Tiki Bar
- Restaurant with liquor Licenses
- Clubhouse
- Large Heated Pool
- 12-person Spa
- Two Bath Houses
- Tennis & Pickle ball Courts

This is a private gated community. 100% occupancy since 2015. 25% full-time renters. Complete with all the staff and equipment necessary to continue its spectacular growth.

Five hundred thousand. Owner financing available with ten percent down.

When I finished reading, Erin said, "That sounds pretty good. I wonder how much the place brings in each month."

Before I could answer, she said, "If they have thirty sites and charge eight hundred a month that comes to twenty-four thousand. You'd have to subtract utilities, insurance, and wages, but it should still be pretty profitable. Might be a fun business to have."

She was smiling while rubbing her chin. Obviously thinking it through.

Just to be sure we were on the same page, I asked, "You think Waldo might be interested in this? Running a clothing optional RV park?"

She shook her head. "I'm not sure about Waldo. But it might be something I'm interested in."

I thought she was joking, so I said, "Yeah right. I could see it now. You out there naked in the bright sun, greeting new visitors. But I can't see how it would work. A fair maiden such as yourself would burn in no time.

"Still, if you bought the place, I'd be one of your first customers. As long as you promised to greet me at the gate in just your birthday suit."

She smiled. "You'd like that, wouldn't you? Me running around naked for your amusement. But that's not the way I'd do it. I'd keep my clothes on and let the staff do all the naked stuff.

"You could still come, but you'd have to drop your drawers at the gate."

She grinned. "I might even offer you a discount if you did."

She pulled out her phone, took a photo of the listing and said, "Maybe I'll look into it. It might work as my next business."

I still wasn't sure if she was joking, but whether she was or not, her talking about us seeing each other naked was a step in the right direction.

We didn't find anything else that seemed legit or of

interest to Waldo in the businesses for sale section, so Erin suggested we check the real estate category and limit the search to Florida.

I did the search and found eighteen listings in the Saint Augustine area. Most were for vacant lots or tax lien properties. There was a six-plex for sale at what seemed like a reasonable price, but in the photos, it looked like a real dump that needed a lot of work.

Still, I asked Erin about it. "How about this one? You could fix it up, rent out the apartments, and have a steady stream of income. Maybe this would work for Waldo?"

She nodded. "You're right. It might be something he'd be interested in. But I don't see how it fits his 'getting in on the ground floor' thinking. But we should follow up on it, just in case. Send the seller a message. Just like the one we sent before. Find out where the building is and if it is still available."

I typed up the message and sent it off.

That meant we had at least two promising leads. Three if you included the clothing optional RV resort.

We scanned the other real estate listings and didn't find anything else of interest. It looked like the video game parlor, the six-plex and the clothing optional RV resort were the three most likely candidates.

We weren't sure that any of them would appeal to Waldo or work within his budget. But eBay and Craigslist weren't the only places he might have looked.

"You said you used to work in a real estate office? Do you think any of your contacts there could tell us if he made an offer or bought anything around here? If he has, it would make it a whole lot easier to find him."

She looked at the clock on her phone and said, "Their office closed at five, so there won't be anyone there now. I can call in the morning and see what I can find out. If the deal has closed, they can give me the details. But they won't be able to tell me anything about pending offers. Those stay confidential."

She leaned back, crossed her arms, and smiled. I was pretty sure she was still thinking about the RV park we'd found on eBay. Maybe she was serious about it. If she were, I'd be happy to go with her to check it out.

I started to tell her this, but my stomach growled. We hadn't eaten since lunch and it was fast approaching dinner time. Erin beat me to the question I was planning to ask. "Dinner? Are we going to eat here or go out?

Before I could answer, she said, "I vote we go out. We can cross the bridge, park at the fort, and walk through old town. Maybe we'll see a sign for a new business getting ready to open. Or something about a ground floor opportunity.

"Either way, there are lots of cafes and restaurants there and we can grab dinner."

She stood and said, "I'm going to go freshen up. Then it'll be your turn. After that, we go."

Chapter Thirty-Six

Ten minutes later, we were in Raif's white ex-police car, heading toward Saint Augustine's historic district. Public access to the fort at Castillo de San Marcos had ended at five and we didn't have any trouble finding a parking space in its large lot.

Erin locked up the car and we crossed over San Marcos and made our way up to Fort Alley. From there, it was a short walk to Saint George, one of the oldest streets in the country.

Narrow and cobble-stoned, it had been turned into a pedestrian-only walkway. Both sides were lined with structures that looked to have been built two hundred years earlier. Most had been converted into cafes, bars, ice cream parlors, and gift shops. But many retained the flavor of the swashbuckling era.

The storekeepers and others walking around in pirate costumes helped seal the illusion. Had the street not been packed with modern-day tourists with their fancy gadgets and immodest apparel, it would have been easy to believe that one had somehow stepped back in time.

But the gaggle of tourists, along with contemporary music being pumped out from a number of the taverns that lined the street, gave it more of the vibe of a Disney-theme park, than a true historical site. Still, it was a pretty interesting place.

As we weaved through the crowds, Erin grabbed my hand and said, "If Waldo was going to open a tourist business, this would be the street to be on. We should walk to the end, looking for signs about new businesses about to open or ground-floor opportunities."

A walk sounded good to me. We'd spent half the day either in bed or on the computer. With the day's heat fading and the cool breezes coming off the Matanzes River it was near perfect weather for walking.

Still holding my hand, Erin led the way through a maze of tourists, many of whom were paying more attention to the buildings around them than the people in front of them. Several times we had to come to a full stop to avoid being hit by a cone licker looking at their phone instead of watching where they were going.

Had I been in a hurry or had a place I needed to be, the throngs of tourists blocking our way would have bothered me.

But not that day. The weather was perfect, Erin was holding my hand, and the buildings around us were interesting. I was tempted to pull out my phone and shoot a few photos of our surroundings. Just like a tourist. But I resisted. Erin had my phone hand, and I wasn't going to let go.

As we walked, we kept to the right side of the street, slowing at each store-front, looking for signs about new business openings or business opportunities. There was no shortage of signs but most were promoting in-store discounts, upcoming events, and second-floor accommodations. None that we saw were what we were looking for.

We stayed on Saint George, crossing over the side streets of Hypolita and Treasury. Both were similar to St George. Cobblestones, pedestrian-only, lined with historic buildings and shops. I wanted to explore them further, but Erin said we needed to wait. She said if we came back the next day, we could catch a ride on the Old Town Trolley. It would take us to many of Saint Augustine's historic sites, including the streets we were on and the fabled Fountain of Youth.

The trolley tour sounded like a good idea. We could visit all the attractions and not worry about traffic or parking. If Erin was still up to it, we'd do it the next day. In the morning before it got too hot.

When we reached the crosswalk at Saint George and the fast-moving traffic on Business One, we turned around and walked back the way we had come, staying on the right side of the street, still looking for new businesses and ground-floor opportunities.

Just about every storefront had vendors outside hawking their wares, handing out discount booklets or playing music. It created a festive, carnival-like atmosphere, and I could see why the place attracted so many tourists.

It was kind of like Bourbon Street in New Orleans but without all the drunks.

About halfway back to Fort Alley, Erin stopped in front of the Taberna Del Caballo restaurant. She pointed at the menu taped on the front glass and asked, "See anything you like?"

Before I could answer, she said, "The Avocado Goddess Salad with grilled chicken. That's what I'm having."

She'd already made her decision. We were going to eat at the Taberna Del Caballo, whether I liked it or not.

I was wearing cargo shorts and a fishing shirt and I was worried I might not be dressed well enough for a fancy restaurant. Stepping inside, I quickly realized that how we were dressed wouldn't be a problem. Especially after I saw a sign that told what Taberina Del Caballo meant; the Tavern of the Horse. The sign explained the place had once been a stable.

Inside it did look like a stable that had been converted into a tavern. One from the seventeenth century. With dark wooden beams spanning the low ceiling. White plastered walls that looked older than they probably were. Wooden picnic tables, both inside and out on the patio, provided plenty of seating.

Erin told the greeter we were there for dinner and she led us to a table on the patio. She asked if we wanted to place our drink orders, and Erin ordered wine. That meant I'd probably be the one driving us home, so I took the high road. I ordered water.

The waitress soon returned with Erin's wine and asked if we knew what we wanted. Erin had already decided on the Goddess Salad and that's what she ordered. After looking at the menu, I went with something called Carne Asada. I didn't know what it was, but it looked good in the photo next to its name.

When the server left, Erin sipped her wine and said, "It's been a pretty good day for me. We've eaten all our meals out, and I haven't had to make a single taco.

"We may not have found Waldo yet, but it's been fun looking for him."

I nodded, thinking that, yes, it had been fun. But I wondered what would happen when we got back to the RV.

She had told Fay she was spending the night with me.

I wondered how that was going to work.

Chapter Thirty-Seven

The food arrived quickly and both choices looked better than the menu photos. The server refilled Erin's wine and again asked me if I wanted to place a drink order.

Had I not been the one who would be driving us back to the RV, I would have ordered sangria. It would have gone well with the Carne Asada.

We didn't talk much during dinner as we were both too busy eating, and the live music next door would have drowned out any conversation we might have had.

Erin finished her meal and had another glass of wine after the server cleared our table. When the check came, I paid with a credit card and left a twenty-dollar tip.

Going back outside, the sun had set, and the party on the street was starting to gear up. Unlike the family friendly tourists we had seen earlier, the night time crowd was mostly twenty-somethings. A little better dressed than the people we had seen during the day.

I asked Erin if she wanted to join the party-goers or head home.

She shook her head and said, "I think I should have stopped on the third glass. The fourth one might have put me over the limit."

She reached into her pocket, pulled out the car keys, handed them to me and said, "You're driving."

It took us about ten minutes to get back to the car in the

Castille de San Marcos parking lot. I helped Erin in on the passenger side, and took my seat behind the wheel.

I pulled out of the lot, and ten minutes later we passed through the gates at Anastasia State Park and soon were parked in front of our motorhome.

After helping Erin out of the car, I escorted her to the front door and helped her up the front steps. As expected, Bob was waiting for us at the door and he wasn't happy. He meowed over and over while walking in circles around us. I bent down to pet him, but he ran off toward the back of the motorhome.

Erin plopped down on the couch and I went back to see what Bob's problem was. He was standing in front of the bathroom door, which for some reason was closed, meaning he couldn't get to his food. Apparently, either Erin or I had shut it before we left for the evening.

I opened the door and Bob rushed in. He ducked his head into his food bowl and started chowing down. While he was doing this, I went back up front to talk to Erin.

She was still on the couch but no longer sitting. She was lying on her side, her hands under her head, acting as a pillow.

I didn't know if she was sleeping or not and I didn't want to wake her if she was. As quietly as I could, I opened the storage compartment above her head, pulled out a blanket and pillow, and set them on the end of the couch. I started to walk back to my bedroom, but Erin stopped me by reaching out and grabbing the back of my shorts.

In a sleepy voice, she said, "You're not going to leave me here, are you? I need to get out of these clothes and into bed. Will you help me?"

Anytime a woman asks me to help her get out of her clothes, I'm happy to oblige. But if she's too drunk to do it herself, that's as far as it will go. I won't be sleeping with her.

I decided I'd be sleeping on the couch, away from temptation.

I helped her up and guided her to the bathroom. I opened the door and gently pushed her in. She mumbled, "Close the door," and I did.

A few minutes later, I heard the toilet flush and I stepped back away. She stumbled out, wearing just bra and panties. Grinning at me, she pointed to the bedroom and mumbled something that sounded like, "Bed. Sleep."

It was easy to figure out what she wanted, so I guided her into the bedroom, got her up on the bed, and covered her with a sheet. Her eyes were closed, but I was pretty sure she was still awake, so I asked, "Anything else?"

She opened her eyes and asked, "Don't I get a goodnight kiss?"

She didn't have to ask twice. I bent over, kissed her on her forehead, and said, "Sleep well. If you need anything during the night, let me know."

I was leaving the room when I heard her say, "Wait." When I turned back to see what she wanted, her eyes were closed. But in what looked like slow motion, she patted the empty space beside her on the bed.

I knew that if I lay down next to her, there was a good chance we'd both regret it in the morning. Still, I have to admit I was considering it. Maybe it wouldn't be so bad. Maybe I should crawl into bed and watch over her, at least until she falls off to sleep.

It could have been that Bob was picking up on my

thoughts because he came into the room and effortlessly glided onto the bed and curled up against her. He looked up at me and blinked his eyes twice, almost as if to say, "You missed your chance, buddy. You should have moved in instead of thinking about it."

He might have been right, but, then again, he's a male cat and might not be the best one to listen to when it comes to advice about women.

With him snuggled up against Erin who was snoring softly, I turned off the light and headed up front to the couch. It's not my favorite place to sleep, but it's better than sleeping outside. I stripped down to my underwear, covered myself with the sheet and lay down.

As I was dozing off I started thinking about how strange it was that Erin, the woman whom I had just met the day earlier, was sleeping in my bed.

It was about to get a lot stranger.

Chapter Thirty-Eight

I was still sleeping when Erin came up front, wearing one of my tee-shirts and nothing else. She gave the couch a pretty good kick with her bare foot and said, "I'm heading to McDonald's in ten minutes. If you want to go with me, you need to get ready."

She turned and shuffled back to the bedroom, closing the door behind her. If she was getting dressed to go out to get breakfast, I figured I needed to do the same.

Since my clothes were in the closet in the bedroom and Erin had closed the door, I had to make a choice. Either barge in on her with the excuse of getting to my clothes or wear the same ones I had worn the day before.

They were in a pile at the end of the couch and within easy reach. I could get them on and be ready to go when she came out.

Fifteen minutes later, we were sitting in the same booth at the same McDonald's we'd eaten breakfast at the day before. Erin ordered pancakes with extra butter and syrup along with a medium Coke to wash it down. I ordered the same.

While we were eating, she stayed quiet. She didn't ask any questions about how she ended up undressed in my bed the previous night. She just ate her pancakes and smiled.

As we were getting ready to leave, she asked, "Do you have scissors in your RV?"

"Yeah, in the bottom drawer next to the sink. Why do

you ask?"

She smiled and said, "When we get back, I'll show you."

I turned right out of the McDonald's parking lot and headed back to our site in Anastasia State Park. As we approached the turn-off, Erin said, "Keep going straight. We've got to make another stop first."

I did as she asked. Two minutes later, she had me make a left onto the bridge to the mainland and then, a left at the light at US 1. Less than a quarter-mile later, she had me pull into the parking lot of a Goodwill store. She smiled and said, "We're here."

"What do you mean we're here? What are we doing at a Goodwill store?"

Instead of answering my question, she opened her door and said, "Follow me."

She went inside the store, and I stayed close behind. We were met by a greeter, who, with a lot of enthusiasm, said, "Welcome to Goodwill." I heard him repeat the same welcome to every other customer that came in. It was a nice touch, a good way to prepare us for what we were about to see.

The store was packed wall-to-wall with inventory. To our right used furniture. Couches, chairs, tables, beds, and lamps. Further back, electronics. TVs, stereos, computer monitors, printers and modems. Mostly obsolete things that had been donated.

Erin led me past all of these and headed over to the men's clothing department. She looked at me for a moment and said, "I'm guessing you're a thirty-six long, right?"

I was hesitant to answer. I was afraid of what that might lead to. But I had to say something, so I said, "I don't need any new clothes. I've got all I need back in the RV, and I like my style."

Totally ignoring me, she thumbed through the racks until she found a pair of long black pants with a thirty-six tag. She pulled them off the hanger, handed them to me and said, "Try these on."

I started to object, but she pointed to a dressing room just steps away and said, "Humor me. Try them on."

I took a deep breath. I didn't want to try on pants, especially used ones from Goodwill. But if it would make her happy, I would.

In the dressing room, I took off my shoes and stepped out of my cargo shorts and into the slightly used pants. They fit, but it felt weird to be wearing them. It'd been a long time since I had worn long pants. In Florida, I didn't need them.

As I was standing in the dressing room, looking at my reflection in the mirror, there was a tap on the door, followed by Erin asking, "Do they fit?"

"Come in and see for yourself."

I was surprised when she opened the door, stepped in, and closed it behind her. She had a white button-up shirt on a hanger in her right hand, a black blazer in her left, with a black tie draped over it.

She held the shirt out to me. "Try this. Let's see how they look together."

I didn't try to talk her out of it. I could tell she was planning something, and she wanted me to dress a certain way.

I put the shirt on and it fit. Seeing me in it, she smiled and said, "That'll work. Now the blazer."

I put it on over the shirt, and even though it felt weird to be wearing a blazer, it looked good on me.

She smiled and said, "That's the look I'm going for. Now put on your old clothes and bring the new ones out with you."

When I came out of the dressing room, she was holding another pair of pants, a white shirt, and a sports jacket. All three looked too small for me. I shook my head. "Nope, I'm not going to wear those."

She smiled. "Don't worry, these are for me."

On the way to the checkout, she grabbed a thin black belt in my size. Behind her, but not out of earshot, I said, "I hope you're getting these for a costume party because I'm not wearing them in public."

If she heard me, she didn't say anything. When we reached the checkout, she gave the clerk our clothes and had me pay. Total for two shirts, two pairs of pants, a tie, two blazers, and two belts was twenty-eight dollars. A real bargain if you didn't mind wearing used clothes.

As we were leaving, the same man who had welcomed us when we came in said, "Have a nice day."

Again, it sounded like he meant it, so I said, "You too."

Out in the parking lot, on the way to the car, I asked Erin, "Okay, tell me. Why did we get the clothes?"

She looked me over then down at my shoes. "Do you have something a bit more formal than the sneakers you're wearing?"

I didn't, and I didn't want her to know. I feared she'd drag me back into the Goodwill store to go shoe shopping. But she'd already made up her mind. "We need to get you some dress shoes. Follow me."

She went back into the store, and again I followed. She led me to the men's shoe section and picked out a pair of well-worn, black dress shoes. "Try these on."

I did, and they fit. We paid and went back to the car. With me behind the wheel, I asked, "Where to next?"

She said, "Walgreens. It's about a mile on your right. Pull in when you get there."

I wasn't going to ask why she wanted me to take her to a drug store. My plan was to get her there, sit in the car while she went in and still be there when she came back out.

Surprisingly, she was okay with that. In fact, she suggested I stay in the car. She said she wouldn't be gone long. I didn't argue. I stayed in the car and waited for her return.

Five minutes later, she came back carrying a plastic shopping bag that looked to be nearly empty.

As soon as she got in the car, she said, "Home, James."

Chapter Thirty-Nine

When we got back to the RV, Erin had me grab the clothes and shoes from Goodwill and take them inside. She gave Bob a few pets and then emptied the bag of goodies from Walgreens onto the kitchen table. There were two pocket-sized notebooks, two ball-point pins, and a comb.

Looking into the bottom drawer by the sink, she found the scissors, came over to me and said, "Have a seat. I'm going to cut your hair."

"No, you're not. I like my hair the way it is. I'm not letting you cut it."

She snapped the scissors and said, "I like the way it is, too, but it's too long for what I have planned for us today. I promise I won't cut too much. It'll look good."

She had me take a seat at the table and draped a dry towel from the bathroom over my shoulder. She picked up the comb and said, "Stay still, this won't take long."

As I sat there listening to the snap of the scissors and watching locks of hair fall into my lap, I wondered what I had gotten myself into. I'd only know her for two days, and she was already changing my wardrobe and cutting my hair. I didn't want to think about what she might want to change next.

A few minutes later, she was done. She put the scissors down and said, "Go look in the mirror, tell me what you think."

When I stood to go check myself, I could feel cool breezes around my ears, places where hair had been before. Same with the back of my neck. There was coolness there that I hadn't felt since my days in the military.

Fearing the worst, I went to the bathroom and looked into the mirror. I was shocked at what I saw. Instead of hair that had been touching my ears, I now had whitewalls, about a half-inch of bare skin above each ear.

The hair on top of my head had been cut back to about an inch in length and resembled a crew cut that had gone wild. The somewhat shaggy hair that previously touched the back of my collar was no more. Now there were two inches of bare skin topped by ruler-straight line.

I no longer had the look of a laid-back surfer dude. Instead, I looked like a boot-camp reject.

When I went back up front, Erin had changed into the black pants and white shirt she'd bought for herself at Goodwill. She was holding a palm-size notepad in her hand.

She said, "Tell me what I look like."

My first thought, which I probably should have kept to myself, was, "Meter maid."

Instead of being offended, she smiled. "Good guess. Now it's your turn. Put on the pants and shirt."

Rather than argue, I dropped my shorts, pulled the newly used pants out of the Goodwill bag and put them on. I followed up with the new, used, white button-up shirt and belt.

When I picked up the tie, Erin came over and said, "Let me do it."

She leaned in, close enough that I could feel her breath

on my neck. It felt good, and I hoped she would take her time getting the tie around me. But she didn't. She did it quickly, and when she was done, she stepped back and admired her work. Then she said, "Put on the jacket and pick up the notepad and flip it open."

I didn't know what kind of game she was playing, but I decided to play along. I put on the jacket, flipped open the notepad and asked, "Now what?"

She pointed to the bathroom. "Go look at yourself in the mirror. Tell me what you see."

I was pretty sure I already knew what I looked like. A fool that had let a red-headed Irish woman take charge.

Still, I had to go see. Looking at my reflection in the mirror, I thought I looked like a cop. In fact, I looked a lot like the detective that had interviewed me about the incident at the Pump & Munch.

I went back to Erin and she asked, "So, do you get it? You know what I'm going for?"

I nodded. "Yeah, you want us to look like cops. But why?"

She pointed over her shoulder to where I had parked the car. "When people see us driving around in that white police special, they already think we're cops. Putting on a jacket and tie will help sell the illusion."

I could understand what she was saying but didn't know why it was important. "So why do you want people to think we're cops? How is that going to help us find Waldo?"

She had her answer ready. "We're going back to his place at Shady Haven to conduct our own search. If the goons who trashed his place are waiting for his return and they see us roll up, they'll think we're cops investigating the break-in. If they think that, they won't bother us."

"Okay, it makes sense. When are we going?"

She grabbed the car keys, tossed them to me and said, "Right now. You're driving."

I put on the black shoes she'd bought me at Goodwill, tightened my belt, grabbed my sunglasses and we headed out.

I hoped we looked like the guys from *Men in Black* but was afraid we looked more like the Blues Brothers.

Chapter Forty

We rolled up to Waldo's trailer in Shady Haven around eleven that morning. There wasn't a car in his drive, and the lights in the trailer were still off as they had been the day earlier.

We both got out of Raif's white police special and stood in the street. Erin pulled out her notepad, flipped it open and looked at the blank pages as if she were reading a police report.

I did the same.

After a few moments, she closed the notepad, shoved it into her blazer's inside pocket, and came over to me. She said, "I'm going to point down the road. When I do, act like I'm telling you something important. Then do a slow three-sixty, checking out our surroundings. Look for any sign of the bad guys."

I nodded and did as she instructed. After doing a full visual sweep and not seeing anyone watching the trailer, I said, "Looks like the coast is clear. Are we going in?"

Instead of answering, she walked to the trailer, went up the steps and knocked on the door. We were both pretty sure that no one was inside, but if other residents of the park were watching, we wanted to give the impression that we were cops doing everything by the book.

No one answered, and Erin knocked again. No one came out to see us.

She tried the doorknob and it was still unlocked as it had been the day before. She pushed the door open and said, "Anyone in here?"

No one responded and she went in. I followed.

The place was still a mess. Furniture turned over, cabinet contents dumped on the floor, fridge door open with food rotting inside.

Acting like the lead detective, she said, "You do the living room. Look for anything that might help us figure out what Waldo was planning to do. Look for business for sale ads, computer printouts, real estate magazines. Anything like that."

She used her thumb to point over her shoulder toward the back of the trailer. "I'll do his bedroom then make my way back up to you. If you find anything, let me know."

I nodded, thinking that real cops probably put on latex gloves before they did a search. We didn't have any with us, so I was hoping that maybe I'd find some under the kitchen sink.

I looked, but there were no gloves. Just a spray bottle filled with green liquid, which I figured was cleaning solution. Sitting next to the bottle was a well-used sponge. The place could use a good cleaning, but it wouldn't be me who'd be doing it.

Thinking about what Erin had said about maybe finding paperwork that could lead us to Waldo, I headed to a large stack of newspapers near the turned-over couch. I got down on my knees and started going through them, page by page.

The first one was dated two months earlier. That was probably right before he moved out. I scanned the pages looking for anything that might tell us where he went.

Nothing did. I doubled-checked the classified section hoping to find ads that were circled or highlighted. None were.

I did the same with the rest of the papers. Each search had the same results. Nothing circled or highlighted.

Next to the pile of newspapers were four takeout menus. Three from Tina's Taco Palace, and one from China Delight. We already knew why Waldo would have the ones from Tina's. He was thinking of buying the place and would want to know what they served.

Maybe he'd picked up the menu from China Delight for the same reason. Maybe he was thinking of buying it. We'd have to follow up.

I cleaned off a space on the floor next to where I was sitting and started a "keep" pile. The China Delight menu would be the first thing in it.

Continuing my search, I looked through the contents of a wastebasket that had been turned over near a recliner. It was mostly household trash, but there were a few other things. Cash register receipts from McDonald's, Burger King and Wendys. Nothing unusual about that. A single guy living in a new town had to eat. Fast food was the easiest and cheapest way. Maybe not the healthiest but better than starving.

Under a used takeout bag from China Delight, I found a Florida state map. Someone had used a yellow marker to highlight the route from Key West to Saint Augustine. There was also a Saint Augustine city map. It had a circle around Tina's Taco Palace and Shady Haven. But nothing else.

It was too bad Waldo hadn't marked a route to his new place. I still put the map in the "keep" pile. It was the only thing I found that had his writing on it.

I continued to go through everything in the room. But I didn't find anything else to put in my keep pile.

Maybe Erin was having better luck. I stood and headed back in her direction but slowed when I heard her voice. Thinking she might be on the phone, I stopped and waited. I didn't want to intrude if she was making a personal call.

But the more I listened the less it sounded like a phone call. Instead, it sounded like she was talking to herself. Wanting to see if she was, I walked up closer and saw she was down on her knees, going through a stack of girlie magazines.

She was saying, "I can't believe I'm doing this. Digging through someone else's trash. There's got to be a better way."

Her back was to me, so I tiptoed over and tapped her shoulder. In my gruffest voice, I asked, "What are you doing here?"

Instead of jumping up, she shook her head and said, "You didn't scare me. I saw you coming. Did you find anything?"

"No, just a takeout menu from China Delight and a highway map showing how to get to Saint Augustine. How about you? Find anything?"

"No, not unless you think this pile of nudie magazines I found under his bed is important. I don't think they are. But maybe you should take a look. Maybe you can see something I missed."

She held up one of the magazines so I could check out its cover. That was all I needed to see. I said, "It looks like you're doing a good job with the magazines. I don't think I need to get involved."

"I didn't think you would. But there is something you can do for me. His bathroom. I haven't checked there yet."

I could tell she didn't want to go through his bathroom and I didn't want to either. But it had to be done. So I said, "I'll do it. But then I'm going to wash my hands and leave this place forever."

I went to the bathroom and was happy to see it was pretty clean. All the drawers were empty, as was the medicine cabinet. Under the sink, I found four rolls of unused toilet paper, a toilet bowl brush, and a plunger. Nothing else.

There was a small, white plastic trash can next to the toilet. It looked to be filled with used tissues and yellowed ear swabs; not the kinds of things I looked forward to handling, especially without gloves.

But I'd told Erin I'd check the bathroom, and I needed to do it well. I dumped the trashcan's contents onto the floor and used the toe of my shoe to separate each item. I didn't want to touch anything that had been in it, but near the bottom of the pile, I saw the corner of a business card. A wadded-up tissue covered most of it, making it unreadable.

I called out to Erin, "I think I found something. Come take a look."

Chapter Forty-One

When Erin joined me in the bathroom, I pointed to the business card on the floor next to the pile of tissues. "That might be important. Pick it up."

She shook her head. "Nope, I'm not going to touch it. You found it, you pick it up."

We both stood there, staring at the corner of the card, knowing it might be the lead we were looking for. But neither one of us wanted to touch it.

I gave in and used my shoe to try to move the tissue off the card but without any luck. It was stuck to it. Best case it would be fluid from Waldo's nose on the tissue. Worse case, fluid from a lower part of his body.

Whatever it was, neither Erin nor I wanted to touch it. I turned to her and asked, "You have any gloves?"

She shook her head. "No, I don't. But I bet Raif does. Let's go see."

His place was next door, so it wasn't much of a walk. Just a few steps. I expected to see him out on his deck, maybe partaking in medicinal herbal relief, but he wasn't there. I hoped that, unlike our previous visit, he wasn't in his bedroom, entertaining his soon-to-be live-in girlfriend, Fay.

Erin knocked on the door and took two steps back. I stayed behind her, doing my best to look like a cop trying to interview a neighbor about a nearby break-in.

No answer on the first knock, so Erin raised her arm to

try again, but before her knuckles hit the door, Raif opened it, wearing only boxer shorts and a T-shirt. He looked at us and said, "Let me guess, you're Crockett and she's Tubbs."

I smiled at the *Miami Vice* reference, but Erin didn't. Maybe she didn't know about TV's most famous Florida cop duo, but I did. I pulled out my notepad, looked at Raif, and said, "Sir, we'd like to ask you a few questions about your next-door neighbor."

He shook his head and turned to Erin. "You did this, right? It was your idea to dress him up as a cop. It sounds like something you'd do. And it's probably best I don't ask why."

Erin smiled and changed the subject. "Where's Fay? I figured she'd be the one answering the door. She did the last time we were here."

Raif grinned. "She's in the back taking a nap. I can wake her if you want."

"No need. We're here to see you. Would you happen to have some latex gloves we could borrow? We found something in Waldo's trailer, but neither of us is willing to pick it up without gloves."

Raif looked at me. "I warned you about her. You hang around too long, and it'll be nothing but trouble. Looks like the trouble's already started, her having you dress up like a pretend cop."

I shrugged. There was nothing I could say. Fortunately, before the silence between us became uncomfortable, he looked at Erin again and said, "I've got gloves. Wait here, I'll get them for you."

He left us at the front door, me still standing behind Erin, trying my best to look like I knew what I was doing. She turned to face me. "He warned you about me? What'd he say?"

I hesitated, then came up with what I thought was a good answer. "The best I can remember is he said you were an angel and I should treat you like one. Yeah, that's it. He said you were an angel and I needed to treat you right."

She looked into my eyes and said, "That's good advice. Treat me right because you don't want to see me when I get angry."

I smiled but didn't tell her that's what Raif had actually told me. That I didn't want to see her get angry.

He soon returned to the door with a box of disposable latex gloves. "Take what you need, and when you're done, put the box on my porch. Don't tell me what you find because I don't want to know.

"But you better not get caught impersonating cops. If you do, I won't be able to bail you out. It's a serious offense."

He leaned in, kissed Erin on the forehead and said, "Be careful. Don't do anything that'd get Walker or the both of you arrested."

After he had gone back inside, Erin handed me the box. "Glove up."

I shook my head. "No, you first."

She smiled, pulled out two gloves, and put one on each hand. Then she poked me in the chest with her gloved hand and said, "Now it's your turn."

With both of us wearing protection, we went back to the bathroom in Waldo's trailer. Erin stood behind me, a sign that she expected me to be the one who moved the tissue and pick up the business card.

It wasn't something I wanted to do, but with the gloves

on, I didn't have a good excuse not to. I took a deep breath and held it in, then bent over and carefully peeled the soiled tissue away.

After picking the card up, I held it so Erin could see the front side. She pulled out her phone, snapped a photo and said, "We've been here long enough. Time to go."

She didn't have to tell me twice. We left the trailer with me leading the way. I got in behind the wheel of Raif's car and she climbed into the passenger's seat. I started the engine and we pulled away, heading back out the same way we came in.

As we approached the manager's office, Erin said to pull over and park. She wanted to go in and ask whoever was in there that day a few questions.

The answers she got were not what we expected.

Chapter Forty-Two

We were still sitting in the car, parked across from Shady Haven's manager's office. Erin spoke first and said, "So here's the plan. We go in and ask if Waldo has moved out. If he has, we ask for his forwarding address. If they want to know why we're asking, we'll tell them we're investigating the break-in at his trailer.

"You go in with me, but don't say anything. Let me ask the questions. If the woman who checked you in is there, we don't want her recognizing you."

We got out of the car and headed toward the office. On the way, Erin pulled out her little notebook and flipped it open. I did the same and followed her in.

The woman sitting at the desk was not the one I had dealt with when I checked in. This one was younger, probably in her mid-twenties, Caucasian, short, brown hair, button-up white shirt, dark blue shorts. Phone in hand, earbuds in. She glanced up at us, removed her earbuds and gave us her full attention. "Can I help you?"

Erin stepped forward. "I'm Donnely. He's Walker. We're here to follow up on a report of a break-in. Before we start, I need your name."

The woman hesitated then said, "Cory. Cory Stokes."

Erin smiled. "Cory. That's a beautiful name. Your parents did well choosing it for you."

Cory, who had been nervous about giving her name,

seemed to relax after hearing Erin's compliment.

She continued her questioning. "Cory, Waldo Raines filed a report of a break-in at his trailer here and we're trying to reach him.

"We've been to his residence, but it looks like he may have moved out. He's not answering his phone either."

Erin paused to see if Cory had any questions. She didn't. But I did. I had one for Erin. I wanted to ask if her last name really was Donnely. She hadn't mentioned it during the three days we had been together. I reminded myself to ask her about it when we got back in the car.

Erin continued with her questions. "Did Mr. Raines give notice that he was moving out?"

Cory shook her head. "I only work here part-time and never met Mr. Raines. But I can look in his folder and see what his status is."

She turned to the file cabinet behind her desk and when I looked at Erin, she winked. Her plan was working.

A few moments later, Cory turned back to us holding a manila folder. She opened it, scanned the first page and said, "According to this, Waldo Raines rented the trailer in site seventy-three. He paid in advance for three months.

"His contract runs out on Friday of this week. He has not let us know whether he plans to renew or not."

She looked up to see if we had any questions. We didn't, so she continued. "There's a note in here that says on Monday this week, two men stopped in and asked about Mr. Raines. They left a phone number and said to call if we saw him. Were those men with you?"

Erin shook her head. "No, they aren't part of our

investigation. But since the break-in occurred Monday morning, about the time the two men were in the park, we'll need to talk to them. Can I have their number?"

Without hesitation, Cory held up the page with the phone number. Erin jotted it down in her notebook. Then she asked, "Do you have any other contact numbers for Mr. Raines? No one answers the one we have."

Cory frowned. "Everything we know about him is on his rental agreement. The number he gave us is at the bottom of the page."

She held it up so Erin could see it. She looked at it, jotted it down and said, "Thanks."

She turned to me and asked, "Detective, you have any questions for the young lady?"

I shook my head. "No, I think you pretty much covered it."

Erin thanked her and we turned to leave, but Cory said something that stopped us. She asked, "You're cops, right?"

Erin smiled and said, "Look at the way he's dressed. Only a cop dresses like that."

Cory smiled and said, "I know what you mean. His haircut too. Only a cop would walk around looking like that."

Erin nodded in agreement and we stepped outside, leaving Cory behind.

When we got into the car, I asked, "Is your last name really Donnely?"

She smiled. "It's actually Davies Donnely MacKenna. Donnely is my mother's maiden name. You want to write that down in your little notepad?"

I didn't. It was a name that I wouldn't soon forget.

Chapter Forty-Three

After leaving Shady Haven, Erin pointed the car in the general direction of Anastasia State Park where our RV was. On the way, she said, "Check your email. See if any of the people we found on Craigslist got back to you."

I checked and both had left a message. The seller with the video game gallery said it was still for sale and he could show it anytime. He included a phone number.

The other seller, the one with the six-plex, said it was sold. He didn't include a phone number.

I read the messages to Erin and after hearing them she said, "Call the guy with the video gallery. See if he can show it to us today."

I made the call and he said if we wanted to see it right away, he'd meet us at the building where the equipment was stored. He gave us the address and we headed in that direction.

On the way, I asked Erin how she wanted to play it. Did we want to act like we were interested or did we just want to ask questions?

She smiled and said, "It was a man who answered, right? How old did he sound?"

I shrugged. "I don't know, maybe in his forties?"

"Good, let me do the talking. Men usually will talk more openly to a woman."

She was probably right. I knew that on many occasions I had given up a lot of personal information to women, simply because they'd asked. The kind of info I would never give a man.

It took us about twenty minutes to get to the building where the video gaming gear was stored. I was surprised to see it was a real business in a retail store-front. According to the large graphic on the plate glass window overlooking the sidewalk, the place was called "GameTastic."

A sign on the door said, "Closed."

We got out of the car, Erin leading the way. When we reached the door with the closed sign, a man from inside came out to greet us. He looked to be in his mid-forties, slightly overweight, balding with a Fu Manchu. He was wearing a *Call of Duty* Black Ops tee-shirt.

He smiled when he saw Erin and welcomed her in. I followed. He looked at me and asked, "You a cop?"

I shook my head. "What do you think?"

He smiled. "You're dressed like a cop. Your car looks like a cop car. So you probably are one. Are you here on business or is this about the gaming gear?"

Before I could answer, Erin stepped up to him and said, "I'm Donnely, he's Walker. Your name is?"

The man tweaked one of his whiskers, looked around and said. "Look, we operate on the up and up here. Nothing illegal is going on."

Erin smiled again. "Don't worry; we're not investigating you or your business. I just need your name so I can include it in my report."

The man looked at her and mumbled out, "Ian. Ian

Perez."

She wrote the name in her notepad. "Ian, we're looking for someone who may have been interested in buying your equipment. His name is Waldo. Waldo Raines. Sound familiar?"

Ian nodded. "Yeah, I know him. Big talker. But when it came time to put money on the table, he bailed. You know how I can reach him?"

Erin smiled. "I was going to ask you the same thing. Seems the last phone number we had on him goes unanswered. When was the last time you heard from him?"

Ian shook his head. "Two months ago. He said he wanted everything in the store. Even said he wanted to rent the space. We agreed on a price, he signed a sales contract, and then he didn't show. I figured something had come up and he'd get back to me, but he never did.

"I called and called and never got an answer. I left voice mails, sent him text messages, even drove around looking for his car. But I never found him. So, thirty days later, I tore up the contract and put the listing back on Craigslist. If you catch up with him, tell him the deal's off."

Erin nodded. "We'll do that. And thanks for talking with us. Good luck selling the video gear. Looks like a great opportunity for someone."

Ian nodded. "It is. Maybe even for you. Come back when you get off, and I'll show you around."

Erin smiled and said, "Maybe I will. But I'll have to ask my husband first."

She turned and we headed back to the car. As soon as we got in, I asked, "Your husband? You're married? Really?"

She laughed and said, "I was married once. Didn't work out. He was the wrong guy and I was the wrong woman. It happens. Same with you, right?"

I nodded and quickly changed the subject. "So, where to next?"

She didn't have to think about it. "First we eat lunch then we call the number on the business card we found in Waldo's bathroom. Maybe we'll get lucky."

Chapter Forty-Four

Erin was driving. She headed north on Dixie Highway for a mile then pulled into the parking lot of a Chick-fil-A. The line at the drive-thru was long, but dressed as we were, she felt we probably should stay in the car. Didn't want to risk going inside and having real cops see us. They might wonder what we were up to and ask questions we didn't want to answer.

The line moved quicker than expected and when it was our time to order, Erin went with the bacon BBQ sandwich and I got the grilled chicken club. We both ordered iced tea.

Ten minutes later, with our orders in hand, we parked in the Home Depot lot behind Chick-fil-A. I was pretty hungry and finished my sandwich first. Erin was only halfway through hers when she saw me shove my sandwich wrappings back into the empty Chick-fil-A bag.

She finished chewing, pointed to my phone and said, "Check Zillow. See if you can find a six-plex that was recently sold in Saint Augustine. If it was ever listed on the MLS, it should still show up there."

I brought up Google on my phone, went to Zillow and entered Saint Augustine as the area I wanted to search. Entering the keyword "six-plex", Zillow returned four listings.

Three of them were still available, and one showed "under contract". I clicked the map icon for it and saw that it was right off A1A, about four miles south of the Home Depot parking lot.

I showed the listing to Erin. "Think we should drop by, see if Waldo is there?"

With sandwich in hand, she shook her head and said, "Not until I finish eating."

A few minutes later, we were on our way to the address Zillow had shown for the six-plex. It took us south, away from old town, down MLK Avenue. Just before we reached Eddie Vicker's Park, Google had us take a left. The six-plex was three doors down on our right.

Even though the street was narrow, several cars, including a few that looked abandoned, were parked on the grass in front of an older two-story home. A sign out front read, "Apartment for Rent."

Erin pulled over onto the grass on the opposite side of the street and asked, "What do you think?"

I shook my head. "It's not the kind of place I'd buy. But maybe Waldo thought differently. You want me to go see if anyone in there knows him?"

She nodded. "Better you than me."

I got out of the car and walked the broken concrete path that led to the front door. Brown and blue tarps in the yard covered several randomly placed boats and cars. Probably all needing work.

When I got to the front door, I started to knock but was met by a young woman with a hardened face. She looked me over and asked, "You a cop?"

"No, I'm looking for Waldo."

She asked again. "You're a cop, right? You're dressed like a cop. You got a cop's haircut."

I pointed across the street to the car we had rolled up in. "Does that look like a cop car to you?"

She nodded. "Yeah, it does. Who'd you say you were looking for?"

"Waldo. Waldo Raines. I'm wondering if he is the new owner of this place."

She thought for a moment then said, "Ain't no one around here named Waldo. If there was, I'd remember him. The new owner's name is Francis. Not sure what her last name is."

She looked across the street at Raif's car. "If you're not cops, why you pretending to be?"

Instead of answering her question, I said, "Have a good day," and headed back to the car where Erin was waiting.

When I got in, she asked, "Learn anything?"

I shook my head and pointed to the woman I'd spoken to. She was still at the front door, watching us. "She said the new owner's name is Francis. She's never heard of Waldo."

Erin frowned. "You believe her?"

"I do. She didn't flinch when I mentioned his name. Nothing in the way she reacted would suggest she'd ever met him."

Erin took a deep breath. "It doesn't look like the kind of place Waldo would be interested in. It's certainly not a ground-floor opportunity."

She started the car and retraced our route until she got us back on business one. When we reached the bridge at A1A, she took a right toward Anastasia. About a mile later, she pulled into a Circle K and parked at the gas pumps. She turned to me and said, "Fill her up."

While I was pumping gas, she went inside. A few minutes later, she returned with a small plastic bag and got into the car on the driver's side. When I finished filling the tank, I slid in on the passenger side.

She handed me an antibacterial wipe and said, "Use this. Never know what diseases might be hiding on that pump handle."

She was probably right. The person who pumped before me could have had an infectious disease or drugs or some other nasty thing on their hands and it could have transferred to the pump handle and then to me. I used the wipe and said, "Thanks."

Instead of pulling out of the Circle K, Erin pulled into a parking spot to the right of the building. She got out her phone and brought up her photo gallery. She pointed to the picture of the business card we had found under the tissues in Waldo's bathroom and said, "I'm going to call this guy. He's a Realtor and maybe he remembers giving Waldo his card."

She made the call and I listened as she spoke into her phone.

"Yes, I'd like to speak to Matthew Phillips about a property he has listed."

"If you're sure, I can meet him there in twenty minutes."

"Will do. Thanks."

She ended the call and turned to me. "He's out of the office at an open house. The receptionist said he would be there until four and if we needed to talk to him, going there would be the best way. You up for it?"

I was, but I wanted to stop by the RV first. "Let's stop in and see how Bob's doing. We're only a few miles away. Then we can go see the guy."

Erin put the car in gear and we headed back to Anastasia State Park. When we got there, the ranger at the entry station saw we had the camping receipt taped to the windshield and waved us through. Two minutes later, we pulled up to the RV.

The people who had been camping in the space next to us were gone. Their trailer had been replaced by a large tent. Six college-age males were outside, drinking beer. Their music was loud but at least it was classic rock. Could have been a lot worse.

When we went into the RV, Bob was waiting for us at the door. He meowed once, letting us know he was happy we were back. I bent down to pet him, but he wasn't interested in getting pets from me. He wanted to be next to Erin, who had taken a seat on the couch.

He trotted over, tail high, and jumped up next to her. He rubbed his big head against her leg then eased into her lap. She immediately began stroking his back, and I could hear his deep purr from where I was standing.

Looking at them both, I decided it was an image worth keeping. I pulled out my phone and shot a few photos. I got the first one before Erin realized what I was doing. After that, she made a face each time I held my phone in her direction.

I took the pictures anyway.

I loosened the tie I'd been wearing since early that morning and asked, "Do I really need to wear this all day? The guy we're going to see probably won't care how we're dressed. We don't need to impress him."

Erin nodded. "You're probably right. Change if you want to."

I went to the back bedroom and changed into a pair of tan cargo shorts and a light blue button-up fishing shirt from Bealls. I didn't think I'd have to be dressing like a cop again but was worried that Erin might be upset if I just piled the cop outfit on the floor. I went to the closet, grabbed a hanger and hung the pants on it. I put the shirt over the pants and put the jacket over the shirt. As a final touch, I draped the tie around the neck of the jacket.

If I had added a balloon to the top of the hanger, from a distance it might have looked like a real person. One without much of a lower body. Just empty pants legs hanging down.

When I went back up front, Erin was standing in the living room in her bra and panties. Her cop outfit was piled up on the floor. Bob was lying on top of it.

She saw me and said, "You're not supposed to be looking. You're supposed to be back there changing clothes. You sure were quick about it."

I nodded. "I've had a lot of practice, it doesn't take me long. But here's the question. Since your clothes are in your bag in the back, how did you plan to get by me without me seeing you in your underwear? Or did you do that on purpose?"

She shook her head and said, "You're a prevert, you know that?"

I laughed. Her uncle Raif had misspoken the word the same way. Prevert instead of pervert. I was pretty sure I was neither, but I didn't mind looking at Erin standing in my living room in just her bra and panties.

She pushed her way past me, muttered the word "prevert" again, and headed to the bedroom to put some clothes on. It made me a bit sad. I preferred her the other way. Unclothed.

Chapter Forty-Five

When Erin came back up front, she was wearing dark blue shorts and a white button-up shirt and no longer looked like a cop. Instead, she looked like the kind of person any man would be happy to talk to.

She looked at me and said, "Take a picture, it'll last longer."

I pulled out my phone and shot several photos. The first one was the best; the rest had her giving me the middle finger salute while making faces.

When I put my phone away, she said, "If you're through fooling around, we have an open house to get to. You ready?"

I was.

Since Erin knew the streets of Saint Augustine and I didn't, she drove. I didn't mind. I kind of liked being chauffeured around by a beautiful woman. It was something I could get used to.

Ten minutes after leaving the RV, we reached the open house. Not wanting to block the seller's driveway, we parked at the curb and got ready to go in. Erin unbuttoned another button on her shirt, revealing intriguing cleavage. She pointed at me and said, "You know the drill. I do the talking. You just listen."

I nodded. If she wanted to do all the work, I was totally on board. It would give me time to admire her shirt, or what was peeking out from under it.

As we walked toward the house, a young couple with a baby came out followed by an older man wearing a silk shirt and casual slacks. He was saying, "If you folks change your mind, just let me know."

After the young couple passed us by, the man, whom we presumed to be the real estate agent we were looking for, smiled and said, "Come on in, folks. Let me show you around."

Erin went in first, I followed. The man introduced himself as Matthew Phillips and asked us to enter our names on the sign-in sheet. It wasn't an unusual request. Most agents want to get the contact info of the people who visit the open houses they hold. It gives them a list of potential buyers and sellers they can reach out to later.

Erin ignored his request; instead, she said, "Mr. Phillips, we're not here to look at your house. We're looking for a friend who has gone missing. Waldo Raines.

"We found your business card in his home and wondered if you remember talking to him."

Phillips smiled broadly at her and said, "Call me Matt. No one calls me mister, it's too formal. I want us to be friends."

We both smiled. Erin stretched, revealing just a bit more cleavage. "That's good to know, Matt. When we get ready to buy a house, we'll come see you first.

"But right now, we're trying to find our friend. Do you remember talking to him?"

Matt smiled again and said, "Normally, I don't share information about the contacts I've made. It's not good for business. But for a pretty lady like you, I'll make an exception. If I've talked to him, it'll be in my notes."

He walked to a nearby table, picked up his iPad and tapped in Waldo's name. A few swipes later, he turned to Erin and said, "Here it is. Two months ago, he came in looking to buy an investment property.

"Said he needed something with good cash flow but nothing to do with food. I wasn't sure why he mentioned food, but that's what he said.

"I went through the MLS and found several commercial properties that might work for him. I showed him the photos along with the details. Some of the places were pretty good deals, but he wasn't interested in any of them.

"He told me he needed owner financing. He said he could make a big down payment but wouldn't be able to get a bank loan, so if the owner wouldn't finance it, he wouldn't be a buyer.

"I told him there weren't many properties in the area with owner financing. Most of those that have it don't show up on the MLS.

"After I explained this, he gave me his phone number and said to call if I found anything that would work for him.

"Later that evening, I got a call from an old friend. A man in his eighties. He told me he was getting too old to work and wanted to sell all his real estate holdings. Three houses, a duplex, and a ratty motor court.

"I took down the information about each of the properties, and when we got to the motel, he told me all about it. He said it was built in the fifties and hadn't been updated since. It was a one-story block building with ten guest rooms and a front office with an apartment for the manager. All the rooms had window air, old-style TVs, and a few had coin-operated vibrating beds. The rooms had no heat and the only view was of the parking lot. There was no pool. Just an outdoor fountain near the office.

"He went on to tell me that he had bought the place in the seventies, hired a manager, and let it ride. After expenses, it made a small profit every month, more than enough to keep him happy.

"But as the place got older, it was hard to attract new guests and hard to keep them once they saw the conditions of the rooms. With rising insurance rates and climbing property tax, the little motel started losing money.

"The manager was having a hard time finding nightly guests, so he started renting the rooms out on a weekly basis. When he did, the quality of the clientele took a nosedive. The only people he could attract were those down on their luck who couldn't afford anywhere else—or were running from the law.

"After too many visits from building inspectors telling him he needed to fix the place up or shut it down, he decided it wasn't worth spending a ton of money on it. So he boarded up the windows, turned off the utilities, and let it sit. That was six years ago. It's been empty since.

"When I told him potential buyers would have a hard time getting a loan on a property like his, he said he'd be willing to offer owner financing, as long as the buyer put a big chunk of money down. He wanted the motel and the headaches it caused him to be gone. He was ready to sell.

"I got all the details, and the next day I remembered talking to Mr. Raines about income properties. I gave him a call and told him about my friend's motor court and how it had owner financing.

"Raines said he was interested, so I contacted the seller,

got permission to show the place, and picked up the master key, which would unlock all the doors. Raines had agreed to meet there the next day, and he was in the parking lot waiting for me when I showed up.

"We went into all the guest rooms and each one was like stepping back into the fifties. Old TVs, the kind with tubes. Busted up furniture. Dusty paintings on the walls, and mold growing in the bathrooms.

"It was easy to see why no one would want to stay there. The rooms were in bad shape. It'd take a lot of money to fix them up.

"The only thing the place had going for it was its location on A1A south on Anastasia Island. But it didn't have a water view, was on the wrong side of the road, and was surrounded by other failing businesses. The parking lot was small, there were no nearby restaurants, and it was hard crossing the highway to get back to Old Town.

"But for some reason, Mr. Raines liked what he saw. He agreed to pay the full asking price of three hundred fifty thousand dollars and he could put forty thousand down.

"I presented the offer to the seller and he accepted it. Since it was an owner finance deal, we had a local attorney draw up the contracts and were able to close two weeks later.

"That was a month ago. I haven't heard from Raines since. He never told me what he planned to do with the property."

Erin nodded and said, "Matt, you're the best. When my husband and I get ready to buy, you'll be the one we talk to.

"But I have one last question. What's the name of the place Waldo bought?"

Phillips smiled and said, "It was originally the Paradise Inn. But that's not what the sign says now. Over the years some of the letters have fallen off, and these days it just says 'die Inn.' It's kind of a local joke. When people ask for directions to Pier Park, we tell them to go south on A1A until they see the Die Inn sign and then take a left at the next light."

Chapter Forty-Six

Our new friend Matt was telling Erin how to find the motor court Waldo had purchased. He offered to draw us a map but said if we got on A1A and headed south, we couldn't miss it. It'd be on our right, about a half mile before the light.

He gave Erin his card and said, "Call me sometime. I'll show you things you might be interested in."

I think I saw him wink at her but couldn't be sure. It didn't matter though. Erin was leaving with me and we knew where we'd be heading.

When we got back in the car, I said, "Well, I guess unbuttoning your shirt worked. Wonder what would happen if you unbuttoned another one. You can test it on me."

She shook her head and said, "Prevert."

After buttoning up her shirt, she started the car and we headed to Anastasia Island. On the way, I asked if there was a flashlight in the car.

"I don't know, look in the glove compartment."

I looked and didn't find one. Instead, I found the chrome pistol that Raif had taken out when he first gave me permission to use the car. At least I thought it was Raif's. But maybe it wasn't. Maybe it belonged to Erin and she had stashed it there when we started riding around together.

I pointed to it. "Is that yours?"

She nodded. "It is. It's loaded so leave it alone."

"No problem. I won't touch it."

It wasn't that I was afraid of hers or any other gun. I had plenty of familiarity with firearms, having carried a pistol and rifle during my time in the desert. Back then, people were shooting at me on a daily basis, and more often than not, I was shooting back.

But riding in Raif's car with Erin beside me, I had no intention of shooting anyone or getting my fingerprints on the pistol in the glove compartment. I didn't think she'd be firing the gun anytime soon, but if she did, I didn't want my prints on it.

I closed the door and said, "If the Die Inn is as bad as Matt says, we should stop and get some gloves. And a flashlight. And maybe more wipes."

Erin nodded and kept going south on A1A. When we passed the Die Inn on our right, she didn't pull into the lot. She kept going. When I asked her why, she said, "There's a hardware store about a mile ahead. We can stop there and get what we need."

We pulled into the Ace parking lot, locked the car and went inside. We quickly found what we needed. Gloves, a flashlight for each of us, and anti-bacterial wipes. On the way to the checkout, Erin grabbed a roll of silver duct tape. I couldn't figure out why, so I asked her about it. "Duct tape? You think we'll need some?"

She shrugged. "We might. You never know when having a roll of duct tape can save the day."

She was right. Duct tape can sometimes be a lifesaver.

When we reached the checkout, a tall, skinny guy, sporting a man bun, was in front of us. Not having anything else to do, I watched to see what he was buying.

Rope, plastic gloves, a shovel, and two bottles of bleach. Everything a person would need if they had kidnapped someone and wanted to bury the evidence. He didn't look like the kidnapper type, but you never know.

He paid with cash and left the store. After the door closed behind him, I stepped over and snapped a photo of his car, with the license plate clearly visible. Just in case the cops needed to find him later.

We paid for our things, bagged them up and went back out to the car. As before, Erin drove.

Three minutes later, we pulled into the Die Inn parking lot. There were no other cars there and no sign of life. With all the windows boarded up, we couldn't look inside to see if maybe Waldo was around. But since we didn't see his car, which Erin described as an old Camry with peeling silver paint, we figured he wasn't there. At least not yet.

It was mid-afternoon, and if he was still in town, he might be at Home Depot or Lowes, gathering up the tools he'd need to rehabilitate the place.

Even though his car wasn't there, Erin said we should get out, walk around, and see if anyone had started fixing things up.

We went to the office first. A small glassed-in room with the word "Closed" painted on the outside wall with what looked like white shoe polish. Erin tried the door and neither of us was surprised to find it was locked.

Leaving the office, we walked the sidewalk around the horseshoe-shaped lot, checking the doors of each unit as we passed. Like the office, all were locked. After reaching the end of the sidewalk, we checked behind the building. There were a couple of dumpsters in a small fenced-in area. Nothing more.

Back around the front, Erin pointed to the water fountain that Matt had told us about. It was about six feet tall, made of what looked like concrete, and had a brass-colored spigot near the top. A healthy stream of water flowed from the nozzle to the drain in the pavement below. With the utilities turned off, I would have thought the water would have been off as well. But apparently it wasn't.

Erin headed to the fountain to get a closer look. I followed. The first thing she did when she got to it was to put her hands under the running water. She smiled and said, "It's cold. It shouldn't be, but it is."

I circled the fountain to see if I could find where the water pipe was coming in. But I found nothing. The base of the fountain went down below the surrounding pavement, suggesting it was in place before the lot was paved. Maybe it was there even before the Die Inn was built.

While I was checking out the base, Erin stayed near the front, intrigued by the water flow. To me, the fountain looked like a large seashell turned on end, with the spigot at the top and water falling directly into the drain below.

When I came back around to tell Erin that I thought the fountain had been there longer than the parking lot, she nodded and said, "Check this out."

She pointed to a brass plaque about the size of a playing card. It had turned black as brass left out in the weather for a long time will do. I reached up and rubbed my finger against the top of the plaque and some of the black came off. But not enough to read the words that had been engraved on it.

I turned to Erin. "Can you read what it says?"

"No, the letters are too dark. But I know how to fix it."

She went to the car and returned with the pencil I'd seen earlier in the glove compartment along with the sales receipt from Ace.

She put the printed side of the receipt against the plaque and started rubbing the pencil on the backside. Soon words started to appear. The first three were, "Fountain of Youth."

Chapter Forty-Seven

"You know there's no such thing as the Fountain of Youth. Ponce De Leon wasn't looking for it and he never mentioned it in his journals.

"The whole thing was made up to get more people to move to La Florida in the new world. Those that made the trip found swamps filled with alligators, voracious clouds of biting bugs, unbearable humidity, and no Fountain of Youth."

Erin was right. I'd read up on it. There was no Fountain of Youth. It didn't exist. Except in the minds of tourists hoping for something that would help them recover from old age.

I reached out and touched the water pouring from the fountain. It had a smooth velvety feel. Being so cool to the touch could mean the water came from a stream or artesian well. Perhaps one that had been there before the motel was built. Rather than try to cover it up, they built a structure over it and called it the Fountain of Youth.

A lot of tourist motels in the area probably had similar fountains. The one at the Die Inn wouldn't be the only one. Still, it was an interesting feature at an otherwise depressing location.

We hung around the Die Inn for two hours, hoping Waldo would show. But he never did. Erin was getting hungry and we decided to get something to eat then come back and wait for his return.

Since the motorhome was close, we stopped there first. As usual, Bob met us at the door. This time with a surprise. A dark green lizard with a white stripe down its back hung from his mouth. The lizard was still alive, but I knew it wouldn't be for long.

Bob would soon drop it on the floor and chase it until it didn't have any chase left it in. He'd eat half of it and, later on that evening, throw it all back up.

Erin watched as he played with the lizard. She said, "He is quite a character. He slept with me most of the night. Every time I rolled over, he would reach out with his paw and let me know he was there.

"When I woke this morning, he was playing touch with my ear lobe. At first, I thought it was you, trying to wake me. But when I heard the purring, I knew it was him."

When he disappeared in the bedroom with his lizard, Erin went to the bathroom to freshen up. When she was done, I did the same.

We discussed our dinner plans and decided to get Chinese to go. We'd eat in the car while waiting for Waldo to return.

Thirty minutes later, we pulled into the parking lot of Vapeville, across the road from the Die Inn. We figured that if Waldo saw a car in his lot, he might get spooked and not return. The Vapeville lot was dimly lit, so we weren't worried about being seen.

We sat in the car for two hours watching customers come and go. Most were middle-aged women, going in empty-handed and coming out with a smile and a shopping bag. After a while, we got bored watching the customers and spent the next hour and a half looking at the screens on our phones.

We'd been sitting in the car for almost four hours when Erin said it was time to call it quits. It was nearly midnight and Waldo hadn't shown. She said we should go home, get some sleep and check back in the morning. It sounded like a good idea.

We left Vapeville and headed back to our campsite at the state park. It was a short drive, no more than six miles. When we pulled into the park, the front gate was closed, keeping us from going in any further.

Erin shook her head. "We're locked out. And I'm too sleepy to go find another place to stay. Guess we'll have to sleep in the car."

There was no way I was going to sleep in the car, especially since I knew how to get through the gate. I told her, "Pull up to the gate. I know how to get us in."

She inched the car forward until the front bumper was almost touching the metal gate. She looked over at me and said, "Okay Houdini, how do we get through it?"

I reached over the dashboard and picked up the park pass the ranger had given me when we checked in. It had our site number and the date we were leaving printed in large letters.

Below that, in a much smaller font, were seven numbers. Four three four one one nine three. I knew what they were for. Erin didn't.

I pointed to the left side of the gate, the driver's side. There was a small keypad on a pole. I said, "Punch in this code. It'll open the gate."

She tried, but the car was too far from the keypad for her to reach it from her window. She needed to get out and step over to the pole.

It was dark in the park, Florida dark, with the possibility of gators, bears, pythons and other interesting and perhaps lethal wildlife lurking nearby. With her window rolled down, she listened to the jungle noises outside and said, "Nope, I'm not going out there. You do it. When the gate opens, I'll pull through and wait for you."

Getting out of the car wasn't something I wanted to do, but being a gentleman, I didn't argue. I opened my door, stepped out and crossed behind the car to get to the keypad. With Erin watching, I made a show of entering the gate code and then a "ta-da" motion with my hand when the gate started to lift.

When it reached its full height, Erin pulled the car through and waited for me on the other side. At least that's what I thought she was going to do.

But as the gate came back down and I started walking toward the car, Erin leaned out her window and said, "Watch out for gators," and drove off.

I'd left my flashlight in the car, and with her a hundred yards down the road, it had gotten Florida dark again. I was pretty sure she was just playing and would come back, but she didn't. She waited for me to walk the distance from the gate to the car.

It wasn't a long walk and was kind of refreshing after spending the last four hours on a stake-out. Still, it was Florida and walking in the dark, especially in a game preserve, was always risky. So I hustled in her direction and just as I was about to reach the car, she pulled away again, this time stopping about fifty yards ahead of me.

I was pretty sure she was enjoying her little game, but I was quickly growing tired of it. It had been a long day and I wanted to get to the RV and rest.

I was hoping that when I got close to the car again, she wouldn't do the same thing. Drive away and make me walk to catch up with her. If she did, it was going to be a long night.

Fortunately, she decided the game was over. When I reached the car and opened the passenger door, she said, "I don't know what happened. I pulled through the gate, and the car kept going like it had a mind of its own. I'm not lying. That's what really happened."

If she hadn't had a big grin on her face while she was telling me about the car driving itself I might have believed her, but the grin gave it away. She'd done it on purpose. Not out of spite, but to have a little fun at my expense. It really didn't bother me. In fact, it kind of felt good that she was confident enough around me to play games.

After I got in, we made our way to the RV. On the way, we saw two raccoons scurry across the road in front of us. No alligators, bears, or pythons.

When we got back to the motorhome, Bob wasn't waiting for us at the door. It was after midnight, and I was pretty sure he was in the back, sleeping. Or maybe he'd found another lizard.

I turned on the lights and asked Erin, "Which one of us is sleeping on the couch?"

She pointed at me and said, "If you promise not to mess with me, and that means no touching or spooning, you can sleep back there with me. But sleep is all we're going to do. If you try anything else, I'll send you to the couch."

I agreed to her terms and after each of us took care of our nightly bathroom business, we headed to bed. She slept in her bra and panties, with me in my boxers at her side.

Chapter Forty-Eight

When I woke the next morning, Erin was still in bed next to me. She had snuggled up against my back and had an arm around my chest. She was moaning. Or maybe snoring. Either way, it was a good start to the day.

I needed to get up and pee, but I wanted to stay in bed and see what Erin might do next.

Still moaning, she began kissing the back of my neck and with the arm she had over my chest, she pulled me in closer. Then, just as things started to get interesting, she pulled away, pushed against my back with her hand and said, "Get off me, you prevert!"

I rolled over to face her, smiled and asked, "What were you dreaming about? It sounded like you were having a good time."

She made a face and said, "It's none of your business. But you can be sure I wasn't dreaming about you."

She tried to roll over away from me, but her path was blocked by Bob. While she had been spooning me in her sleep, he had been spooning her as well, his belly up tight against her neck.

When she rolled into his direction, her face met his manly parts. He purred even louder until Erin opened her eyes and took in the view.

She sat up, pulling the covers off both of us, and said, "I need to find my own place. I can't stay here much longer."

She pushed me out of bed and I headed to the bathroom. When I came out, she was standing there, a frown on her face. "It wasn't about you. The dream, it wasn't about you."

I grinned and stepped aside so she could go into the bathroom and take care of business. While she was doing this, I put on my clothes and headed to the kitchen. I pulled out the bottle of Simply Tropical juice from the fridge and poured half a glass. I used it to wash down my morning pill.

As I was putting the glass in the sink, Erin came up and joined me. She was fully clothed. She pointed at the juice and said, "Pour me one."

I did and asked, "You want me to fix you breakfast? I've got eggs, bacon, and toast."

"No, we don't have time. We need to get to Waldo's. We can stop at McDonald's on the way."

Ten minutes later, after topping off Bob's food and water bowls, we were sitting in Mickey D's drive-through. Erin ordered an Egg McMuffin, and I got two breakfast burritos.

After paying and picking up our order, Erin pulled out of the parking lot and headed to Waldo's. As before, we pulled into Vapeville and backed into a spot that gave us a direct view of the Die Inn. We didn't see Waldo's car, so we sat and ate our breakfast.

Erin didn't have much to say and I knew better than to ask her about her dream. Even if it were about me, she would never admit it, and it wouldn't do me any good to antagonize her by bringing it up.

We finished our breakfast and sat watching Waldo's place, hoping he'd show up. We had arrived at Vapeville around seven and there weren't any other cars in the lot. Around eight, one pulled in. The driver slowed when he saw us but didn't stop. After parking near the front door, a man who looked to be about twenty-five, dressed in all black, came over to talk to us.

Seeing him heading our way, Erin rolled down her window and met him with a smile. She pointed to the Die Inn and said, "We're watching the place across the street. If you need us to move, we will."

We were in Raif's unmarked police cruiser, and it would have been easy to mistake us for undercover cops, parked as we were.

The man, who we assumed was either the owner or the manager of Vapeville, said, "No problem. Can I get you a coffee? I'll have a pot ready in a few minutes."

Erin shook her head. "Thanks but no thanks. We don't want to do anything that might attract attention."

The man nodded and said, "I don't mind you parking here, but when my customers see a police car in our lot, they might be put off. So, the sooner you leave the better."

Erin nodded. "We won't be here long. Sorry if we created a problem."

The man walked to the front door of Vapeville, pulled out a set of keys, unlocked it and went in. A few minutes later, the inside lights came on and the sign on the door was turned to read "Open."

Erin started the car and I asked, "Are we leaving?"

"Yeah, we're pretty visible parked here. Time to move."

She pulled out of Vapeville and headed north, back toward Anastasia State Park. We'd gone a half-mile when she slowed and took a right on Sixteenth Street, heading east. A mile later, we pulled into the parking lot of St John's

Fishing Pier.

She killed the engine and said, "Let's take a walk. Stretch our legs. Bring your wallet."

She got out of the car, and I did the same. I followed as she headed toward a collection of one-story block buildings, all with teal doors and matching dormers. The structures looked to be made of concrete and designed to withstand the pounding winds of the hurricanes that frequented the area.

With Erin leading the way, we headed to a building with a sign that said, "Visitor Center." Erin pushed open the door, walked up to the counter, pointed to me and said, "Pay the lady."

An all-day pier pass for sightseers cost two dollars a person. I paid for both of us and we followed the boardwalk out onto the pier. Erin grabbed my hand and we walked on the weathered boards over the white-capped waves of the Atlantic Ocean below. Seagulls flew above, and sandy beaches spread in both directions.

Reaching the end of the pier, Erin released my hand, turned to me and said, "Walker, I enjoy your company. And Bob's too. It's been a fun three days and I hate that it has to end. But today is going to be my last day. We either find Waldo or we don't. Either way, I need to find a place of my own. I can stay with Raif and Fay for a few days but not for long.

"I need to find my own place. But first, I need to see if the shop has got my car fixed. After I get it back, I need to decide what I'm going to do next, business-wise.

"You're a nice guy. Too nice for me. The only thing we really have in common is Waldo. After we find him, I don't expect you to stay around. You have a life somewhere else and will want to get back to it.

"So when you leave, whether it's today, tomorrow or the next day, don't worry about me. I have my own life and want to get on with it as well."

She grabbed my hand and said, "Let's go find Waldo."

We didn't say anything on our walk back to the car. I wanted to tell her she was wrong about me moving on but thought better of it. Sometimes silence is the best way to go.

When we got to the car, she slid in on the driver's side and buckled her belt. She waited for me to get in before she started the engine. After I was buckled in, she turned to me and asked, "Aren't you going to say anything?"

I nodded. "I am. You may not like what I have to say, but I need to say it.

"First of all, Saint Augustine is the oldest city in the country and there are lots of things here I want to see. The castle at San Marcos. The pirate museum. The Fountain of Youth. The lighthouse. All the touristy things.

"You promised to show me these places. You promised to go with me on the old town trolley tour. But you haven't yet. You promised to take me with you when you toured that nudist RV park you might buy. You haven't done that either.

"I paid a month in advance for my site at Shady Haven. I plan to stay there until my time's up. You're welcome to stay with me if you want.

"Either way, I'm staying. After that, I might stay longer. Or I might leave. But right now, I'm not planning to go anywhere. Except with you to the Die Inn to look for Waldo."

When I finished talking, I saw her wipe a tear from her

eye. She made a sad face, and I thought she was going to cry. Finally, she smiled and said, "I think I like you."

She started the car, pulled out of the pier parking lot, and we headed back to Waldo's.

Chapter Forty-Nine

It didn't take us long to get back to the Die Inn parking lot. When we pulled in, we saw a faded silver Camry parked near the water fountain. Next to it, a man was standing with his back to us, filling a jug with water from the fountain. On the ground near him were at least ten more plastic jugs.

If he heard us pull in, he didn't act like it. He didn't bother to look over his shoulder to see who we were, nor did he stop filling the plastic jug he was holding. He ignored us.

Erin said, "That's Waldo."

She pulled her car up to the rear bumper of his Camry, making sure he wouldn't be able to leave unless she wanted him to.

When she got out and slammed her car door, it got his attention. When he turned and saw her, he put down the gallon jug he was holding and walked over. He smiled broadly and said, "Erin. I'm glad you're here. I've found something and wanted to tell you about it."

Erin walked up to him and said, "You took my money and I want it back."

He shook his head. "I shouldn't have done that. I just figured that since I worked at the truck for two days, I should get paid. So after you left that day, I went back, found the money box, and took what I deserved."

Erin walked up close to him, poked a finger into his chest and said, "You didn't earn anything. You should have been

235

paying me. I spent two days training you on how to run the business.

"Then you steal my money and send me a text saying you're backing out of the deal. I've had it with you. Pay up."

Waldo looked over at me and nodded like he was acknowledging my presence, the way guys sometimes do. I nodded back.

Erin repeated her demand. "Give me my money."

Waldo reached into both pants pockets and pulled out the lining showing he had nothing in them. "I'm broke. I don't have any money."

She cocked her fist, but before she could deliver a punch, I stopped her. I stepped up to Waldo and said, "Erin here is the least of your worries. You owe a lot of money to Mad Dog. You're behind in your payments and he's sent two guys up here to find you.

"They'll want their money or they're going to rough you up. They might do worse than that. They've already visited your mother and threatened her. If they don't get satisfaction from you, they'll go back and get it from her."

When I stopped talking, he asked, "Who are you? How do you know about my mother?"

I shook my head. "Waldo, your mother sent me here to find you. To somehow get you out of this mess. But if you don't have any money, I don't know how I'm going to do it. Mad Dog takes it seriously when people don't pay. That's why he sent his guys up here. To find you and get what you owe him. And probably break a few bones in the process.

"It only took us four days to find you. It probably won't take them much longer than that.

The color drained from Waldo's face. He looked over my shoulder into the parking lot then back at me. "If Madicof can give me an extension, I'll be able to pay him back and more. Just not right away."

He pointed to the fountain. "This is the real Fountain of Youth. People come from all over the world looking for it, and I've found it. No one else has it."

He pointed to the water jugs on the ground near him. "I plan to sell Fountain of Youth water. Ten dollars a jug. Won't take me long to come up with enough money to pay Madicof."

I looked at Erin and we both shook our heads. She was the first to tell Waldo the flaw in his plan. "You owe him fifty thousand dollars. Plus a late fee. Let's say ten thousand.

"So you need to come up with sixty thousand dollars. Do you know how many ten-dollar jugs you'll need to sell to get that kind of money?"

Waldo nodded. "I've already done the math. I only need to sell six hundred. I can do that down at the farmers' market. It should only take me a day or two."

Erin shook her head again. "Waldo, you need to sell six thousand jugs, not six hundred."

He cocked his head and asked, "Are you sure about that? Because when I did the math, it came out to six hundred. I've already sold ten. Won't take me long to sell the rest."

I was starting to feel bad for him. His math skills were lacking as was his concern about his obligation to Mad Dog. I took a deep breath and said, "Waldo, we don't need to be standing out here in the open. We need to get inside, away from prying eyes.

"Are any of these rooms unlocked?"

He nodded. "No. But the apartment behind the office is. We can go there."

He started to pick up the water jug he had been filling, but I stopped him. "Waldo, you need to get inside. Leave the jugs where they are. No one's going to take them."

He sighed like maybe he was starting to grasp the seriousness of the situation. But I doubted it. He didn't seem too concerned about the guys Mad Dog had sent looking for him.

I was pretty sure he would change his mind as soon as he met them in person.

He led us to the main office and up to the front desk, where guests wanting to check in would go. But there would be no guests, not for a long time. Not without electricity and running water and guest rooms that looked like they were sets for a horror movie.

From the front desk, Waldo took us through a door that led into the manager's apartment. It was dark, hot and smelled like mildew. He stepped over to a table and turned on an electric lantern. A 12-volt car battery was on the floor near his bed and connected to a fan creating a warm breeze. He waved his arm and said, "Isn't this great? A private suite for the manager. When I fix it up, it'll really be something."

Erin shook her head. "You live here now? Without lights, running water or air conditioning? You're not that stupid, are you?"

He had a ready answer. "No, I'm not. I don't live here yet. I plan to as soon as I get the utilities turned back on, but right now I'm staying at a motel down the street. It's not as nice as this place, but it does have everything I need."

Erin asked the obvious question. "If you don't have any

money, how can you afford to stay there?"

He smiled. "I've been cleaning out the rooms here, selling whatever I can find in them. I've already gone through three and made almost eight hundred dollars.

"I can pay you back the same way. Take anything you want from any of the rooms. Whatever you think is fair."

I was pretty sure Erin wouldn't want anything from a motel room that had been closed up for six years. But she surprised me when she said, "Give me the keys. I'll go look."

Chapter Fifty

We grabbed one of the flashlights we'd bought the day before and headed to the locked motel rooms. Waldo said to start with room ten, which was the closest to the office. He said he'd cleaned it and the one next to it.

When we opened the door and stepped in, I wasn't sure he knew the definition of clean. The floors were filthy and an inch of dust covered everything in the room. The mattress on the bed had disintegrated into a sunken pile of cotton, likely infested with bed bugs or worse. We didn't bother checking out the bathroom.

The next room was more of the same. Lots of dirt, dust and spider webs. Unlike the first, the second still had a few paintings on the wall. Erin pointed to one and said, "Get that. I want it."

The painting was unframed and hung onto the wall with a thin wire over a single nail. I had no problem getting it down and out of the room. I did my best to take as few steps as I could, not wanting to get too much of whatever was on the floor on my shoes.

Outside, in the sun, the painting didn't look too bad. Erin used a tissue to wipe the dust off and it revealed a colorful Florida scene of a sunset over a tropical oasis. She nodded and said, "Not bad. Let's see if we can find a few more."

The next two rooms had the same kind of paintings, three

of them in each room. I grabbed them all and we set them next to the first one I'd retrieved.

After she had removed most of the dust from the largest one, I checked the name signed on the bottom. It showed "Albert Hair." The other two were signed by Harold Newton. I didn't have an art background and didn't know if the paintings were valuable, but they were pleasant to look at.

When you looked closely, you could see individual brush strokes, meaning the paintings were probably originals and not reprints. But unlike most paintings, the ones we had found were on backing board instead of canvas.

I remembered something that Katrina, Marissa's daughter, had told me about paintings she used to sell by the side of the road to gullible tourists. They looked like the famous Highway Men paintings, but the ones she sold were fakes. Still, she had studied the real ones enough to know the difference.

I snapped a photo of each painting with close-ups of the signatures. I sent them to her along with a short message asking, "Are these worth anything?"

A few minutes later, my phone chimed with an incoming call. The caller ID said it was from Kat. I answered on the third ring and before I could say hello, she asked, "Where did you find them?"

I told her about the old motel rooms and she said, "That sounds about right. If they're originals, they are worth between two thousand and five thousand each. Are there more?"

"Yeah. Probably ten or fifteen."

As soon as I answered, she asked, "Where are you? If

you're anywhere close to Daytona, I can come and help you sell them. Or buy them myself. It won't matter whether they're real or not. I can sell them either way."

I didn't think it would be a good idea to get Marissa and Boris's daughter involved in what could be selling fake paintings. It might come back to haunt me, so I thanked her for her time and said, "The paintings are not mine. I was checking for a friend. If anything changes, I'll let you know."

I ended the call before she could ask more questions. Erin was standing near me and asked, "What'd you find out?"

"They might be worth something. Let's check the other rooms, see how many we can find."

Thirty minutes later, we were knocking the dust off our shoes while standing next to sixteen paintings, all in the same style as the first ones. Erin had picked the three she liked best and put them in the backseat of Raif's car.

I snapped a photo of each one just so I'd have a record of what we had found.

We went back to the manager's apartment where we'd left Waldo. He was sleeping on the bed, taking a nap. One of the water jugs he had filled from the fountain was on the floor next to the bed. Half-empty.

Not wanting to bother him while he slept, we went outside to talk about our next move. Erin spoke first. "Should we tell him? About the paintings?"

I nodded. "We have to. If they're worth what my friend thinks they are, selling them might help him get square with Mad Dog. He was a fool for getting in so deep, and again when he bought this dump of a motel. If it were just me, I wouldn't do anything. But I'm doing this as a favor for a friend of his mother and she is depending on me to keep him from getting roughed up.

"So yeah, we need to tell him about the paintings. Let's do it now before I change my mind."

We went back into the manager's apartment. Waldo was still where we'd left him. On the bed, sleeping. I walked over, kicked the bed and said, "Wake up. We need to talk."

He didn't move. Not a muscle.

I said it a second time. "Wake up. We need to talk."

Again, no response.

Not wanting to waste much time, I picked up the water jug off the floor, flipped open the cap, and poured about a third of it on his face. His eyes opened and he struggled to sit up.

When he was finally upright, he used the bottom of his T-shirt to wipe the water off his face. "What'd you do that for?"

"I couldn't wake you and was worried you were in a coma or something, so I dumped a little water on your face. If that hadn't worked, we would have called 9-1-1."

He wiped the sleep from his eyes. "I got sleepy all of a sudden. I sat down on the bed, and the next thing I know, you're splashing me with water. You didn't need to do that. You could have just left me alone."

Looking into his eyes, I could see that the pupils were dilated. That along with his deep sleep and difficulty in waking suggested he might have taken something.

I asked him about it. "Waldo, what did you take?"

He shook his head. "Nothing. I didn't take anything. Now leave me alone. I'm sleepy."

He started to lie back down, but I grabbed his arm and kept him upright. "Waldo, if you've taken something, tell me what it is. I'll need to know if we have to call 9-1-1. It might save your life."

He shrugged. "I took a pill to help me relax. Got it from the guy in the room next to mine at the motel. He said it wasn't dangerous. It would just help me relax. You guys were stressing me out, so I took it when you went to check the rooms."

I nodded. "So this guy with the pill, did he give it to you or did you have to pay for it?"

Waldo rubbed his chin like he was trying to remember. Finally, he said, "I think I paid him ten for it. Maybe twenty."

Chapter Fifty-One

"This guy who sold you the pill, did he tell you what it was? Can you remember if he called it something?"

Waldo shook his head. "I can't remember. It doesn't matter. I feel fine. I'm just sleepy."

I looked over at Erin and asked, "What do you think? Should we call 9-1-1?"

She looked at Waldo, checked his eyes and said, "He doesn't look that bad to me. It was probably Xanax. If it was, he'll sleep it off and be fine in a few hours."

Waldo nodded. "Yeah, that's what he said it was. Xanax. He said it wasn't dangerous."

I nodded. "Okay, let's assume that's what it was. How many did you buy, how many did you take, and how many do you have left?"

Waldo held up one finger. "One. I just bought the one. Or maybe two, I don't really remember. So far I've only taken one today. I took one last night and still have one left. So I guess it was three."

He was still sitting on the bed, woozy but awake. I decided to tell him about what we'd found. "The paintings in the guest rooms. They might be valuable. Maybe worth enough to pay off your loans to Madicof."

I thought he would be happy to hear this, but he wasn't. Instead, he said, "I've already checked. They're fakes. I took one to Night Shade, a pawnshop on the other side of town, and the guy there looked at it. He said it was a fake. A good one but still a fake. He offered to give me a hundred for it, so I sold it to him.

"I told him about the others, and he said he'd pay me a hundred for each one. He even offered to come pick them up. I didn't want him coming here, so I told him the paintings were in Daytona, in a storage building.

"He wanted to go look at them, but I told him I had other things to do and promised I'd come back with the rest in a few days. At a hundred dollars each, I'd get a little over a thousand in cash. I could use the money to buy more jugs."

He mumbled something I couldn't decipher. Then his eyes rolled back and he fell onto his mattress. In a matter of seconds, he was snoring.

I looked over at Erin. "Think we should maybe go by Night Shade? See what they're asking for the painting Waldo sold them?"

She nodded. "Yes, we should. Then we should take one over to the Lost Art Gallery downtown. They might have someone there who can tell us if it's authentic or not and what it's really worth."

We left Waldo sleeping on his bed. I made sure the fan was blowing directly on him. Without air conditioning, the room would get warm. But being in the shade, it would be cooler than being outside.

Erin knew where the pawnshop was, so she drove. She claimed she'd never been inside and I had no reason not to believe her.

After going through what some would say was the bad side of town, we pulled up in front of the pawnshop. The squat block building had steel bars over the heavily tinted windows. No doubt to keep out would-be thieves. A pawnshop would be a gold mine to a burglar who knew how to get in and get out without getting shot.

A bright yellow banner hung from the roof of the building with the word "Pawn" in a large all caps font. Below it, evenly spaced on the sign were the words, "Cash, Gold, Jewelry, Guns." It looked like they had it pretty much covered.

We headed for the door and saw a sign advising customers to "Unload your guns before entering." It was probably there to remind those who had a gun to pawn to unload it before going inside. Below that sign was another one with the words, "SMILE. YOU ARE ON CAMERA."

Below that was a graphic of a loaded pistol the way you'd see it if it were pointed at you. Below the pistol, the words, "Shoplifters and Thieves, do not expect a warning shot."

It was clear that anyone planning to rob the place would be a fool or have a death wish. We weren't armed and didn't plan to shoplift, so we were good.

Erin stepped in first, and I followed. Inside, to our right, was a long glass counter filled with guns and watches. Behind the counter, a large, heavily tattooed man with a bald head held a pistol and a cleaning rod.

When he saw us, he put the gun down and asked, "You folks looking to pawn something?"

Erin shook her head and said, "No, we're here because we heard you might have a painting we'd be interested in."

He grunted, looked over his shoulder, then back at her. "You heard we had a painting? From who? Who told you we had paintings here?"

"A friend. Said he was in here a few days ago and saw a

painting of a Florida sunset. You still have it?"

"Yeah, we do. You want to see it?"

Erin nodded.

The man stood, walked over to what looked like a bank vault at the far end of the counter and pulled the six-inch-thick door open. From where we were standing, we could see several canvases stacked vertically on the middle shelf.

The pawnshop guy flipped through them, found the one he was looking for and pulled it out. He held it up. "This the one?"

"That's it. How much are you asking for it?"

He turned the painting over, looked at the price tag taped to the back, and grunted. "Five thousand."

He started to put the painting back, but he stopped when Erin said, "I might be interested. But I need a closer look."

Instead of bringing the painting over to where we were standing, he said, "You want to see it? You need to come over here. I ain't bringing it to you."

She walked over and he held the painting up so she could see more details. When she pulled out her phone, he shook his head. "No pictures. We don't allow it. You can look all you want, but no pictures."

Erin shrugged. "Okay, no pictures. Do you have a certificate of authenticity?"

The guy frowned and said, "Look, lady, if you want the painting, it's five thousand. You get what I'm holding. Nothing more."

She took a deep breath and said, "I don't think I'd be interested in it without the certificate. Thanks for your time."

She headed for the door, but just as she reached it, the pawnshop guy said, "Wait. Four thousand. Today only. You walk out without buying it and the price goes back to five."

Erin shook her head, opened the door and we both went out. When we got in the car, she said, "They think it's real. They wouldn't price it that way if they didn't."

She started the car and we headed to the Lost Art Gallery to talk to the curator.

Chapter Fifty-Two

On the way to the gallery, I pulled up their website on my phone and it said that their curator, Victoria, was an accredited appraiser with the International Society of Appraisers with more than twenty years of experience. She sounded like the kind of person we needed to talk to.

I called ahead and asked to speak to her. I was told she was there but not able to come to the phone at the moment. I said I'd call back.

The gallery was in old town on St. George Street, a narrow cobblestone affair with very limited parking. We were fortunate to find a meter just a few steps from their door. Erin parked and had me grab one of the paintings from the back seat. I flipped through them and picked the one that had two palm trees on a rustic beach overlooking the ocean. It was signed in the lower right corner by Harold Newton.

Going into the gallery with me carrying the painting under my arm, we were greeted at the door by a nicely dressed woman who looked to be in her mid-thirties. She pointed at the painting and asked, "Are you here to consign or get it appraised?"

Erin and I answered at the same time. "Appraised."

The woman nodded, picked up her phone and punched in a number. She whispered a few words, hung up, and turned to us. "Victoria will be out in a moment. Feel free to look around while you wait."

Still carrying the painting, I followed Erin as she walked into the gallery. Soft lighting and cool air gave it a mystical feel. The art hanging from the wall, with pinpoint lighting highlighting each piece, was impressive. Even though I don't know much about art, I thought what they had was pretty amazing. As were the prices shown on the info cards below each piece.

After we had viewed most of the paintings, a well-dressed woman who looked to be in her late forties came over and introduced herself as Victoria. She pointed at the painting I was carrying and asked, "Is that the one you want me to appraise?"

I nodded and held the painting up so she could see it. She leaned in, saw the artist's signature and said, "Interesting. Very interesting."

She pointed to the back and said, "Follow me."

She led us into a separate studio and had me put the painting on a vertical easel. A ceiling-mounted light aimed directly on the easel brought out the painting's true colors.

Victoria put on a pair of white cotton gloves, picked up a large magnifying glass, and moved in close to see more detail. As she moved the magnifying glass across the painting, she would stop, look closer and repeat what she had said earlier. "Interesting. Very interesting."

Fifteen minutes later, she pulled out a camera and snapped a photo of the artist's signature. She then went to a nearby computer and pulled authenticated samples of the artist's previous works.

When she was done, she came back to us and said, "I'm pretty sure this is a real Harold Newton. Everything checks out. The board it's painted on, the subject matter, the size, the direction of the strokes, and the signature.

"This is just my opinion, and I would need to do more work to be sure, but I think it's real. Are you interested in selling it?"

Erin nodded. "We might be. What do you think it's worth?"

Victoria looked at her computer again. "One like this recently sold at auction for thirty-five hundred dollars. The one you have would probably sell close to that.

"We would be happy to take it in on consignment if you're interested."

Erin took a deep breath and said, "I didn't think it would be worth that much. When I decide to sell, I'll bring it back to you."

Victoria thanked us for bringing it in and said we'd be welcome to return any time. She mentioned that if we found other similar pieces, she would be interested in them as well.

When we started to leave, she said, "Please don't carry it like that. You'll damage it. Let me wrap it for you."

We gave her the painting and she wrapped it in what looked like tissue paper, only heavier. When she was done, she said, "Be sure to store it in a dry place, out of direct sunlight."

We said we would, and just as I turned to head to the door, Erin said, "We have two more in the car. Would you like to see them?"

"Yes, please. Bring them in. Let me see what you have."

Erin sent me to the car to retrieve the two paintings we'd left in it. Back in the gallery, the curator examined each one and said they looked to be authentic. According to recent auctions, each one would be worth around three thousand.

As before, she offered to take them in on consignment. Erin thought about it for a moment, then said, "Pick the one you think will do best."

Victoria chose the first one we had shown her, the one signed by Harold Newton. She explained the consignment process and the percentage the store would get from the selling price. She had Erin sign a contract, gave her a copy, and thanked her for bringing the paintings in.

As we were leaving, she said, "Don't be surprised if it sells quickly. There are a lot of people who collect these Highwaymen paintings. I wish I had more."

I carried the two paintings we hadn't consigned back to the car. This time, I was careful when I put them in the back seat. I didn't want to damage them in any way.

Erin started the car, pulled away from the curb and got us back out onto US One. After clearing traffic she said, "I don't think we should tell Waldo. I think we should buy all that he'll sell us. We can rent an air-conditioned storage unit and store the paintings there.

"It's not that I want to keep them for myself, it's just that I don't think Waldo is going to take care of them. He's already been snookered by the pawnshop. No telling what he might do next.

"If we get them, we can make sure they don't get damaged. We can get an estimate of what they're worth and maybe figure out a way to give Waldo some cash. What do you think?"

I didn't have to think long. She was right about Waldo. He'd hadn't proven to be the kind of person you'd want to hand over fifty thousand dollars of fine art to.

"You're right. The best thing to do is to take the paintings somewhere they'll be safe. Let's do it."

We stopped at Anastasia Self Storage, rented a five-by-nine air-conditioned unit, and headed back to the Die Inn.

Chapter Fifty-Three

When we pulled into the Die Inn parking lot, Waldo was back outside by the fountain, filling water jugs as he had been doing earlier that day. Like before, he didn't hear us coming, and it bothered me. If Mad Dog's associates were pulling into the lot instead of us, they could grab him and drag him off before he knew it.

I needed to warn him. To make sure he understood the seriousness of his situation. Mad Dog's collectors weren't playing games.

We got out of the car and walked over to him. When he saw us, he smiled and asked, "Did you bring me lunch?"

Erin shook her head. "No, we didn't. But if you want, we can go get you something. But first, we need to talk."

She pointed to the paintings we had laid out against the wall. The ones we had retrieved from the guest rooms. "You said you needed money. Walker and I have been thinking about it, and we don't want you dealing with a pawnbroker. You said you thought you'd get a thousand for the rest of the paintings.

"That's probably a good price. But Walker will pay you more. He can give you fifteen hundred for all of them and pay in cash. All you have to do is say, 'Yes.'

"If you do, we'll go get the money, bring you back lunch, and get the paintings out of your way. What do you think?"

Waldo grinned. "I think I'm getting the better end of that

deal. So yeah, you can have them all for fifteen hundred. Bring me back a Big Mac, fries and a large Coke."

He turned back to the fountain and began filling another jug. He still didn't understand how being out in the open like he was would make it easier for the collection guys to find him.

I shook my head. I'd already warned him about it, and he hadn't changed his ways. Telling him again probably wouldn't make any difference so I followed Erin back to the car. Inside, after she started the engine and put the air conditioning on high, she asked, "Can you come up with fifteen hundred? Or do you need me to spot you?"

I didn't have that much cash on me, I rarely did. But I knew where to get it. I smiled at Erin and said, "Take me to the bank. I'll cash a check."

The bank I use has branches all over Florida, and finding one in Saint Augustine was easy. There was one just a few minutes from Waldo's place, and we got there quickly. Inside, there wasn't a line, and after looking at my ID, the teller counted out fifteen one-hundred-dollar bills. She put the money in a small white envelope, handed it to me and said, "Have a nice day."

With cash in hand, we headed to McDonald's to pick up a burger and fries for Waldo. While there, I got a southern-style chicken sandwich and Erin ordered a walnut vinaigrette salad.

When we got back to the Die Inn, Waldo was sitting in the shade in front of room number three. When he saw us, he hustled over to our car and asked, "Did you get me lunch?"

I showed him the McDonald's bag and the large Coke.

took both, thanked us and went back to his perch in the shade.

After pulling up two of the metal chairs that sat near the fountain, we joined him and ate our lunch. When we were done, I pulled the cash from my pocket and peeled off fifteen one-hundred-dollar bills. I handed them to Waldo and said, "Don't spend the money on anything except food and shelter. No drugs."

He nodded and took the cash. After recounting it, he folded it in half and put it in his back pocket. Then he stood and said, "I've got to fill ten more jugs. If I can sell them at the farmers' market tomorrow, I'll have a five-thousand-dollar day."

I didn't understand what kind of new-age math he was using to come up with the five thousand number, but I didn't ask him about it. I didn't care.

We went back to the car, opened the back doors and trunk and made room for the paintings I had just bought. Remembering what Victoria had said about being careful not to damage them, I asked Waldo if there were any old towels around that we could use.

He said, "Check the bathrooms. You'll find towels in every one of them. I don't know if they're clean or not, but if you want them, you can have them."

Erin got the towels out of rooms one through eight and I got the rest. We'd go in, hold our breath, run to the bathroom, grab the towels, and run back out. When we were done, we had twelve. Enough for what we needed. We put one between each painting as we loaded it into the car.

Ten minutes later, we were back at Anastasia Storage, moving the paintings from the car into the unit we had ıted.

When they were safely stored away, I asked Erin, "What next?"

She shrugged. "We found Waldo. The three paintings he gave me will more than cover what he owes me. So from here on, it's your show. Whatever you want to do is fine with me."

I decided we should go back to the motorhome and check on Bob. While there, I'd call Marissa and let her know I'd found Waldo and that, so far, Mad Dog's guys hadn't gotten to him. But I suspected they would soon.

We pulled into our site at Anastasia and saw that the tent campers who had been next to us when we left that morning had moved on. For the moment at least, we had no neighbors. That would probably change as we got closer to the weekend. But we'd be gone by then. Our reservation was only good for two more days.

Inside the RV, Bob was lounging on the couch, licking his paws. He looked pretty contented. I figured he'd either just eaten or pooped. I went back to check his bowls and could tell by the smell that he'd just made a deposit in his litter box.

Being a big cat, he doesn't poop out raisin-sized nuggets. He drops the big ones. In the clumping litter I use, they end up being tennis ball sized.

I grabbed the litter scoop from under the counter and one of the plastic bags I saved when I bought food. Getting down on my knees, I started cleaning his box. When I felt warm breath on my back, I figured it was Erin checking in on me.

It wasn't. It was Bob. He was making sure I got the job done to his satisfaction. He likes a clean box and likes to watch when I scoop out his leavings.

After taking the bag of poop out to the roadside trash bin, I came back in to find both Erin and Bob on the couch. He was sitting in her lap and she was petting him.

"Looks like he's got you trained."

She nodded. "I think he has."

I grabbed my phone off the counter and said, "I've got to make a call. I'll be right back."

Back in the bedroom with the door closed, I punched in the number for Marissa's burner phone. She answered on the third ring and asked, "Have you found him?"

I told her we had and he was safe for the moment. I also told her he'd spent all the money he'd borrowed, and he didn't have any way to pay it back.

The bad news was that two of Mad Dog's goons were in town looking for him. They wouldn't be happy when they learned he didn't have any money.

After hearing my report, Marissa said, "Anything you can do to get him out of this mess, do it. But not if it means you getting hurt or using your own money to pay off his loan. Waldo got himself into this, and if he hadn't involved his mother, I'd let Mad Dog's men teach him a lesson."

She ended the call by saying, "Call me when things change one way or another."

When I went back into the living room, Bob was still sitting in Erin's lap. She had her phone out and was saying, "Okay, I'll come get it. Thanks."

She ended the call and said, "That was the repair shop. My car is ready. We need to pick it up today before they close at five."

I checked the time and saw that it was nearly four. "I can go as soon as you're ready."

I grabbed two bottles of water from the fridge and handed one to Erin. She twisted off the top, took a sip and said. "If we leave now, we might beat rush hour traffic."

I didn't think a small town like Saint Augustine had a rush hour, but it did. Probably mostly tourists heading back to their hotel rooms after a day of viewing the sights. With the traffic, it took us fifteen minutes to get to the small auto repair shop where Erin had left her car. It was located well south of old town, a few blocks west of the Walmart Super Center we had visited earlier.

There were several cars in the shop's lot. A few classics, including a nice fifty-seven Chevy and a sixty-four low rider. There were a few newer cars as well, including a Volvo station wagon and a late model Mercedes. The outside of the shop looked clean, the building looked well kept, and the cars they were working on looked to be the kind that people with money would own.

Seeing the classics and the late model luxury cars, I wondered which one was Erin's. She had gone inside to pay and told me to wait in Raif's car. I guessed I'd soon find out which car was hers.

A few minutes later, she came out of the shop's office carrying a receipt and car keys. She walked to the side of the building and climbed into a teal-green Ford Focus wagon. After getting it started, she pulled over to where I was parked and said, "Follow me back to the RV. We'll leave Raif's car there and go get dinner in mine."

It sounded like a good plan to me.

Fifteen minutes later, we reached the gate at the park.

Because Erin's car didn't have a sticker showing she was a registered camper, she had to purchase a day pass. Good for two days.

With the park pass taped to the inside left corner of her windshield, the ranger waved us through. When we got to the RV, Erin stayed in her car as I pulled into our site and parked Raif's.

It'd been less than an hour since we left the RV, and I didn't feel the need to check on Bob. He had plenty of food, a clean litter box, and plenty of places to sleep. He'd be fine, so I didn't go in.

When I slid into the passenger seat of Erin's car, she was smiling. "I missed having my own car. It's nice to have it back."

Then she asked, "Where do you want to eat dinner?"

I shrugged. "You know this town better than I do; you choose."

We ended up eating at the Mellow Mushroom, the place I had gotten takeout the first night I'd been with Erin.

This time, we had a sit-down meal. For starters, we each ordered their house salad, and for our main course, we went with a thin crust buffalo chicken pizza.

Our food was brought out quickly. The salads first and a few minutes later our pizza. We ate, enjoying the laid-back atmosphere as well as each other's company.

When we finished, Erin suggested we cruise by Waldo's to make sure he hadn't gone crazy with the money I'd given him. Knowing how he had quickly gone through the fifty thousand he had borrowed from Mad Dog, it wouldn't have been a surprise if he'd already blown through the fifteen hundred he'd gotten from me.

It was almost dark when we reached the Die Inn. The parking lot was empty. Waldo's car was gone. So were all the water jugs he had been filling from the fountain. Maybe he had taken them into town in search of gullible tourists willing to fork over a ten-spot for a jug of water.

If he had, good for him. At least he'd be trying to generate income. It was a start. But it wasn't much and he'd have a long way to go.

Since his car wasn't in the lot, Erin kept going south on A1A. About six miles later, she pulled into a strip mall across from a row of high rise condos. She parked in front of the Island Ice Cream Cafe and asked, "You in the mood for ice cream?"

I hadn't really been thinking about it, but if Erin was having some, so would I. She ordered a cup of almond praline and I went with the maple walnut. After I paid, we sat at the table closest to the window and watched the traffic go by as we enjoyed our cool confections.

When we were done, we got back into her car and headed north. On the way, I looked for Waldo's car in the parking lots of the small motels we passed. He had said he was staying in one but didn't tell us the name.

If his next-door neighbor, the one who had sold him Xanax, was selling drugs from his room, the place probably wouldn't be much better than the Die Inn. Except for the part about it having electricity and running water.

I checked all the lots on my side of the road and didn't see his car. When we passed the Die Inn, it wasn't there either. I should have been worried about it, but I wasn't. I'd told him about the trouble he'd be in if Mad Dog's guys found him. If he didn't want to listen to my warning, that was up to him.

Chapter Fifty-Four

That evening, Erin and I watched a movie on Netflix before going to bed. She said I could sleep with her as long as I followed the same rules she had given me the night before. No spooning, no touching, nothing of a sexual nature. We were in bed to sleep. Nothing more.

I didn't like the rules, but I was going to abide by them. I didn't want to spend the night on the couch. It was made for sitting, not sleeping.

The next morning, I woke with Erin's arm over my chest, holding me tight against her warm body. She wasn't moaning like she had been the previous morning, but she was breathing deeply. I could feel her hot breath on the back of my neck.

Since we'd already found Waldo and didn't need to get up early, there was no reason for us not to sleep in. We stayed in bed for another hour. I was wide awake, needed to pee and was hungry. But I wasn't going to get up. Not until she woke and explained how her arm had somehow gotten around my chest.

Unfortunately, that never happened and it was Bob's fault. While she was still sleeping, he jumped up on the bed and made his presence known by tapping her ear with his paw. It didn't take many to get her attention.

She rolled over away from me, saw Bob and whispered, "Is it time for some petting?"

He didn't answer, but if she had asked me, my answer would have been a definite "Yes."

With the spell broken, I rolled out of bed and took care of my morning business. When I went up front, I was surprised to see it was a little after nine. The day was moving along, leaving us behind.

Erin soon joined me, rubbing her eyes with one hand and trying to tame her bedhead with the other. She squinted at the bright light streaming in through the skylight and said, "Turn that thing off. It's too early to have the lights on."

I tried not to laugh but couldn't hold back. "Erin, I can't turn it off. It's the sun. Get dressed and I'll take you to breakfast."

She shook her head. "I'll stay here. You go get it for me. Egg biscuit and a Coke. No Cheese."

Without waiting to see if I was going to agree to her request, she turned and wobbled back to the bedroom. Since I was hungry too and breakfast from McDonald's was the quick and easy way to get fed, I decided to go get it.

Erin's car was parked behind Raif's, blocking it in and there was no way I was going to ask her to move it. So I found her keys on the kitchen counter, locked the RV behind me, and headed to Micky D's.

When I got back with the food, Erin was sitting at the kitchen table waiting. She looked like she had showered and changed into clean clothes. I needed to do the same, but it would have to wait until after I ate.

While we were eating, she asked if I slept well and I told her I had. I asked her the same, and she said, "Not really. Sometime during the night, my side of the bed got hot. I didn't want to get up, so I just lay there. Hot and sweaty."

I smiled. "Yeah, I know. You were plenty sweaty this morning when you had your arm wrapped around me.

"Maybe tonight you should sleep naked. You'd be cooler that way."

She smiled and said, "That's not going to happen. We're both keeping our clothes on. Those are the rules."

Disappointed with her answer, but not surprised, I took a shower and got ready for the day.

An hour later, riding in Erin's Ford wagon, we pulled into the Die Inn parking lot. There were several official-looking cars already there. Three men in long pants and ties stood in front of the fountain. One of the men was holding a clipboard.

Behind them, the door to guest room three opened, and a man with a camera came out. He checked his camera then walked over to room number four and went in.

To me, it looked like police investigating a crime scene. The only thing missing was yellow crime tape and the coroner's wagon. Maybe they'd already cleared the scene.

Erin and I were in shorts and tees, and to the officials standing near the fountain, we probably looked like nosy neighbors wanting to see what was going on.

But that didn't stop us. We got out and walked to the man holding the clipboard. He saw us coming and nodded. Before he could tell us to leave, I asked, "Where's Waldo?"

I was half expecting him to tell me that he was dead or in the hospital having been badly beaten. But instead he said, "He's in the office."

When I turned to go there, the first thing I noticed was the lights. They were on. Not just a lantern but real lights. I wanted to find out why.

Entering, I saw Waldo sitting in the chair behind the check-in counter with a stack of papers on the desk in front of him. I noticed that the room wasn't hot like it had been the day before. The air conditioning was on.

Waldo saw us coming and stood. He walked up to the counter and said, "Guess what."

I couldn't think of any reason the electricity would be back on and the parking lot filled with county officials so I shrugged and said, "I don't know. Divine intervention?"

Waldo nodded. "It seems that way. I was filling jugs at the fountain when the first car rolled up. A guy got out and said he was from the county. Said they were looking for a facility where they could place single mothers that were homeless.

"They had checked around and found that this place was empty. After inspecting the rooms he said the county would pay me seven hundred a month for each room. They'd also pay to get the utilities turned on and keep them on.

"And they promised to put new beds, carpet, and TVs in all the rooms.

"I couldn't believe it. They were in a hurry and didn't want to waste time. He said they had single moms sleeping in cars with their kids. They needed a place to stay and the county wanted to help.

"All I had to do was to sign a contract, and they'd take care of the rest. They even said I could move into the apartment behind the manager's office and live there rent-free.

"So I said, 'Yes,' and within the hour this place was swarming with people. Two men from the power company, another from water and sewer, and two guys with cameras shooting photos of the rooms so they'd know what needed to be done to get them ready.

"They told me they'd be updating everything in the coming week, and people would be moving in soon after."

He grinned and said, "Can you believe it?"

If I hadn't seen it with my own eyes, I wouldn't have. I knew Florida was serious about helping with the homeless problem. They had recently passed legislation to speed up the flow of state and federal funding to get those with young children off the street.

But seeing the money flow in Waldo's direction, especially that quickly, was hard to believe.

Still, if the county could use the empty motel rooms to provide a safe place for single mothers and their children, I was wholeheartedly for it.

Chapter Fifty-Five

I was happy for Waldo. Somehow, his investment in the Paradise Inn looked like it was going to pay off. He still had the Mad Dog problem and that wouldn't be as easy to resolve.

Erin congratulated him on his good fortune and we went back out into the parking lot. It was starting to warm up and I suggested we visit old town before it got too hot. We could walk the streets then go to the pirate museum to cool off.

She thought it was a good idea but said that, since she had her own car, we should take Raif's back to him so as not to leave him without a set of wheels. He needed a way to go somewhere if Fay got on his nerves.

We headed back to our campsite, picked up his car, and then, with me following Erin, headed to Raif's. On the way, I remembered what he had said about bringing the car back with a full tank; I checked the gas gauge. The needle was just about E. It was nearly empty.

I flagged Erin down at the first stop sign and let her know I needed to get gas. She nodded and said, "I figured you would. I'll stop at Pump and Munch. You can fill it there."

Ten minutes later, I was standing near the back of Raif's car, pumping gas. When it was full, I stepped back to Erin's car, which was near the pump behind me, and filled her tank as well. If I was going to be riding around with her, the least I could do was pay for gas.

With the tanks in both cars topped off, we headed to Raif's. Erin led the way, I followed.

After going by the office, I slowed to see if the site I had paid for was still vacant. It was. That was a good thing because I needed to be out of my site at Anastasia by noon the following day.

When we reached Raif's, Erin parked on the street. The same baby-blue Subaru, the one I figured belonged to Fay, was already parked in the drive. I pulled up behind it.

As soon as I got the car parked, Raif came outside to greet us. He looked at Erin and asked, "You still hanging around with that bum? I thought you had better taste in men."

She nodded. "I do, but sometimes you can't be choosy."

They were both smiling, waiting for me to say something. I didn't disappoint. "You're right; she can do better than me. As long he isn't bothered by her snoring."

Raif laughed. Erin had been bunking in his place for a few months and there was no doubt he knew what I was talking about. She snored. Sometimes loudly.

She was shaking her head. "I don't snore. And Walker, if it bothers you, you can sleep on the couch tonight."

Raif said, "Ooh, burn."

He pointed to his car and asked, "You fill it up?"

I nodded a yes.

"Good. How's it running?"

It was a question most men will ask after letting someone else drive their car. Especially a special car like Raif's.

I gave him the answer he wanted to hear. "It runs like a

new one. A really nice ride. Erin got it up to eighty and it didn't miss a beat."

He turned to her and asked, "Have you been hot-rodding my car again? I warned you, next time you get a ticket I'm not going to take care of it."

She shook her head. "You know he's kidding, right? We never left town, I never got it up to eighty. I know how much you care about that car, so I drove like a little old lady. Slow and sure."

He nodded and changed the subject. "So, did you find Waldo yet?"

The question was directed at both of us. Erin answered first. "Yes, we found him. He bought a run-down motel on A1A south. The Die Inn."

Raif shook his head. "So they found someone foolish enough to buy that place. I sure hope he didn't pay too much. I don't much care for Waldo but would hate to see him get in over his head with that thing."

Still looking at Erin, he asked, "Did you get your money back?"

"Not in cash but in a painting worth a lot more than he owed me."

"A painting? You sure it's valuable? Not a fake?"

"It's not a fake. We took it to the appraiser at the Lost Art Gallery and she said it was real and thought it might sell for three grand. Since I didn't have a place to keep it, I put it on consignment in her gallery."

Raif nodded. "Hope you didn't take advantage of poor Waldo. If he gave you a painting worth three thousand to cover the nine hundred dollars he owed you, it sounds like you might have."

Erin shook her head. "Nope, not at all. He'd already taken one to Night Shade and they told him it was a fake worth around a hundred. He was more than happy to give me one and sell the rest to Walker for the same price, a hundred each.

"Waldo is pretty much broke except for the money we gave him. He hasn't paid his loan shark and he took on another loan from the owner of the motel.

"The guys who are looking for him are still in town and they want their money. We tried to warn him that they would be coming after him, but he didn't seem too worried. He thinks he can get an extension."

Raif turned to me. "What do you think? Any chance the guy who loaned him the money is willing to renegotiate the terms?"

I'm sure Raif already knew the answer to his question. "No, I don't think he's the negotiating type. The people working for him don't negotiate either. They either collect what is owed or start breaking bones."

Raif nodded. "So, let me guess. You're going to try to be a hero and figure out some way to get him out of the mess he's in."

I sighed. "I don't want to be anyone's hero. But I don't want to see him get hurt too badly. Maybe I can come up with a way out for him."

Raif shook his head. "Don't get between him and the loan shark. If you do, he might decide to come after you when they find out he can't pay."

He turned to Erin. "You're done with this, right? You got what you wanted from Waldo. There's no need for you to see him again. Right?"

Erin nodded. "Yeah, I'm mostly through with him. I'm going to see him one more time this afternoon, and after that, it's over."

"You're going to see him? Why?"

Erin smiled. "You're not going to believe this. The county agreed to fix up the Die Inn. They're going to replace all the carpets, furniture and bedding. Even repaint the rooms. And they're not going to charge Waldo anything.

"All he had to do was to agree to rent all the rooms to the county to house single mothers.

"The only reason I want to go back is to see if there are any paintings we missed. If there are, I'll buy them from him."

Raif shook his head again and turned to me. "You're going with her, right? You're going to make sure she stays safe. Right?"

I nodded. "Yes, I'm going with her. And I'll do my best to keep her safe."

He turned back to her. "You find a place to live yet? If not, your old room is still available. You can move back any time. I kind of wish you would, I miss having you around."

Erin smiled. "I miss you too. But I have a plan. Waldo's lease is up next door and since I already know the neighborhood, I'm thinking about renting his place for a month or two while I look for something more permanent.

She looked at me and winked. I'm not sure why but maybe because she hadn't bothered to tell me she'd be moving out of my RV that soon.

I thanked Raif for letting me use his car and we left with

Erin driving hers. I didn't bother asking where we were going. I was pretty sure we were heading back to the Die Inn.

Chapter Fifty-Six

Twelve minutes later, we pulled into the parking lot of the Paradise Inn, the motel that Waldo had bought. The place was humming with activity. A large dumpster had been brought in and workers were there ready to strip the rooms down to the bare walls.

We found a place to park in front of the office, next to a Cool Today air conditioning truck. Erin got out and headed to the open guest rooms, in search of wall art we may have missed. I went into the office to talk to Waldo, who was sitting behind the check-in desk with his feet up on the counter.

He saw me coming but didn't bother to get up. I walked over and said, "You look pretty comfortable. Does that mean you're not worried about Madicof's guys finding you?"

He shook his head. "No need to worry. I called him and told him I was broke. Told him I couldn't pay. I said I'd be making a little money starting next month, and I'd be willing to pay him some then."

"So you called him? What did he say after you told him you couldn't pay?"

Waldo smiled. "He was real nice about it. He said he'd be happy to talk to me. Said he'd be in town tomorrow and we could get together."

"And you're not worried about meeting with him?"

"No, why should I be? I'm willing to pay him what I owe; I just can't do it on his schedule. After I tell him my situation, I'm sure he'll understand."

I couldn't believe Waldo was so naive. He owed Madicof a lot of money and hadn't made any payments. Madicof was coming all the way from Key West to Saint Augustine to meet with him. No way that was a good thing.

I only had one question. "Did you tell him where you live?"

Waldo shook his head. "He asked, but I told him I was moving around and didn't know where I'd be when he got into town. I told him to call and we'd get together."

I nodded. "You still staying in that motel you talked about? The one with the drug dealer living next door?"

"Yes, I'll be there until they get my apartment fixed up here. They're going to pull the carpet and furniture out today. They're supposed to paint it tomorrow.

"It should be ready for me to move into by the middle of next week."

I should have asked him the name of the motel, but I didn't. I really didn't care where he was staying.

I wished him good luck and headed outside to see if Erin had found anything of value. She wasn't in the parking lot, but her car was still there. She hadn't driven off and left me behind.

I started checking the rooms and it wasn't until I got to room twelve that I found her. She was in the back, standing on a rickety chair, trying to pry a small painting off the wall. It looked like she could fall any second.

I walked over, wrapped my arms around her waist, lifted her out of the chair and set her safely on the floor. Before she turned around, she said, "You better not let my boyfriend see you do that. He's the jealous type."

She turned and laughed. "I found three more paintings. They're smaller than the others but looked to be the same kind. Florida scenes painted on board.

"I was able to get the first two down, but not the one in here. I think it might be nailed to the wall. You want to see if you can get it down for me?"

It didn't look like the chair she had been standing on would hold my weight, so I didn't bother to use it. Instead, I grabbed the painting from the bottom and, rather than trying to pull it off the wall, I pushed it up toward the ceiling. I figured it was hung by a wire over a screw and if I pushed up, it would likely come loose. It did.

Erin was surprised to see how quickly I was able to get it down. She looked up at me and said, "My hero," then she took the painting out of my hands and headed for the door.

I followed her to the car where she put the painting in the back seat with the other two she'd found. When she was done, she said, "I'm taking them to the storage building. Whenever you're ready, we're leaving."

We had just pulled back on the street when Erin's phone chimed with an incoming call. She answered and after a few moments, the call ended. "That was one of the new people working at the Taco Palace. He said an inspector from the health department was there and had a question that none of them could answer. Something about the taco oven.

"He said the inspector was going to shut the place down if he didn't get an answer right away, so I agreed to go over and help them out.

"It might take a while, so I'm thinking I can drop you off at the RV before I go. That way you won't have to wait around for however long it takes me to explain things to the inspector. Is that okay?"

There were a few things I needed to do back at the motorhome, including dumping the tanks. I was pretty sure Erin didn't want to be around when I did that. "Yeah, drop me off. Call me when you get done."

Fifteen minutes later, I was alone in the motorhome. Not the first time and certainly not the last.

Chapter Fifty-Seven

While Erin was talking with the health inspector at the Taco Palace, I kept busy in the RV. I washed a few dishes, made the bed and in general cleaned the place up.

Going outside, I unhooked from shore power, stored the power cord and locked up the lower compartment. Back inside, I looked for Bob and found him in the back bedroom taking his afternoon nap.

While he was safely on the bed, I went up front and pressed the button to bring the two front slide rooms in. Then I checked on Bob again. He was still sleeping on the bed. Not wanting to disturb him, I watched to make sure he didn't move as I brought the bedroom slide in. It didn't seem to bother him, he slept right through it.

With the slides in and everything else taken care of, I fired up the engine and let it warm up for a couple of minutes. Then, after rechecking the campground map, I headed for the dump station. It was less than a quarter-mile from my site and easy to find.

When I got there, I was happy to see there wasn't a line; no one else was dumping their tanks ahead of me. Dumping can be messy, especially when newbies are involved. If they don't know what they are doing, all kinds of bad things can happen.

Trying to drain forty gallons of poop water from a holding tank using a flimsy plastic hose isn't that difficult and doesn't have to be messy. But if the hose leaks or if the tank connections aren't secure, you could end up with a lot of poopy water on the ground around you.

It doesn't happen often, but when it does, the person responsible is supposed to clean it up. But a lot of times, they don't. They just drive away leaving a nasty surprise for the next person who shows up.

Most communal dump stations at state and national parks have wash down hoses readily available to clean up spills. These hoses usually hang on a spring-loaded hook above and off to the side of the dump hole. They usually have a high-pressure nozzle making it easy to clean away any mess and make it nice for the next person.

Of course, it doesn't always work that way. Sometimes the mess isn't cleaned up. That's why I always stop before I pull up to a dump station. I want to get out and take a look before I commit. If there's a mess, I don't want to be walking through it while I dump my tanks. I'll clean it up first.

Being mid-afternoon, well past checkout time, the RV'ers who'd left early and dumped their tanks before they pulled out were long gone. The park's maintenance workers had cleaned up the area, and it was safe for me to use it.

I pulled up to the sewer hole and got ready to empty the tanks. The first step was to unlock the compartment where I stored the dump hose and put on a pair of rubber gloves. Then it was just a matter of connecting one end of the hose to the RV and the other into the dump station's sewer hole.

When everything was connected, I pulled the handle on the black tank and let it rip. When the sound of rushing lumpy water inside the hose subsided, I closed the black tank handle and pulled the one for the grey tank.

The grey tank contained mostly shower and sink water, which meant it flowed faster than the black tank's contents and would tend to flush the sewer hose on its way out. When the grey tank was empty, I closed the tank handle and double-checked to make sure both were secure. I then disconnected the sewer hose at the RV end and used the station's water hose to wash it out.

When it was clean, I put it away and pulled off my rubber gloves. After locking the storage compartment, the only thing left to do was to wash my hands and go back inside.

It had taken me less than thirty minutes to get to the dump station, dump the tanks, and get back to my site. I backed in, hooked up to shore power and ran the slide rooms back out.

With the tanks empty, the slides out, and the place cleaned up, there wasn't much for me to do except wait for Erin to return. I figured she'd be gone at least an hour, maybe more.

I decided as a reward for cleaning the place and dumping the tanks, a nap was in order. I joined Bob in the back bedroom and dozed off.

Three hours later, I woke and was surprised to see that Erin hadn't returned. I figured maybe after answering the health inspector's questions about the taco oven she decided to stay until the full inspection was over, just in case other questions came up.

An hour later, it was nearly six, dinner time, and she was still gone. I was starting to get worried. Maybe her car had broken down or for some reason she wasn't able to get through the park's gate. I decided to call and see if there was a problem or if there was any way I could help.

I punched in her number and made the call. After ten rings, it went to voice mail.

I left a message. "Call me when you get the time."

A few minutes later, my phone chimed with an incoming call. It looked to be from Erin, but when I answered, the voice on the other end wasn't hers. It was instead a man's. He said, "Mr. Walker. We need to talk."

Chapter Fifty-Eight

"Is Erin okay?"

"Yes, I can assure you she is. She's here with me right now. Would you like to speak to her?"

"Yes, put her on the line."

I could hear someone whisper something then I heard Erin say, "Walker, Mr. Madicof is here with me, and he's trying to find Waldo. He hasn't hurt me in any way, but he wants me to stay with him until Waldo shows up. So if you could find him and arrange a meeting this evening, it would make both of us happy."

When she paused, I asked, "Where are you? Where is he holding you?"

She didn't get a chance to answer. The man who I had spoken to earlier was back on the line. He said, "Mr. Walker, we haven't had the pleasure of meeting, but I hope to get together with you soon. My name's Madicof and I came up here from Key West to meet with a friend of yours.

"He borrowed a bit of money from me and, for some reason, hasn't been able to make his payments on time. He called me today and said he would meet with me, but now that I'm in town, he's not answering his phone.

"Before I made the loan, he told me he was going to use it to purchase the taco truck business from Ms. Donnely. Since we are unable to find Mr. Raines, we thought that maybe she knew how to reach him. So we arranged to meet up with her this afternoon and we've since had an interesting conversation.

"She says she doesn't know where Waldo is and doesn't know how to reach him. She claims he also owes her money and he's been avoiding her as well.

"She suggested that perhaps you might know where he is and might be able to arrange a meeting. If you were able to do that, I would appreciate it. I'm sure Ms. Donnely would as well.

"Mr. Walker, I assure you that no harm will come to her. We are not in the business of hurting women and will not hurt her in any way. But as she said in her brief talk with you, she will be staying with us until we are able to meet with Waldo, face-to-face.

"I'm hoping you can make that happen. And soon."

He paused, and I said, "Madicof, I know about your business. And I know about your associates, but you don't know me or what I might do to get Erin back. My suggestion is you let her go before this thing gets out of hand."

There was silence on the other end, then, "Mr. Walker, we do not wish this to as you say, get out of hand. We simply need you to set up a face-to-face meeting with Waldo. After that, you and Ms. Donnely can go free."

I thought about what he was saying. He wanted me to give him Waldo in return for Erin. It was an easy decision. I would do it. But first, I needed to see if I could strike a deal.

"Madicof, I'll try to find Waldo and set up a meeting. It may be difficult as he hasn't told me where he's staying. But I will look for him and do my best to find him.

"You should know that he is broke. He owes us all

money and the chances of any of us getting paid back in full anytime soon are slim to none.

"But there might be a way for you to recover your investment. I have gained possession of an asset with a cash value somewhere in excess of fifty thousand dollars. I might be able to make it available to you for the immediate return of Ms. Donnely, regardless of whether I find Waldo or not.

"Are you interested?"

While waiting for his reply. I could hear voices whispering in the background, then, "Mr. Walker, what is this asset you speak of, the one that you say is worth more than fifty thousand dollars?"

I didn't answer right away. I wanted him to think that I might have changed my mind about the trade. So I said nothing, I knew that in negotiations when the question of price comes up, he who speaks first often loses.

Finally, Madicof asked, "Mr. Walker, are you still there?"

I smiled. It sounded like he was interested in maybe doing a trade.

"Yes, I'm here. I was just thinking that maybe I'd rather keep these things for myself. I wouldn't need to offer them to you if I could find Waldo. In fact, I think that's the better plan.

"I'll find him and turn him over to you. He doesn't have any money and you won't get anything out of him. I'll keep the asset and walk away free and clear with Ms. Donnely."

I knew this wouldn't sit well with him; I'd teased him with the lure of something worth fifty thousand dollars and knew the hook was set. I waited to see what he'd say next. I was pretty sure how it would go.

He didn't disappoint. "Mr. Walker, tell me more about this asset that you think is worth fifty grand."

I smiled, he was interested. "Paintings. I have ten of them. Each worth at least five thousand. Originals signed by well-known Florida artists. Perhaps you've heard of them. Highwaymen?"

Madicof paused then said, "I know about them. What makes you think the ones you have are worth so much?"

I lied. "I had them appraised by a local gallery. They said each was worth at least five grand. Maybe more."

I was expecting his next question. "If the paintings are worth so much, why would you consider giving them to me? It doesn't make sense."

I was ready with my answer. "I'm quite fond of Ms. Donnely and I'm not sure I can find Waldo. If I am unable to do so, I would rather have Ms. Donnely than the paintings."

There was a pause on the line and again I could hear voices whispering in the background. Then Madicof said, "Okay, I'm interested in the paintings. Have them with you when we meet with Waldo. If they are what you say they are, I'll release Ms. Donnely to you."

I waited for a moment, then said, "I have a better offer. I bring the paintings to you now and you release Erin to me. That way, even if I can't find Waldo, you still have the paintings."

Madicof wasn't buying it. "Mr. Walker, I'm not a fool. I know that when I release the woman, I'll probably never hear from either of you again. If the paintings turn out to be fakes and you don't bring me Waldo, I gain nothing. So no deal. Find Waldo and call me when you do."

He hung up.

Chapter Fifty-Nine

I didn't have a car. We had returned Raif's and Erin had taken hers. My motorhome was my only option. It wouldn't be the best vehicle to use to find Waldo. It was too wide and long to get into small parking lots or drive on many of the narrow streets in Saint Augustine.

I was pretty sure I could get it into the Die Inn though. If luck was with me, Waldo would be there. I could pick him up, go to the storage building where the paintings were, put ten of them in the motorhome, and call Madicof to set up a meeting.

Before I could do any of that, I needed to bring the slide rooms in and unhook from shore power. I did it quickly, and because I had secured everything when I went to the dump station, I was ready to roll.

I started the engine and left Anastasia State Park. When I got to A1A, I turned south heading for the Die Inn where I hoped to find Waldo.

I'm not much of a fan of driving the motorhome after dark through city streets, but it had to be done. I stayed in the right lane and when I got to Waldo's place, I pulled in, hoping to see his silver Camry in the parking lot.

It wasn't there. Neither was Waldo. He had left for the evening. He was either in town trying to sell jugs of water, or back at the motel room he had mentioned earlier.

Since the county had solved his money problem, I figured

he didn't need to raise cash selling water, and had gone back to his motel room.

Problem was I didn't know the name of the motel, or where it was located. Trying to find it while driving the motorhome after dark with just me as the lookout wasn't a winning strategy.

I only knew one other person in Saint Augustine, and while still parked at the Die Inn, I gave him a call. He answered on the third ring.

"Raif, they've taken Erin and won't let her go until I bring them Waldo."

Before I could explain the situation, he asked, "What do you mean they've taken Erin? Who's taken her? How'd you let that happen?"

I answered his questions the best I could. "The loan shark from Key West and his two goons. They've got her. One of them called pretending to be a worker at the taco truck. They told her there was a problem and they needed her help.

"She dropped me at the motorhome and took her car to meet with them. If I'd been with her, I would have stopped them. Or died trying."

Raif was silent for a moment then asked, "Where are you? I'll come get you."

"No, don't do that. I'm only a few minutes away. I'm coming to your place in my RV. I'll be there in ten minutes."

I turned the motorhome around, pulled back out on A1A and headed to Raif's. Traffic was light and I got there quicker than expected. He was outside waiting and when he saw me pull in, he headed in my direction. As he got closer, I could see he was wearing a shoulder holster. I assumed there was a loaded gun in it.

I was hoping we wouldn't need it. But if we did, it was good to have it ready.

His fists were clenched and he had a sour look on his face. I half expected him to take a swing at me for letting Erin get sucked into this mess. But he didn't. Instead, he said, "What do we need to do?"

"Pick up the paintings. They're in a storage building not far from here."

"Paintings? What paintings? Why are they more important than getting Erin back?"

I explained it to him. "The paintings are my backup plan in case we don't find Waldo. Madicof might give us Erin if I give him the paintings."

Raif nodded. "Okay. Let's go get them."

He tossed me his car keys and said, "You're driving."

He knew how to get around Saint Augustine a lot better than I did, and it would have made sense for him to drive. But since he didn't want to, my guess was he had been enjoying some herbal relief when I called. He may not have trusted himself behind the wheel.

With me driving and Raif in the passenger seat, it took us nine minutes to get to the storage building. We burned another ten minutes unlocking the unit and grabbing the first ten paintings. I stacked them in the trunk, using the towels from the motel as padding.

With the paintings taken care of, the next step was to find Waldo. I was hoping it would be easy. But I wasn't expecting it to be.

I brought Raif up to speed. "I looked at the Die Inn and he wasn't there. He told me earlier he was staying in a motel close by, but he didn't tell me the name of the place. All I know is it is somewhere off A1A, rooms are cheap and there's a drug dealer in the room next to him."

Raif thought for a moment. "I know a few places that fit that description. Let's hope he's at one of them."

Four minutes later, we were on A1A south, checking the parking lots of cheap motels trying to find Waldo's car. I drove slowly, scanning the lots on my left, with Raif scanning the ones on the right.

When we got to the Die Inn, I pulled in and again checked to see if Waldo was in the office or any of the rooms. I was hoping he had gone to get dinner and had come back. But he hadn't. The place was still locked up. No lights and no cars in the lot.

Leaving the Die Inn, we drove south for about ten miles, checking every place we passed. When we reached a row of expensive high rise condos, it was time to turn back. Waldo wouldn't fork over what it would cost to stay in one of those places.

Raif had me pull in the same parking lot where Erin and I had eaten ice cream the night before. "What else did Waldo tell you?"

I shook my head and tried to remember. "All he said was the motel was a few miles south, and the guy in the room next to him was selling drugs."

Raif nodded. "So he didn't actually say it was on A1A? That means it could be on one of the side streets. Turn around. Let's check."

We'd been on the road for twenty minutes when my phone chimed with an incoming call. The caller ID was the same as before. Erin.

I answered. "This is Walker."

Madicof asked, "You find him yet?"

I shook my head. "No, but I'm looking for him. I'll call you when I do."

I didn't wait to see what he might say next. I hung up.

Raif looked at me. "Was that him?"

I nodded.

He shook his head. "If they hurt her in any way, I'll kill them. All of them."

I was certain he would.

Chapter Sixty

Raif was telling me that when he was a cop, they got a lot of calls about one place in particular. The Romar Motor Court. Most of the cases there were drug-related, but they were also known for prostitution. It wasn't the kind of place that most people would want to stay. At least not voluntarily.

But the rates were low and a newcomer like Waldo might not know any better. We decided to check there first.

Raif gave me directions and we pulled into their parking lot a few minutes later. A group of about ten youths loitering in the lot saw the ex-cop car we were in and quickly headed for their rooms. Whatever they had been doing, they didn't want the police to know about it.

We didn't bother going to the front office. Raif said it was the kind of place that didn't keep track of who was staying there. As long as customers paid in cash, there were no questions asked. The management didn't care who you were or what you did as long as you paid the going rate.

We cruised the parking lot twice before finding Waldo's Camry. It was on the side of the building, between two cars that looked like they had been abandoned.

Finding his Camry meant Waldo was probably at the Romar in his room. The problem was we didn't know which one he was in and didn't think knocking on doors of likely drug dealers and pimps would get us anywhere. They were firm believers of following the "snitches get stitches" rules of conduct. If Waldo's neighbors thought he was friendly with the PoPo, they might want to shut him up. We didn't want that. We needed to find him alive and unharmed.

Raif asked the obvious question. "How do we know which room he's in?"

I shook my head. "I don't know. But Waldo did say the guy in the room next to his was selling drugs. If we could find him, Waldo's room would be close by."

Raif wasn't overly happy with my answer. "There's a good chance that more than one person is selling drugs out of a room here at the Romar. Could be that everyone here is in the same business, except Waldo.

"We might as well start knocking on doors until we find him."

I didn't agree. "Raif, don't take this wrong, but you look like a cop. And we're in a cop car. Nobody here is going to tell us anything. We're leaving."

I pulled out of the parking lot and instead of turning left to get back on A1A turned right into a residential neighborhood. I drove a block and pulled over in front of a vacant lot.

I turned to Raif and said, "You stay here, out of sight. I'm going to go back and start asking questions. I'll start with the desk clerk and a hundred-dollar bill.

"If I learn anything, I'll call you."

Raif didn't like the idea of me going in on my own, but he knew we needed to find Waldo if we wanted to get Erin back. It might be dangerous to start asking questions at the Romar, but both of us were willing to take the risk for Erin's sake.

As I was getting out of the car, Raif asked, "You want a gun?"

"No, I don't think I'll need one. I'm hoping that cash will get the job done. If it doesn't, we'll go to plan B."

I didn't know what plan B was, but between the two of us, I was pretty sure we'd come up with something.

After I got out of the car, I bent over and grabbed a handful of dirt from the side of the road. I rubbed some on my pants and a little more on my shirt. I roughed up my hair and did my best not to look like a cop. I wanted to fit in with the crowd we had seen in the parking lot and none of them looked like they were working for John Law.

My plan was to look like a junkie with cash-in-hand looking for a quick fix. A drug dealer's dream customer.

I headed back toward the motel and when I got close, I started my act. I hunched over and walked slowly, mumbling to myself like maybe I had too much to drink or smoke. I added a limp to help sell the illusion.

Not wanting to take a chance of knocking on random doors, I headed to the office. I opened the door and stepped into a small dirty room that reeked of sweat and cigarette smoke. A man who I figured to be the night clerk sat in a small cubby, separated from the lobby by bulletproof glass. He had his feet up on the desk and was watching porn on a small TV.

When he saw me come in, he shook his head and said, "We're full up. Go somewhere else."

I didn't leave. Instead, I walked up to the glass barrier, pulled a hundred-dollar bill out of my pocket and said, "My friend Waldo told me to meet him here. You know which room he's in?"

The clerk looked at the hundred, thought about it for a few seconds and then said, "We've got a lot of Waldos here. Not worth me getting up out of my chair for just one Benjamin."

When he smiled, showing a few missing teeth, I knew what he wanted. More money.

I pulled out another hundred and held it up to the glass.

This time he got up and walked over to me. We were still separated by the bulletproof partition. He looked at the two bills and said, "We don't keep a register here. Can't look up guests by name. Tell me what he looks like. I might be able to help."

I nodded. "White guy, early thirties, about five-seven, a little overweight. Drives a Camry. Silver with fading paint."

The clerk smiled. "Yeah, I know him. Didn't know his name was Waldo though. We just call him the fat white guy."

He pointed to the two hundreds I was holding and waited. I slid one through the narrow opening at the bottom of the glass. The clerk snatched it up and put it in his pocket.

"Room sixteen. Maybe seventeen. Not sure which, but it's one of those."

I pushed the other hundred under the glass. "If you're playing me, you won't like it when I come back."

He moved back to his chair, "You won't need to come back. He's in room sixteen. Or seventeen. One of the two."

Leaving the office, I noticed that the group of youths who had been in the lot when we pulled in in Raif's car were back. I checked to see if Waldo was with them. He wasn't, or at least I didn't see him. He would have stood out if he was with them. There was no way I would have missed him.

One of the men in the group saw me looking in their direction and yelled, "What do you want, homie?"

I didn't answer. No need to get them riled up. I turned and headed back to where Raif was waiting.

When I got to his car, he asked, "Any luck?"

"Yes, the guy in the office said he's in room sixteen, maybe seventeen. Not sure which, but he's in one of them. I'm going to go see if I can find out."

I started to go back to the Romar, but Raif stopped me when he said, "I've got a better idea."

Chapter Sixty-One

We were still sitting in Raif's car. About a block behind the Romar. We had learned that Waldo was in room sixteen or seventeen. But we didn't know which one.

I wanted to go back and knock on doors. Find out which room he was in. If he wasn't in sixteen, I'd check seventeen.

I thought it was a good plan. Raif didn't.

He said, "Look, we saw Waldo's car. So we know he's there. That's all that really matters. We'll let Madicof figure out which room. We'll let him knock on doors.

"All we have to do is make sure Waldo doesn't leave before Madicof gets there. We don't know which room Waldo's in, but we do know what he'd be driving if he wanted to leave.

"So go back to his car and pull the coil wire. That'll keep him there."

I started to get out, but Raif wasn't finished. "Don't go the same way you did before. This time go in on the backside, near Waldo's car. Keep low and don't let the guys in the parking lot see you. Call me if you get into trouble."

Raif's plan sounded good. But it would only work if Waldo's car was unlocked. If it wasn't, I wouldn't be able to open the hood to pull the coil wire unless I was willing to break a window.

I was definitely willing to do that but worried the sound of breaking glass might attract the wrong kind of attention. I was hoping to get lucky and find the car unlocked.

I left Raif behind and headed to the Romar. Going the back way, there were no street lights. The poles were there, but the lights weren't working. They'd probably been busted out by people not wanting others to see what they were up to. I didn't want to be seen either, so darkness worked in my favor.

Judging by the odor of urine and feces that grew stronger the closer I got to Waldo's car it looked like the side street was being used as an outdoor toilet. It was close and convenient for guests and visitors who didn't want to go back into their rooms and handy for those partying in Romar's front lot.

I was hoping none of them would feel the urge as I made my way to Waldo's car. I didn't want to be lurking on the side of the road when they pulled their pants down nor did I want them to see me.

Fortunately, no one did. I got to Waldo's Camry unseen. Staying low, I went to the driver's door and tried it. Surprisingly, it was unlocked. Either Waldo was dumber than I thought or he figured it was better to leave the car unlocked so thieves wouldn't have to break a window to get inside.

It was something people living in South Florida quickly learned. If there is nothing inside a car worth stealing, it's better to leave it unlocked. Replacing a broken window is expensive. Especially if you have to do it more than once. It's cheaper to leave the doors unlocked so thieves don't have to break glass to get in.

When I opened his door, the dome light flickered on. Not wanting to draw attention, I quickly found the hood latch, pulled it, and shut the door.

I waited a few seconds to see if my actions had attracted any attention. They hadn't. The loud music coming from the front parking lot along with whatever the crowd was doing to stay entertained covered any sounds I made.

Going to the front of the car, I lifted the hood and looked for the coil. But like a lot of newer cars, it was buried deep underneath a plastic engine cover. There was no way I could get to it quickly. So instead of trying to get it out, I found the battery and pulled the positive cable. It came off easier than it should have. A sign that Waldo hadn't been much on keeping up with basic car maintenance.

Without battery power, the car wouldn't be going anywhere any time soon. I quietly closed the hood and headed back to where Raif was waiting.

As soon as I slid onto the passenger seat, he asked, "Any problems?"

"No. It's done."

"Good, now what do we do?"

I'd thought about it on my walk back to the car and had worked out a plan that might have a chance of working.

"I'll call Madicof and tell him I found Waldo. I'll tell him to meet me at the Romar and to bring Erin with him so we can end this thing."

Without waiting to see if Raif had anything to say, I hit redial on my phone. After three rings, Madicof answered. "You find him yet?"

"Yeah, he's here with me. At the Romar motel off of A1A south. Meet me at the office. I'll take you to him. Bring Erin or there's no deal."

There was a pause on the line and I could hear Madicof

tell someone in the background to bring his car around.

Returning his attention to me he said, "We're on our way. Remember, no tricks, no cops."

He ended the call.

I turned to Raif. "He's coming. But he warned me about not getting the cops involved. If he sees your car, it could be trouble for Erin.

"So, you stay here in the car where it can't be seen. I'll go to the office and wait for him. When he arrives, I'll turn my phone on so you can hear everything.

"He won't come alone. He'll bring his two goons. I'm hoping he'll have one go into Waldo's room with him and leave the other in the car with Erin. That'll be our best chance to get her. When there's only one guy to deal with.

"But maybe we'll get lucky. Maybe Madicof's meeting with Waldo will go off without a hitch. If it does, maybe he'll give up Erin without a fight.

"But if it goes south and you hear me say 'Avocado,' meet me at Waldo's car. We'll grab Erin and disappear."

Raif nodded. "You sure you don't want the gun?"

"No. Madicof's guys will search me. If they find a gun, they'll take it. You wouldn't get it back. So no gun. I'll try to outsmart them instead."

Raif shook his head. "Good luck with that."

Chapter Sixty-Two

I headed back to the Romar. My plan was to stay out of sight near the office until I saw Madicof's car pull up. I'd show myself and make sure Erin was safe. Then I'd tell him where to find Waldo.

A few minutes later, a black SUV with heavily tinted windows pulled up under the awning in front of the Romar office.

I took a deep breath and stepped out of the shadows. Almost immediately, the back driver's side window slid down, revealing the face of a man who I presumed to be Madicof, with Erin sitting to his right.

He asked, "You Walker?"

I nodded.

He looked around. "No cops, right?"

I nodded again.

He pointed to the other side of the SUV and said, "Get in."

I did as I was told. I opened the heavy door and slid in beside Erin. I took her hand and asked, "Are you okay?"

"Yeah, just peachy."

She started to say something, but Madicof interrupted. "Where's Waldo?"

I pointed to the row of rooms in front of us. "He's here. I'm not going to tell you which one he's in until you let Erin go."

Madicof laughed. "You think I'm a fool? Do you think I'm going to take your word? She's not going anywhere until I talk to Waldo."

I nodded. "Okay, call him. Ask him if he's staying at the Romar and if he's in his room. Don't tell him you're coming to visit. That might scare him off. Just tell him you'll get together with him tomorrow."

Madicof looked at me and said, "You better be telling the truth. If you're setting me up, I won't be happy."

He pulled out his phone, found the number that Waldo had used when he called earlier that day, and hit redial. He put the call on speaker so we could hear what was being said.

Waldo answered, "This is Waldo."

Madicof nodded at me and said, "Waldo, I'll be in town tomorrow and would like to get together with you. Are you still at the Romar?"

Waldo answered, "I'm here tonight but not sure where I'll be tomorrow. Call me then, we can set something up."

Before Madicof could ask him which room he was in, Waldo ended the call.

I smiled and said, "I told you he was here. Now let her go."

He didn't. Instead, he asked, "What's the room number? If Waldo's in it, I'll think about letting the girl go. But not before."

I didn't like his answer. Instead of saying he was going to let her go, he said he was thinking about it. That didn't sound good. Maybe he was planning on keeping her, using her as a way to get the paintings after he got Waldo.

He repeated his question. "What's the room number?"

Without thinking it through, I said, "Sixteen, he's in room sixteen."

But I wasn't sure. He could have been in seventeen. That's what I should have told him. That he was either in sixteen or seventeen. That way, if he didn't find him in sixteen, he'd know where to look next.

There was a fifty-fifty chance the first room would be the right one. There was also a fifty-fifty chance it wouldn't be, and I wasn't feeling lucky. At least not yet.

Madicof told the thug behind the wheel to park across from sixteen. As the car started moving toward the crowd of revelers still in the parking lot, they quickly dispersed. Most went into nearby guest rooms. A few ran toward the back of the building where Waldo's car was parked. Two headed into room sixteen. That probably meant Waldo was in seventeen. But I wasn't going to tell Madicof. Not yet. I wanted to give him a reason to keep Erin and me around and unhurt.

The SUV slowly cruised the lot, the driver counting off the room numbers until we reached sixteen. There was already a car in the parking space nearest the door, so Mad Dog's driver pulled to the street side and parked.

From the back seat, Madicof told him to stay in the car with us. He had his other goon get out and they both headed for sixteen. When they got to the door, Madicof's man reached into his jacket and pulled out a black pistol.

Then, instead of knocking, he kicked the door in, going for the element of surprise.

Going in that way, without knocking, was a big mistake. Two men inside the room were counting money, with stacks of bills on the floor. Another was sitting in a chair near the door, sawed-off pump shotgun in his lap. Still another was near the bathroom door at the back wall.

When Madicof's guy kicked in the door, the men inside the room must have thought they were being robbed. So they did what most in their trade would do. Fight back.

From outside in the car, we heard three gunshots. Boom, boom, boom. Probably from the shotgun.

Madicof fell backwards out of the door onto the sidewalk, blood pouring from a nasty chest wound. The man who had gone in with him backed out of the door, still firing his gun.

The driver who had stayed in the car saw his boss on the ground bleeding and went to his aid. When he did, I said, "Avocado, avocado, avocado."

Erin looked at me like I was crazy. Wondering why I was repeating the word "avocado" over and over. She didn't know it was my signal to Raif.

Before she could ask about it, I grabbed her hand and pulled her out of the SUV. Ducking down, we ran to the backside of the lot, next to where Waldo's car was parked. I knew the doors were unlocked; I opened the back one and pushed Erin in. "Stay here until you see Raif."

I handed her my phone and said, "Tell him you're in Waldo's car. Tell him not to wait for me."

I went back around to check on Madicof. He was lying on the sidewalk, blood pouring out onto the pavement beside him. The SUV and the two guys who had been in it with him were gone. They'd left him behind.

The door to room sixteen was open and I didn't see anyone inside. The guys who'd been in it had gathered up their money and bailed. Most likely they didn't want to be around when the cops arrived. Neither did I.

I walked back to Waldo's car to check on Erin. She was gone. Raif had come to her rescue. If I hadn't given her my phone, I would have called and asked him to come rescue me as well.

But I couldn't call anyone and didn't have a car. I only had two options. Knock on room seventeen, hoping that Waldo was there and ask for his help, or walk away. As fast as I could.

I decided that walking was the better choice.

Seven minutes later, I heard the sirens. Followed by flashing blue lights. I hid behind a palm as four police cars sped by. Soon after, an ambulance followed.

Thinking the scene would keep the cops busy, I stepped out on the sidewalk and started walking toward the Die Inn. It was about three miles ahead of me, and I figured that when Raif and Erin came back looking for me, that's where they would check first.

I was wrong.

Chapter Sixty-Three

I had walked about two miles when the cop car pulled up behind me. A uniformed officer got out, gun drawn, and told me to get down on the ground. I didn't argue. I dropped to the pavement and lay on my belly, arms spread.

While the first officer kept his gun trained on me, the second rushed over and cuffed me. He helped me to my feet and patted me down for weapons. I was glad I wasn't carrying any.

The first officer read me my rights and put me in the backseat of his car. Eight minutes later, I was brought into the St Augustine police station, where I was patted down again then led into an interrogation room.

They put me in a seat facing what I knew was a one-way mirror and connected my cuffs to a chain bolted to the table. One officer left and the other remained, standing near the door.

After about fifteen minutes, a detective came in and the interrogation began.

His first question was, "Where is the gun?"

Followed by, "Why did you shoot him?"

And then, "Who else was there with you?"

I kept my mouth shut. I couldn't answer without telling them about Waldo, Erin, and Raif. I didn't want to drag them into it, if it could be avoided.

After seeing that I wasn't going to answer his questions, the detective said, "You're only making this worse. Tell me what happened and it'll go easier on you."

I shook my head and said nothing. The detective took a deep breath. "I tried to help you, but you're not talking, so I'm done. Murder will get you life in prison. Hope you enjoy it."

He left the room.

Fifteen minutes later, a second detective came in. He nodded at the officer standing in the corner and took a seat across from me. He looked to be about fifty, wearing a rumpled white shirt with a thin, black clip-on tie. He looked tired. I could see it in his eyes and, later on, hear it in his voice.

After introducing himself as Detective Booker, which I thought was a good name for someone in his line of work, he asked if I would like something to drink. I was thirsty but I was going to pass on the refreshments until I found out how long I'd be in the station.

"No thanks. I won't be staying long."

He smiled, then reread my rights. When he was done, he asked if I understood them. It was the third time I'd been read my rights that night. I understood them each time. "Yes, I understand them."

The detective, who was acting a lot friendlier than the first one, smiled and said, "Good."

Before I was put in the cop car earlier that evening, I'd been frisked and they'd found my wallet. It was now sitting on the table in front of me. The detective opened it and pointed to my driver's license.

"Mr. Walker, you're here because there was a shooting. We

have an eye witness who saw you when it happened. He said he saw you standing in the doorway of the room where the shooting occurred and saw you leave when the man inside came out bleeding.

"Our witness did the right thing. He called 9-1-1 and stayed at the scene. He told us everything; that's why we picked you up. You were the guy with the gun.

"But that's not all. When we searched the room, we found physical evidence that clearly showed you had been inside. Probably doing a drug deal.

"The only thing we don't know is what you did with the gun. You want to tell me about it?"

I decided to talk. "I didn't shoot anyone and didn't have a gun."

The detective frowned and said, "Look, we know you ditched it. If a kid finds it and hurts himself or uses it in a crime, it'll be on you. You don't want that. So tell us what you did with it."

They had the wrong guy, but I didn't have an alibi. I was at the Romar. I was seen by a lot of people, including the man in the office. The cops had picked me up walking away from the scene of the crime, and I couldn't tell them why I had been there.

I was pretty sure there was no way a witness saw me go into the room with a gun. It hadn't happened that way. I'd been outside in the SUV when the shooting started. When the witness recanted, I'd be home free.

The detective continued to ask questions, and I repeated the answers I had given earlier. "It wasn't me. I didn't shoot anyone and I didn't have a gun."

Twenty minutes later, Detective Booker left the room.

The officer who had been standing watch left as well.

An hour later, Booker returned. He had good news. The liquor store across the street from the Romar had a security camera. It was pointed at the Romar lot and recorded everything that went down.

Booker was holding a tablet and asked me to watch the video. He clicked play, and the video started with Madicof's black SUV rolling up to room sixteen. It showed Madicof and his associate getting out of the car and going over to the room. Then his goon pulling a gun and kicking in the door.

It showed people in the room firing at Madicof and him stumbling back out with a chest wound, with the driver of the SUV running over to check on him.

At that point, Booker stopped the video. "Now, I need you to explain this next part."

He pressed play again, and the video showed me getting out of the SUV with Erin close by. It showed us running away to the backside of the parking lot. We were on screen for less than three seconds.

He stopped the video and asked, "What were you doing in the SUV?"

I decided to tell him.

"We were being held hostage. By a guy named Madicof. He thought we knew the location of a guy who owed him a large sum of money. He had grabbed the girl earlier and was holding her against her will. He told me he'd let her go when I found his guy.

"I'd asked around and he was at the Romar. I told Madicof and he had me meet him there. Soon after, he showed up with the girl and his two goons. He had me get in the car and wait while they checked out the room they thought their guy was in.

"The video shows what happened next. As soon as the shooting started, we ran. Next thing I know, I'm getting arrested for something I didn't do."

Booker nodded and said, "I'm pretty sure that's not the whole story. But the video does show you weren't the shooter, and you tried to get the woman to safety. That keeps you from being locked up tonight.

"But the investigation is just getting started. Don't leave town until it's over."

He unlocked my cuffs and called in an officer who escorted me to the door. I stepped out into the night air and was happy to be free. It had been a long day and I was ready to go home. But without my phone, I didn't have a way to call Raif or Erin to come pick me up.

The police had given my wallet back and I had enough cash to make a call if I could find a phone.

I walked a mile and found an all-night convenience store. I called Raif, and he agreed to come get me.

Chapter Sixty-Four

Raif showed up a few minutes after I called. He was alone. Erin wasn't with him.

His first words were, "She's pretty shook up. She's never been in a gunfight before. She saw the man she had spent the evening with die right in front of her. She didn't like him, but she didn't want him dead.

"She's blaming it on you. The kidnapping, the shootout, the police. She said it's your fault. She said she'd be better off if she had never met you.

"She's back at my place. She'll be spending the next few days there until she sorts this thing out. You need to stay away. She doesn't want the kind of trouble you seem to attract."

I wanted to say it wasn't my fault. It was Waldo's or Mad Dog's, or the drug dealers in room sixteen. But the truth was, if I hadn't gotten involved, none of it would have happened. Erin wouldn't have been kidnapped, and she wouldn't have been caught in the middle of a shooting war.

But she had. And she was right. It was my fault.

Raif dropped me off at my RV, and as I was getting out of his car he repeated what he said earlier. "Stay away from her. I mean it. She doesn't want to see you. She doesn't want to talk about it. Leave her alone."

He returned my phone, the one I'd given Erin the night before, and drove off without saying anything else.

Inside the motorhome, Bob met me at the door. He wasn't happy I had left him alone most of the day. I bent over and stroked his back then headed to the bathroom where I washed the dirt off my face and hands. I filled Bob's bowls and went to the bedroom and flopped down on the bed.

While I slept, the same dream repeated over and over. Erin was on a raft, heading for a waterfall, and there was nothing I could do to keep her from going over. Two thugs held me back and laughed as they watched her disappear in the mist.

Each time the dream replayed, I tried to figure out a different way to save her. And each time, I failed. She always went over.

I was still trying to figure out a way to save her when Bob woke me up around six the next morning. He was on the bed and had nestled his warm body up against mine. His paw was on my shoulder and he was purring. He either knew how bad I felt and was trying to console me or he was just being a cat and didn't understand what was going on.

I'd missed dinner the night before and my stomach growled, reminding me I needed to eat. My first thought was McDonald's. Erin had taken me there for breakfast after our first date. We both had pancakes and it was the beginning of our relationship.

I wanted to return to that happy place in my life. But I couldn't. Erin didn't want to talk to me, and I didn't have a way to get to McDonald's unless I drove the motorhome. I wasn't going to do that.

Instead, I scrambled some eggs, toasted two slices of bread and poured a glass of juice. I moved my food to the table and ate alone. I don't know if it tasted good or not. I'm not even sure if I remember eating.

I was still missing Erin. Still in shock from the events from the night before. Still wishing things had turned out differently.

After breakfast, I put the dishes in the sink, not bothering to wash them. I didn't feel like it would matter. Nothing did.

Having fought through the dream reruns the night before, and not getting much sleep, I went back to bed. With nothing else to do, I planned to stay there for the rest of the day. Maybe the next day as well.

Bob snuggled up beside me. Sometime later, while I was lying there, trying to come up with a way the night could have gone differently, my phone chimed with an incoming call. I'd left it on the kitchen counter, and I didn't want to get out of bed to go get it. But I was worried that it might be Erin, and if it was, I didn't want to miss it.

On the third ring, I ran to the kitchen and grabbed the phone. When I answered, a woman's voice said, "Walker, tell me what happened."

The voice belonged to Marissa Chesnokov, the woman who had sent me to find Waldo. If the events of the previous night were anyone's fault, they were hers. If she hadn't asked me to find him, Erin wouldn't have been upset with me. But if Marissa hadn't sent me to Saint Augustine in the first place, I would have never met Erin. That would have been the real tragedy.

"Walker, you still there?"

I didn't want to talk, but she needed to know.

"Yeah, I'm here. I'm not feeling well. Didn't get much

sleep last night."

I was hoping she'd get the message. That I didn't want to talk to her or anyone else except Erin. I just wanted to get back in bed and be alone.

But she still wanted to talk. "Walker, we heard a rumor that Mad Dog was in Saint Augustine. Do you know anything about that?"

It was a question I didn't want to answer. But Marissa needed to know.

"Yeah, I was with him last night. He had kidnapped the woman I was with and forced me to tell him where Waldo was. I didn't want Waldo to get hurt, but I wasn't going to let Mad Dog keep the girl.

"It wasn't my fault he got shot. They should have just knocked on the door instead of kicking it down. Things would have gone differently if he had. But he didn't. That's why he got shot. It wasn't my fault."

There was silence on the other end of the line. Then, "Walker, are you saying Waldo got shot? And you were there? Did Mad Dog shoot him?"

"No, it wasn't Waldo who got shot, he's fine. But Mad Dog is dead. He won't be coming back to Key West or anywhere else. I doubt his two associates will either."

There was a pause on the line as I let Marissa think about what I had just said. I waited to see what she would say.

Finally, after a few seconds of silence, she asked, "The woman, the one you said Mad Dog kidnapped? Is she okay?"

"Yes, she is. But she saw it go down and blames it on me. She wants me out of her life."

Saying it out loud didn't make me feel any better. I didn't want her out of my life. I wanted to be around her. Even though it had been a few hours since I last saw her, I already missed her.

"Walker, I'm sorry it turned out this way. It wasn't my intention to put you or the people around you in danger.

"I can tell you don't want to talk about it now, so we won't. But Boris will find out. He'll want to know why you were up there and what you were doing. I think it's best he hears it from me. I'll tell him everything today.

"If you need anything or someone to talk to, call me. I'm here for you."

She ended the call.

Chapter Sixty-Five

I wanted to talk to Raif to see what his buddies down at the station had learned about the shooting. I wanted to know if they knew Erin was the woman in the SUV and if she was in any kind of trouble.

But I was pretty sure Raif wasn't in the mood to talk, at least not to me. He had said to stay away from Erin, and since she was staying with him, I didn't want to give him another reason to want me gone.

I checked the TV to see if there was any news about the shooting. The closest channel was in Jacksonville, and they didn't have anything to say about an overnight shootout in Saint Augustine. Maybe the local paper covered it.

I pulled on my shoes and sunglasses, grabbed my keys and started walking. Ten minutes later, I crossed the street at the light and went into the Pump and Munch. The man who had been behind the counter the last time I visited was still working there.

I wondered if he remembered I was in the store when the kid tried to rob it. I doubted it. He probably saw hundreds of customers a day, and unless one of them did something memorable like pulling a gun, he wouldn't remember them.

I grabbed a can of Coke from the cooler, a Kit Kat bar from the candy rack, and a copy of the St. Augustine Record. The front-page headline said, "Police investigate shootout at local motel."

Below it, a photo of room sixteen at the Romar. Police tape blocking the door. Below the photo, a three-column article that I thought I probably should read to make sure my name wasn't in it.

I paid at the register and took my Coke, candy, and newspaper outside. Instead of heading back to Shady Haven, I went around to the back of the store and took a seat on the same bench Raif and I had sat on after he stopped the kid with the gun.

I pulled the tab on the Coke, took a long swallow, and started reading the headline story in the paper. It didn't take me long to figure out whoever wrote the piece didn't have many details. He didn't know who was shot, why they were shot, or who else was involved.

Since the reporter didn't have any facts to go on, the article mostly dealt with the long history of problems at the Romar. There was a list of recent police calls and quotes from nearby residents mostly saying it was past time for the city or county to get the place cleaned up.

After reading the article, and happily not seeing Erin's, Raif's or my name mentioned, I relaxed a little. I unwrapped the Kit Kat bar and ate it while I read the rest of the paper.

I had gotten to the comics section when I heard footsteps.

Looking up, I saw Raif heading in my direction with a coffee cup in hand. I was sitting on his bench and knew it was time for me to leave.

When he got close, I stood, nodded a hello and said, "I never wanted this to happen."

I started to walk away, but he stopped me. "I know it wasn't your fault. Erin told me how it happened. How

Madicof's guys called and pretended they needed her help at the taco stand.

"When she got there, they scooped her up and took her to Madicof's suite. They held her but didn't harm her. They even had room service bring her dinner.

"She told me she wasn't scared. She knew you would come to her rescue. And you did. The problem was she didn't expect a gun battle. She just thought you'd give Waldo to Madicof and she'd go free.

"The shooting freaked her out. When she saw Madicof stumble out of the room with his guts hanging out, she thought maybe you had planned it to go that way all along.

"I don't think you did. Instead, I think the desk clerk gave you the wrong room number. Maybe on purpose. Maybe he knew the people in sixteen had cash and drugs and were ready to start shooting if anyone tried to break in.

"We'll probably never know for sure. The clerk disappeared after the shooting and hasn't shown up for work."

I nodded. Raif was talking to me. He didn't sound upset that things had gone so wrong. I didn't want to interrupt his train of thought, so I kept quiet.

"I talked to a friend at the station. They have a video. It shows what happened, and it matches the statement you gave; that Erin was being held hostage and you and she were not involved in the shooting.

"They think it was a drug deal gone wrong. They're looking for the shooters who were in sixteen and Madicof's associates. They don't think they'll ever find them.

"Both parties were long gone before the police got there, and no one expects them to come back."

He took a deep breath and said, "I was wrong about Erin. She doesn't hold you responsible. She doesn't want you to leave town either. She says you have some unfinished business with her. She wouldn't tell me what it was."

He reached into his pocket and pulled out his car keys. "Erin's car is still parked near the taco truck. She needs someone to take her there to get it. I think maybe it should be you."

I took the keys and said, "Thanks."

Five minutes later, I pulled up in front of Raif's trailer. Erin was sitting outside reading a book. She was in the chair that Raif had been sitting in the first time I met him.

She looked up and when she saw it wasn't Raif getting out of the car, she frowned and went back to her book.

Chapter Sixty-Six

I walked over and said, "Raif told me you might need a ride to your car. He gave me his keys and said I should see if you wanted me to drive you there."

She looked up from her book. "I'm reading. Go away."

I stood there for a moment, trying to think of something to say, but I couldn't come up with anything. I thought about leaving until I remembered what was in the trunk of Raif's car.

I walked over, unlocked it, and pulled out one of the paintings. I took it over to Erin and asked, "What do you want me to do with these? There are ten of them in the car."

She looked up, thought for a moment, then asked, "Why are the paintings in the trunk?"

I pointed over my shoulder and said, "I was going to trade them for you."

She smiled. "So you think I'm only worth ten of them? What were you going to do with the rest?"

Then she laughed. It warmed my heart when she did.

She stood, put the book she was reading onto the chair and said, "Don't go anywhere. I'll be right back." She went into the trailer and I waited to see if she was really coming back.

A few minutes later, she returned wearing different clothes and a funky hat. She climbed down the steps, walked over to me and said, "I'm still mad at you. But I know it wasn't your fault."

She got into the car and had me go to the storage building and put the ten paintings back where we had stored the others.

Then, instead of having me take her to her car where it was parked at the taco truck, she asked, "Are you in the mood for pancakes?"

Epilogue

A month later, I was still living in the site I had rented at Shady Haven. I had paid for another month and wasn't sure when I would be leaving.

Erin had rented Waldo's trailer. The one between mine and Raif's. Before she moved in, she had it cleaned, replaced all the furniture and generally fluffed it up.

The police questioned me again, and I gave them the same answers I had given before. This time, though, they showed me a photo and asked if I recognized the woman in it. I did. It was the woman who had stolen my meds.

"Yeah, I recognize her. I think her name is Sierra. Is she in some kind of trouble?"

The detective who had shown me the photo shrugged. "We haven't figured that out yet. She was in room fifteen at the Romar when the shooting started. She told us an interesting story.

"She said the guys in sixteen were using young women to steal drugs. The women would knock on doors asking to use the bathroom and take whatever they found in the medicine cabinet.

"They'd have the girls bring the drugs back to the guys in sixteen and they'd get paid in either cash or meth. She said she took the cash. She needed it to support her kid.

"The reason I'm asking about her is we found a bag of empty prescription bottles in her room. Two of them have your name on them. You want to tell me how she got those?"

I nodded. "Remember that sinkhole that stopped traffic on I-75 last month? I was stuck there in my motorhome when she came to my door holding a baby. She asked if I had anything the kid could drink.

"I invited her in. She asked to use the bathroom and of course, I let her. That's when she stole the pills. I didn't realize it until a few hours later.

"You can call CVS and they'll tell you I reported the drugs stolen and canceled the prescriptions that day."

The detective nodded. "That fits with what she told us.

"Unless you want to press charges, we're not going to hold her. We'd rather help her get back on her feet. She's applied for a room at the Paradise, and we hope she gets it."

Even though she had stolen from me, I could understand why. She needed the money to support her child. I held no ill will toward her.

They also questioned Erin about being kidnapped, and her story matched mine. Since it looked like we were both victims caught up in the same thing, they said we were free to go.

They never identified or caught the guys from room sixteen. But they learned the names of Madicof's two associates and had warrants out for both. The general consensus was they were no longer in Florida. They were last seen boarding a thirty-four-foot go-fast boat in Key West. The boat never returned.

In their haste, they left the black SUV behind and when it was searched, a ledger book was found in the back seat.

It listed all the loans Madicof had made, along with

payments and contact info of those who had borrowed money from him. After a district judge's name was found in the ledger, the book mysteriously disappeared. It was assumed that since all the loans violated Florida's usury law, they were not valid and would be wiped clean.

Waldo slept in the day after the shooting. He had taken another Xanax after getting Madicof's call, and slept through everything. When he finally got up the next morning, he had to call triple A to come fix his car. It didn't take them long to get it running.

After receiving the first's month rent payment from the county, he had the motel sign repainted so it would no longer be known as the Die Inn. The new sign simply said, "Paradise."

Erin and I decided to split up the Highwaymen paintings. I gave her first choice and she took the ones she wanted. She hung three in her trailer and put the rest on consignment at Lost Art.

I took two of the smallest ones to hang in my RV. I donated the others to a local shelter for battered women. They planned to sell them at a charity auction and use the money to expand their services.

Boris Chesnokov called me from Key West and thanked me for helping his wife. He was especially appreciative that Madicof wouldn't be returning. For that, he said he owed me. He would repay me soon. He also warned me that the next time his wife asked me to do something for her, to clear it with him first.

I wasn't sure I would.

Bob pretty much continued to be Bob. He'd always meet me at the door expecting to be petted. He'd meow loudly when his food or water bowls were not to his satisfaction, and he'd sleep on Erin's lap when she visited.

We still had breakfast at McDonald's almost every morning. It was a good way to start the day, but I had to give up on pancakes for something a little lighter.

I wasn't sure where our relationship was going. She did amend the no touching and no spooning rules in bed. That made life a lot more interesting. But we really hadn't talked about our future together. She was still looking for a business to buy and I was wondering where my next adventure might take me.

I may have gotten an answer when she showed up late August and said, "I can't take the heat anymore. I'm tired of sweating as soon as I step outside. You need to take me someplace cool where I can get out and walk and not feel like I'm in a steam bath. Don't say the mall. That won't do."

I thought about it for a moment, then came up with what I thought was the perfect solution. "I know the place. It's always cool, so cool you might need to bring a sweater. It's half a day away. Go pack and we'll hit the road."

And that's what we did.

Author's Notes

Most of the locations in this book are real, but none of the characters are, except for Bob.

If you plan to visit Florida, one of the places you won't want to miss is Saint Augustine. Its streets and museums are steeped in history, and you'll be able to get a taste of what life was like back in the sixteen hundreds.

Start by visiting the Castillo de San Marcos National Monument. It's a large stone and mortar fort built to protect Saint Augustine from pirates and other invaders. As you walk the grounds you'll see what life in the fort was like three hundred years earlier.

After the fort, you'll want to take a historic trolley tour. There are several available and all provide interesting and insightful details about the history of the buildings and people who lived in early Saint Augustine.

There are plenty of other things to do as well, including many fine restaurants, bed and breakfasts, nearby beaches, and camping at Anastasia State Park.

If you visit the area, look for a motorhome with a big orange tabby cat sitting on the dash. It might be Mango Bob.

Finally, if you like this book, please post a positive review on Amazon. Good reviews keep me motivated to create new volumes of the adventures of Mango Bob and Walker.

As always, thanks for your support.

Bill Myers

The adventure continues . . .

If you liked Mango Motel, please post a review at Amazon, and let your friends know about the Mango Bob series.

Other books in the Mango Bob series include:

Mango Bob

Mango Lucky

Mango Bay

Mango Glades

Mango Key

Mango Blues

Mango Digger

Mango Crush

You can find photos, maps, and more from the Mango Bob adventures at http://www.mangobob.com

Stay in touch with Mango Bob and Walker on Facebook at: https://www.facebook.com/MangoBob-197177127009774/

Made in the USA
Columbia, SC
26 May 2020